Praise for *Miracle at Midlife*

"A wonderful, thoughtful, and inspiring story of love and courage—the kind of tale that teaches us to take chances, and that we *can* overcome our own obstacles."
>—Betsy Stone, PhD, author of *Happily Ever After*

"Roni Beth Tower shares her journey through life with wit, warmth, and insight. *Miracle at Midlife* is written with an eye for detail and the ability to make the reader feel like a participant in this adventure. Following a romantic meeting in Paris, the author describes events that involve two continents. Subsequently, she is able to overcome many obstacles, and to reinvent herself as someone open to love and affection."
>—Dorothy and Jerome Singer, Yale University

"*Miracle at Midlife* is an honest, thoughtful, and authentic memoir about a real love affair in which the intimacies, conflicts, misunderstandings, and resolutions of new love are explored. Roni Beth Tower writes with a compelling command of psychological process and insight, while ably injecting humor in the story of her transatlantic romance."
>—Jeanne Bodin, author of *We, the American Women*
>and *Women Who Work*

"Roni Beth Tower's *Miracle at Midlife* transports the reader across time and the Atlantic to the sights, tastes, and heady romance of Paris. Through a meeting of the minds, and with great passion, Roni rebirths herself and finds her soul mate. Her journey is at once moving, humorous, candid, and a gift."
>—Traci Stein, PhD, MPH, integrative medicine expert
>and award-winning author of *The Everything Guide*
>*to Integrative Pain Management*

". . . a wonderful story (that) needed to be told . . . demonstrates triumph for all of us who aspire, regardless of our age or doubts, and is a reminder . . . to take life by the coattails and fly. *Miracle at Midlife* is a testimonial to pursuing a passion, to doing, completing, persevering, and to embracing life."

—Camille Mancuso, from her Chatterbox column
"Bucks County Herald"

"Roni Beth Tower shares a remarkable story about the renewal of hope after loss, and the elegance of destiny in love. Beautifully crafted and narrated, her story will captivate the senses and awaken the reader to the power of living with courage, vulnerability, and most of all integrity."

—Jennifer Lee, PhD, clinical psychologist and coauthor of
Mindfulness-Based Cognitive Therapy for Anxious Children

"What could be more romantic than a vacationing psychologist falling in love with an ex-pat attorney living on a converted barge in the heart of Paris? A page-turner from beginning to end, Roni Beth Tower's remarkable memoir, *Miracle at Midlife*, offers the reader a chance to experience both the sexual intensity of the romance novel and a clinician's clear-eyed insights into the difficulties besetting many a cross-cultural relationship. The author would have it that we do not fall in love; rather, we remove the obstacles to being in love. And the obstacles are everywhere, from contradictory styles of interaction—she favoring open dialogue and shared feelings, he preferring to avoid conflicts, all the better to enjoy the pleasures of the moment (be it a crispy croissant or a glass of vin rouge)—to differing styles of parenting adult children and managing complex professional and social lives. This Francophile couldn't put it down. Highly recommended."

—Barbara Bracht Donsky, author of *Veronica's Grave*

Miracle at Midlife

Miracle at Midlife

A Transatlantic Romance

A Memoir

Roni Beth Tower

Roni Beth Tower

SHE WRITES PRESS

Published 2016
Printed in the United States of America
Print ISBN: 978-1-63152-123-2
E-ISBN: 978-1-63152-124-9
Library of Congress Control Number: 2016943293

For information, address:
She Writes Press
1563 Solano Ave #546
Berkeley, CA 94707

Cover design © Julie Metz, Ltd./metzdesign.com
Formatting by Kiran Spees

She Writes Press is a division of SparkPoint Studio, LLC.

To David
And to the anonymous Air France reservation agent who
helped him get me back to Paris

Contents

Prologue

More than twenty years have passed since I was first mesmerized by the twinkle in his brown velvet eyes. The American lawyer with the resonant voice—too short, too sophisticated, too foreign, and too addicted to Marlboros—began provoking my transformation on our first encounter in Paris and has continued to this day. Each morning the magic renews, and each night we bring gratitude to each other as we fall asleep. Through each other's hugs, hearts, and conversations, we have grown toward our own unique wholeness, reclaiming parts of our souls that had been lost or abandoned. But I am getting ahead of my story. Today I will just share how it all began.

I

Destiny Delivered to the Doorstep

1

Arrival

*I*t was late March 1996, and the trip to Paris was growing closer. I had sold the jewelry I'd inherited from my mother to finance the cheap winter fare and had enough left over to cover two nights (two more paid for with frequent-flier coupons) at a Hilton near the Eiffel Tower, airport parking, some simple food and sightseeing, and even a much-needed new computer. I met a friend for dinner and confided, "I have that surreal feeling about this trip. I am terrified, but it's another one of those things that I know I need to do—wildly impractical but essential." Going back to school; buying my Maine cottage; adopting my dog, Luke; cross-training in epidemiology—many of my best decisions had not been practical.

Back then, three girlfriends and I met at the local diner for breakfast every two weeks. For two months they had listened to my travel plans unfold while they and their husbands journeyed to sunny spots like Sarasota, St. Martin, Australia. The day before departure, one of them announced, "You really should call David."

"Who's David?" I asked.

"He went to law school with Jim."

"He's in Paris?"

"He lives there. We see him every time we go."

"It doesn't matter, but is he single?"

"I think so."

"It doesn't matter, but is he gay?"

"I don't think so."

"Okay. Will you get me his number?"

In 1996, e-mail was in its infancy and transatlantic phone calls were costly. Auspiciously, I had already promised a friend from Toronto that I would call her cousin, just to say hello. So why not? This trip was all about taking risks, and if I could master the French phone system for one call to a stranger, I could commit to a second. Besides, nothing was going to happen during a weekend journey across an ocean. I had confidence in my armor.

"I'll have Jim call him and let him know you're coming," she volunteered.

I phoned her the next morning to get David's telephone number. Jim never did contact David. But I did.

Cardinal rule of traveling as a single woman: pack light. You always want to be able to manage your own belongings. Almost as a talisman, I chose the red calico tote that had been a present from my closest childhood friend. She was my personal fashion angel, sending gifts that represented beauty, femininity, style. Indulgence. For good measure, I transferred my passport into the Paloma Picasso wallet that she had sent me for my fiftieth birthday. French francs fit in its compartments, and its luxurious leather helped my fingers rub away fears. A skirt and pair of slacks, which matched the forest-green jacket I wore on the plane (extra warmth over a black cashmere turtleneck and leather pencil skirt), were tucked neatly into the cotton bag. Add a white blouse, sensible underwear, a second pair of shoes, some makeup and toiletries, and I could sling the carryall over my shoulder and into the overhead with no strain at all.

So, on March 27, 1996, I left Luke the bichon with Carmella (his groomer), my patients with the name of another psychologist in case of emergency, an away message on my answering machine, my Honda at long-term parking at JFK, and a layer of illusions in Connecticut as I boarded a flight to Charles de Gaulle Airport.

Thirty-three years was a long time to have been away. The nineteen-year-old girl who had claimed Paris as her own in 1963 had had her whole adult life in front of her. She could not possibly have imagined the losses and pain that were going to unfold in her future, nor her own triumphs as a parent and a professional. And she had little she thought she could lose. Puffed up by freedom from a jealous and judgmental mother, she drew courage from her determination to solve problems as they arose and confidence from a belief that we control our future. Now, here I was, middle-aged, going back to the source. Back to the place where I had discovered a softness and receptivity that were later lost in the cultural demands of doing rather than being, of accomplishing rather than exploring, of giving love rather than receiving love myself. Life's external demands can be harder to ignore than internal ones.

Navigating Charles de Gaulle Airport's then-bewildering circular Terminal 1, I eventually found the newsstand that sold phone cards, bought a Museum Pass at the tourism desk, and then joined the queue for Les Cars Air France to the Étoile. Nestled inside the modern bus, I watched the morning landscape as it rolled past on the way into the city. Decorative sound screens lined the highway, graffiti affirmed local talent, billboards advertised international corporations. The construction that was becoming the Stade de France for the 1998 World Cup came into view. Shortly beyond, majestic as always, the luminous and curvy Sacré Coeur perched like a crown atop its small mountain. Spoken French surrounded me, and I prayed that my ear might soon again become attuned to its lilting rhythms and round sounds. The softness of the landscape and the language began to relax my own edges, too long exposed to Manhattan's hard angles. I consulted my *Plan*, the small, worn book of maps, arrondissement by arrondissement, that I had saved all these years, hope of returning never totally buried.

The bus left the Périphérique at Porte Maillot, and then, a short drive beyond, there was L'Arc de Triomphe. As grand and stately as ever, it now presided over a broad avenue, sidewalks wider than some streets, with a center boulevard free of any parking. I gasped. Not quite the same Champs-Élysées that I had left in 1963. The lineup remained as I had remembered it: the Arch, the Luxor Obelisk at Place de la Concorde, the gates to the Tuileries, and then the little arch announcing the Louvre. But it all seemed so much brighter, more orderly. And it was. As in so many places in Paris—the Invalides, the Louvre, Notre Dame, for example—parking lots had been constructed underground; kiosks and street lamps renovated, restored, and freshly painted; boulevards and walkways swept clean of cigarette butts and stray papers. Paris was taking pride in her presentation.

Underground, I bought my first *carnet* and slipped a ticket into the metro turnstile. I had forgotten how large and confusing the station at the Étoile could be; the clear signs pointing out routes to board lines 1, 2, 6, and RER line A seemed unintelligible at first. Eventually I found line 6, eventually the entrance for Nation-bound trains, and eventually I stood on a platform, about to board the metro for the first time in decades. Gone were the massive steel gates that clanked closed at night, the wooden seats filled with a generation of women widowed by the war. Instead, the cars were clean, the billboards lining the station informative or entertaining, and the passengers diverse, courteous, orderly, and often stylishly dressed.

The train rose above ground at Bir Hakeim, and I got off, trying to identify anything that seemed recognizable. This part of the 15th seemed frighteningly unfamiliar, but I studied my maps again. Just a block away, I found the river and followed it. The Eiffel Tower sprang into view, larger than life, breathtaking in its security as one of the world's best-known landmarks. Walking along the Quai de Grenelle, I moved toward it, then turned right onto avenue de Suffren. There, overlooking a pristine soccer field, with its entrance on a tiny side street, lay my hotel, the base camp for my adventure.

Not surprisingly, my room was not available at the early-morning hour. I parked my Vera Bradley tote with the bellman and walked outside to begin to rediscover—to reclaim—Paris. Images had been racing through both waking and sleeping moments ever since I had made the reservation: the flower arrangements at the Rond Point; the steps and views in front of Sacré Coeur; the river and its bridges; the Monet water lilies in their oval rooms; tiny glass elevators; tall, molded ceilings; cafés smelling of espresso and Gauloises. So much to discover, too. The Musée d'Orsay, the Musée Picasso, the Centre Pompidou, and the pyramid in front of the Louvre had not existed in 1963. I was hoping that churches would still host concerts, shops proudly sport enchanting displays, and architecture stun with its grace and occasional whimsy. I yearned for the taste of a perfect croissant, a *sandwich au Camembert, soupe à l'oignon*—staples from student days. But first I needed to get my bearings. I decided to begin where my nineteen-year-old self had left off and headed toward 214 bd Raspail, just south of bd Montparnasse, where I had lived. From there, I planned to follow the street I had known so well toward the river and the Musée d'Orsay.

That first day was a fiasco. My language skills refused to return, and my usually strong spatial orientation was abysmal. I kept getting on the metro going in the wrong direction and then needing to disembark from a train, cross an overpass (or underpass) to the other side, and board one heading the opposite way. Repeatedly, I got lost and then found myself. The unexpected learning curve amplified the expense of my efforts. Learning is more costly (in time, energy, money, and demands on the body) than knowing. But confronting and mastering the unfamiliar can be more rewarding and is often essential to growth.

Jet lag set in, and finally, exhausted, in the late afternoon I made my way back to the hotel, officially checked in, caught my breath, and realized I was famished. This was a metaphor for my life, wasn't it? Lost and then found, exhausted and needing to recover, starving for basic sustenance after sustained effort. I had come to Paris because of some internal demand, and there it was: I needed to recalibrate to a more respectful flow of energy, creating space for abandoned interiors and hidden corners along the way. Years of responding to legitimate needs of others, problems requiring solutions, responsibilities demanding honor, had shifted attention outward. Needs that lived deep in the heart, in the soul, had become buried under the clutter of daily life. Would slowing down, quieting down, scraping away the external demands permit room for those parts of me to speak?

Dinner out that night was beyond my capacity. I had noticed the charming restaurants that lay just across the street on avenue de Suffren, even read the daily specials posted in chalk on the *ardoises* (menu boards) out front. But I was watching each franc (no euros yet in 1996) and too tired to take on a solo meal in a foreign culture, so I headed for the third-floor hotel bar. Staring out the windows that overlooked the Eiffel Tower as it began to glow against the night sky, I sipped a glass of Bordeaux, snacked on a plate of cheeses, and contemplated the phone calls I had agreed to make. That task would be the last I would ask of my overly conscientious East Coast American self, at least until the next day.

I have never liked making phone calls, especially to people I do not know, but my life had been filled with completing tasks I did not like doing and did anyway because they were the right things to do (an RSVP or a call on behalf of the PTA), or because they might be helpful to someone else (a patient in need or a friend in grief), or because they simply needed to be done (repairs to the furnace or updating an insurance policy). And I had made a promise to a friend.

I am mechanically challenged, so conquering the pay-phone system (while trying to understand required steps written in a foreign language, no less) was no small feat and made the accomplishment of calling my friend's cousin a small miracle. When I reached her, she seemed cold and distant and I could hear annoyance beneath her icy politeness. No doubt an endless parade of visitors who had been given her name as a resource had caused her to burn out on the kindness and generosity she once might have displayed to strangers. I extended well wishes, a news report, a promise to take regards back to North America, and hung up as quickly as I could.

Fear of a rerun was insufficient reason not to call David, and so I did. Sitting in that tiny phone booth in the corridor outside the Hilton bar, I sighed with relief when his answering machine picked up, providing first a message in French and then an English translation. His voice—deep, soft, resonant, flawless, undeniably masculine yet smooth—felt like silk slipping over my body; it sent shivers through me. I left my name, my contact information, and a message that I was in Paris for the weekend, first time in thirty-three years, and that our mutual friend had suggested he might have ideas about what activities would be most worthwhile during my short time in the city. I hung up, had that no-turning-back feeling, and settled in early for a deep night's sleep.

The next morning the phone rang with uncanny timing, just as I had climbed out of the bathtub and was dry enough to slide naked under sheets and blankets for the conversation that followed. He had been out to dinner, heard the message upon return, too late to call back, and wanted to reach me before his first client of the day. (Twenty minutes later, I thought, and I would have been gone.) As he reeled off suggestions, from picking up the current *Officiel des Spectacles* to walking rue du Faubourg St. Honoré (special attention to the Hermès windows) to visiting the incomparable Musée d'Orsay, his meeting time drew closer. I asked him a question about some specific choice of visits or sites. He responded, "Depends on your point of view."

"I do that for a living," I bantered.

"You're an optometrist?" he asked, the teasing clear in his tone. I laughed. A few minutes later, he invited me to dinner that evening "to continue the conversation."

I agreed to meet him in the lobby at eight. "I'm middle-aged, have gray hair and glasses, and will be wearing a green suit."

In spite of my determination to make no demands of my trip, this was *not* the weekend I had been expecting. Oops! Planning again, wasn't I? *Slow down, breathe*, I said, but the energy had its own agenda. Besides, I was in Paris. With a long must-do list and now some new entries, I walked toward and over the river, then took the metro to St. Philippe du Roule, a reasonable place to begin a walk down rue du Faubourg St. Honoré. I found a kiosk and bought an *Officiel*, and a bakery, where a cup of coffee and a croissant, each flake crisp and yeasty on my savoring tongue, became breakfast.

I had left home with no perfume. Dinner without perfume with a strange man who had a voice like David's—and in Paris!—was unthinkable. For sure I could buy it at *les grands magasins*, and for sure they would accept my Visa card. But maybe I'd wander a bit first, and then, according to the *Officiel*, there was a noon concert at Église de la Sainte-Trinité, not far from Galeries Lafayette. Sounded like a perfect place to rest from walking, enjoy beautiful music, and prepare myself for the afternoon.

As I walked along rue du Faubourg St. Honoré, my steps became surer and lighter at the same time. Elegant and imaginatively dressed Parisians moved in a manner and at a pace far different from that of New Yorkers. Unconsciously, I slowed down to let my attention be drawn, rather than directed. I began voraciously consuming the carefully constructed eye candy in the windows of the boutiques, one haute couture designer after another. As David had promised, those at Hermès were spectacular. They showed off sculpture-paintings made from monochromatic or two-color arrangements of scarves and saddles, pocketbooks and silk shirts. By the time I reached the Madeleine, where a metro could take me north to Trinité, I had begun to feel the joy of taking in beauty and the internal spaciousness created through moving and stretching.

The church was opposite the metro stop, easy to locate. I sat down in a pew, the familiarity of meditating in an old church bringing comfort, delight, and hope all at once, and slipped into an altered state of consciousness. Soon the concert would begin, and I trusted that it would rouse me. Except that it did not. Noon. Then my watch said twelve fifteen. I approached one of the few women who was entering or leaving and tried my best to question what was wrong. She smiled but clearly did not understand my French. Finally, I pointed to the entry for the concert in the *Officiel*. She nodded. *"Aujourd'hui—ce n'est pas jeudi."* In taking the overnight flight, I had lost track of a day. It was already Friday. Maybe the unexpected date with a mysterious stranger that night had disorganized my usually methodical mind?

Galeries Lafayette was only a few blocks from the church. A salad from the cafeteria in my stomach, and fifty milliliters of Coco eau de toilette in my pocketbook, and I was ready to take on the afternoon. I strolled along the stalls in front of *les grands magasins*, then down rue Tronchet to the Madeleine, pressing my nose against windows featuring pâtés at Fauchon, jewels made out of chocolate at Madame de Sévigny, the wine of the day at Nicolas, *fruits glacés* at Hédiard. Past Baccarat on the corner and then the china and crystal shops that line rue Royale—Villeroy & Boch, Swarovski, Christofle, Bernardaud. I turned right to walk through the Jardins des Champs-Élysées, past the boutique hotel on avenue Matignon where I had stayed with my father in 1960, and reached the Rond Point, with its six matching displays of spring blossoms welcoming the season. Another view of the Champs-Élysées, widened and returned to turn-of-the-century elegance. Across the intersection onto avenue Montaigne and past flagship stores of great *couturières*—Dior and Chanel and Nina Ricci and so many others—down to Place de l'Alma. There, I crossed the river and then turned left toward the Musée D'Orsay, opposite the Tuileries on the Left Bank of the Seine. It had been a train station, sometimes used as a movie set, when I was a student. Now it featured some of France's finest art collections.

I was beginning to feel oriented again. French signs became familiar and then comprehensible. The sounds of the language carried words with meaning, as well as background music. Parallel tracks fueled my hungry consciousness: I wanted to take it all in, become reacquainted with the Paris of my adolescence, the Paris where I had felt so utterly comfortable and able to manage any needs that might arise. At the same time, a refrain kept strumming, a low-level awareness chanting that the fifty-two-year-old me had a dinner date that night with a mysterious friend of a friend.

Attention thus split, I entered the glorious museum. After slowly descending the few steps to the first floor's center path, casually punctuated with major Rodin sculptures, I made my way toward the back to tiptoe across the glass floor covering a model of the neighborhood surrounding Opéra Garnier. I climbed the stairs to the top floor in search of Renoir, Cézanne, van Gogh, Monet and Manet, Degas, eventually Toulouse-Lautrec. The balcony that overlooked the Seine and the Tuileries offered a perfect rail to lean against as I contemplated the beauty inside and outside the building, whose energy was pulsing through my body. The river curved; the streets followed. In the distance, the fountains at Place de la Concorde flowed. I was filling up fast, and everything inside me wanted to relax and open up to the nourishment of balance, color, explorations in light. The air reeked of the end of March—fresh, clear, ready to usher in all manner of new growth.

Here I began to reclaim my Paris, the city I knew, the one that spoke to the creativity of the human spirit and a complementary separation of the sexes. A hundred years before, the impressionists had transformed the artistic landscape. This building that now held so many masterpieces had itself been transformed, from train station with adjoining hotel, to post office, to theater, to museum—evolution according to need. And now I needed to reclaim the soft self who could stop long enough to look at the light, to follow its changes, to see the colors and watch them dance through the sparklies on the river. As the museum approached its six o'clock closing, I made my way back to the river, the heart and soul that organized the city.

I don't remember getting back to the hotel that afternoon. Perhaps I had realized that I was within walking distance—simply follow the river and turn left after passing the Eiffel Tower. But I probably didn't. The 7th arrondissement was not a quartier I had known well, like the Right Bank Golden Triangle of my father's elegant world or the Left Bank Latin Quarter, which had been home when I was a student. Instead, because I was tired and had gained some confidence in getting around the city, I may have just hopped on the RER for three stops and then made my way back to the Hilton. The light was changing quickly as sunset approached; by the time David was due to arrive, night promised to blanket the city with a different kind of transformation and mystery.

Contemplating my "date" with a man I did not know, I was more curious than nervous. After all, nothing beyond a pleasant (or even uncomfortable) evening could possibly result from this encounter. It would merely be an opportunity to learn more about this city I loved from someone who had chosen to devote his adult life to enjoying its inspiration. To discover a "real" French restaurant with someone who knew his way around them. To have a few hours of adventure. Nonetheless, it *was* Paris and I *was* a woman, and so I put on fresh makeup, dabbed on the perfume, meditated for half an hour, and got dressed. Only much later did David confess that my green suit, the newest and most prized possession in my wardrobe, was one of the dumpiest, dowdiest, downright ugliest outfits he had ever seen.

2
Encounter

he phone rang at precisely eight o'clock. He was waiting in the
lobby. Deep breath, and I walked down the hall, into the elevator, toward the unknown. A few floors down, and the doors opened.
Stepping off, I looked to the right and, as though a magnet were pull-
ing me, was drawn to a man leaning against a pillar. He wore an Irish
tweed hat at a jaunty angle, a blue plaid sport coat, and a plaid tie that
complemented, rather than clashed with, the jacket pattern. Holding
a lit cigarette in his hand, he surveyed the elevators. My eyes met
his liquid gaze, and the rest of the lobby faded away. He waited a
moment, seemed to take his own deep breath—was he disappointed
already?—and then, with a slightly surprised look on his face, he
walked toward me, nodding and flashing a smile signaling some kind
of recognition.

David was shorter than the man I had been expecting. And
younger-looking. And definitely cuter. Brown hair, brown eyes, and a
smile that lit up the lobby. He ushered me out to the street and into his
car, a black Ford Escort that, I later learned, was a modest cover for a
limited-edition sedan with 150 horsepower and a two-liter engine, a
model not exported to the United States. Kind of like David himself—
nothing flashy or unusual until you looked inside. And then he was a
laser beam of focus, a true powerhouse. As he settled into the driver's

seat, he seemed a little nervous, alternately sucking on Tic Tacs and his cigarettes. We began to make our way across the 7th arrondissement.

The sun had already set, and night surrounded us.

David asked, "Have you seen the Eiffel Tower yet?"

"No, not yet on this trip. I mean, I've seen it—it's pretty hard not to—but I haven't been near it yet, not really close."

"Let's take a look, then."

David maneuvered his car around cement blocks that formed a kind of barricade, then pulled off the paved roadway. He drove directly underneath the impressive steel structure, all the while talking about *Foucault's Pendulum* by Umberto Eco, a favorite novel of his that reached across time and traditions toward mystical truths and closed with a scene at the Eiffel Tower. I began to feel myself on a journey beyond the realities I knew and yanked myself back.

"Are you allowed to be doing this?" I asked, referring to his driving into clearly forbidden territory.

"There aren't any police around to stop me, are there?"

"Who are they?" I asked, pointing to the window in the office at the South Tower, the one with POLICE written over its doorway and with two astonished gendarmes staring at us.

"Oops!" he said. Flashing that smile, he nodded to them, tipped his hat, and reversed his car back onto the pavement.

As we drove alongside the river, tiny lights twinkled on the opposite bank, forming a high, transparent wall of glitter. I gasped and asked David what they were. I have always loved light, whether natural or artificial, and especially any light that twinkles, shimmers, or blinks on and off. David parked the car alongside the roadway, came around to open my door, casually took my hand, and escorted me across the street, gently navigating a busy thoroughfare without the aid of traffic lights. We stood leaning against the waist-high wall that separated the sidewalk from the Seine below, and he pointed across the water to the home of the Bateaux Mouches, boats that glide up and down the Seine, showing tourists the city from yet another perspective (great for optometrists). The trees above and behind them were strung with countless transparent Christmas-tree lights, elusive stars against a lush background of chestnut trees, the whole display framed by the golden glow of lampposts and monuments that defined central Paris after dark. Reflections danced on the surface of the Seine as though they were Tinker Bells celebrating spring in the balmy night.

Any lingering anxiety that I had sensed in David vanished, and his natural radiance shone through. He was in his city, where he was clearly in perpetual awe and in command. And there it was: an omen. David's most enduring gift to me would be access to light, to sparks, to energy, as we traveled through our years together.

But on that last Friday night of March 1996, we were simply headed to our first shared dinner. Beneath us, the boats glided by, evening dinner cruises under way, an occasional working barge passing through Paris, a private yacht navigating toward its destination. Here, opposite Place de l'Alma, I could spot in the distance the beginning of the houseboat colony that lined the Right Bank at Cours de la Reine and beyond. I had no idea what was about to be revealed.

"You know, I live on one of them," David said casually.

"You live on one of what?"

"Those boats. I live on a houseboat."

"You what?"

"Didn't she tell you? I've been living on a converted Dutch barge since 1982."

I had no response. I had never known anyone who actually lived on a boat before. I'm not even certain that it had registered that people actually did live on boats. Certainly not in the middle of Paris. And now here I was, about to spend an evening with one of those people. How intriguing!

Back in the car, David drove along the river then turned onto rue Surcouf, a two-block-long side street lined with little restaurants. After masterfully parking, he walked me to the end of the street, to rue St. Dominique, and asked me to turn to the right. I gasped at the unexpected. The Eiffel Tower, illuminated with thousands of lights, looked like a pointed bridge made of golden lace that arched across the end of the narrow shopping street. David smiled and then, when I stopped gawking, led me back onto rue Surcouf and through the third doorway on the right.

Du Côté 7ème, the restaurant at that location back then, was a small bistro with a stable clientele, a prix fixe menu, and clearly a long association with David. He was warmly greeted by an elegant woman at a hostess station near the entrance and by Patrick, a maître d' who seemed delighted to see him. I settled onto the crimson velour banquette, David opposite me, and breathed in the ambience of this small establishment that exuded festive but quiet comfort.

What do I remember? David reading the intoxicating menu to me, complete with translations that went far beyond the inaccuracies found on the English version that had been handed to me. The *kir royale* that seemed to appear out of nowhere: bubbly champagne and sweet cassis. "Bon appétit." The Poilâne toast that David lightly buttered and offered to me. The salad with a *crottin de chèvre* surpassing anything I had bought at my finest local market, and a rack of lamb roasted to pink perfection, all accompanied by a bottle of delicious wine from the Dordogne. An *île flottante*, espresso, brandy. The single, perfect floral arrangement on the counter that hid the cash register. The balcony that seemed to be as crowded as the restaurant below. But most of all and through it all, there was David and his electricity—this man who sat across from me, infinitely expressive lines in his rugged face and those soft brown eyes that occasionally danced with secrets shining behind them; a voice that was thrilling to listen to in either language; a command of the situation; and an energy that would come to haunt me.

I know we talked about his grown children and mine, his road to Paris and mine back, and we must have touched on our respective daily lives a bit. I did learn that he was one of only two Americans living in the forty-eight-houseboat community in the center of Paris, a detail for which I had absolutely no frame of reference, and that he practiced international business law, representing mostly French companies at this point in his quarter century of working in Paris. He learned that I was a clinical psychologist and that I was in the midst of trying to downsize now that my children were grown. More recently, we had both had painful romantic relationships that had ended more than a year before. And there we were.

I sensed myself sitting straighter by the minute, shoulders releasing down and back, breathing becoming slower and deeper, aware of all my senses as rarely before, drinking in the moments and the thrill of sharing them along with the Bergerac that slipped so easily across my tongue. Around us, the soft French conversations receded and David became larger, taller, even more compelling. Meanwhile, he was just being David, casting his spell straight through to my unconscious while my conscious internal chatter was running something like, *This is pleasant. The man is interesting; he's led a somewhat untraditional life up to this point. He, too, chose not to pursue fame and fortune. And he really cares about and enjoys his kids. I like that.*

I told David about my earlier visits to Paris, the first during the magical five-week trip to Europe with my father when I was sixteen, newly graduated from high school, and nearing the end of a childhood lived in permanent chaos and often at near-poverty levels with my mother. That was back when my father had his haberdashery made at Sulka in Paris and his suits at Brioni in Rome. It was also when I had discovered escargots and champagne and cheeses as a separate course, the ballet at Opéra Garnier, red velvet and violins at Maxim's, the scanty (or absent) costumes of chorus girls at the Lido, a boat ride on the Seine, lunch surveying the landscape from Jules Verne in the Eiffel Tower, *Winged Victory* presiding over the top of her staircase at the Louvre. We had watched the world go by from front-row seats in cafés, studied windows of haute couture across the luxurious 8th arrondissement, sipped aperitifs and eaten crêpes on Place du Tertre. That was when a haircut had transformed my Midwestern adolescent self into the more sophisticated college freshman she hoped to become the following fall.

Three summers later, I combined the $600 from "child support"—the last year my father owed any legal obligation to help me financially—with $300 more that I had earned babysitting during my junior year at Barnard and used it to take myself back to Paris to study. Two years before, my father had gotten remarried, to a woman with three children of her own to raise. My mother had moved from Ohio to San Francisco, where she would become a secretary and then a locally recognized artist. I had needed a place to live when the spring semester ended; "home" no longer existed. Besides, I needed three additional credits in order to graduate the following spring. I had bought a ticket on a charter flight, enrolled in summer school at the Sorbonne, arranged housing at a women's residence on bd Raspail, packed forty pounds of clothes and miscellany into a single suitcase, and said good-bye to my boyfriend, who had failed to invite me to spend that summer in Connecticut with him and his family. That was the summer of living on *sandwiches au Camembert* and croissants; of walking fourteen miles the evening, night, and morning of Bastille Day; of mustering the courage to enter a tiny shop to buy a navy princess-cut coat when I was miserable because July nights were far colder than I had antici-pated. It was the summer of cutting through the Luxembourg gardens on the way to the stark but privileged classrooms of the Sorbonne. The summer of claiming the city as my own, mastering most of her arrondissements, and taking local trains to Chartres, to Versailles, to the Bois de Boulogne, to the races at Saint Cloud. I confided to David that, on my last day in Paris, I had stood facing the fountains at Place de la Concorde, my back to the gilded gates to the Tuileries, the Jeu de Paume on my right and the Orangerie on my left. I looked up at the Arch and back to the Louvre and vowed I would return to Paris but not until I could come back with a man I loved.

It never happened. Two years later, I was married to my boyfriend from my Barnard years, living in San Francisco, and pregnant. I joined Alliance Française, reluctant to let domestic needs and shifting pri-orities force my language skills into oblivion. But then my daughter was born and life took its turns and the years passed. Jennifer grew. I loved her and loved raising her and decided to have at least three more children.

We moved back to Connecticut and bought a four-bedroom colonial house in a new development behind a Catholic church in a neighborhood that was soon populated by many large families. I learned to manage the homestead, a social calendar, roles in community life. A miscarriage. Then a second daughter, Judith Hope, was born six weeks prematurely. Preemie resources being what they were then, she developed hyaline membrane disease, and, thirty-nine hours after her birth, she died. I was devastated. Two years later, I bore a son, and, after five hours of fighting to keep his tiny heart beating, Matthew Jay died also. He was riddled with congenital defects; had he lived, his inevitably short life would have been a saga of struggle and serial failures. I learned that my own life was not fully controllable—at least not by me. So much for planning. I also learned about grief.

The following summer, when Jennifer was four, we adopted Danny. Jennifer had taught me how my heart would just keep expanding. The more I loved her, the more love there was. It was a first lesson in learning that love is limitless, the ground of everything and not a figure superimposed on it. We don't "fall" in love; we remove barriers to loving. The tricky part is that loving is not always safe. But babies were another matter; loving them could only amplify joy. So I was not surprised when I fell totally and permanently in love with Danny the first time I cradled him in my arms. The mystical ferocity of the gift of connection to this soul who had dropped suddenly and unexpectedly into my life stayed with me permanently and informed and directed what was beginning during this trip to Paris in March 1996.

I knew I would need more internal and external resources if ever again I lost a being I loved. Relying on those who remained placed too great a burden on them and was ultimately insufficient anyway. So, when Danny was three, I went back to school, taking courses to transform my undergraduate religion major into a building block for a career in clinical psychology. When he was six, I began a full-time doctoral program. Skills developed through parenting, homemaking, financial management, and community participation were supplemented by those of research design and data collection, analysis and interpretation, assessment, interviewing, and intervention.

The years passed, bringing thrills and conflicts from watching the children grow and develop; the excitement and rewards of becoming a psychotherapist, a scientist, a competent adult who could make contributions to a larger world; and then the disappointment of shattered dreams and expectations when my marriage of sixteen years failed to survive the competing demands of graduate school, parenting, and professional responsibilities. My first husband and I never made it to Paris. The parts of me that I had discovered on her streets, in her cafés, infused with her language, became buried more and more deeply inside me.

A few years after the divorce, I met Stuart. He brought a brilliant capacity to see both forest and trees, a passionate commitment to whatever he took on, and the understanding and acceptance revealed when he gave me both a briefcase and a bottle of perfume for my birthday. I began to feel loved by a man who shared my worldview and spirit of discovery. Even better, he had the courage to design and build a house and home, create a family, explore new countries. Stuart and I married. Several months later, we sat on the patio of a Puerto Rican resort in February, planning a late-spring trip to Paris with the children in celebration of Jennifer's high school graduation. A month later, in another hotel room, following a Disney World dinner show, as Jennifer and Danny slept in the adjoining room at the Contemporary Hotel, this man whom the universe had uncannily brought to me began to turn blue in front of my eyes while I waited for the EMTs to arrive. After dinner, he had commented on discomfort in his neck and shoulder. He resisted my attempts to call the desk for a doctor, but finally I ignored him. I told him an ambulance with medical help was on the way. "Don't you think that's a bit much?" he protested. No. It was too little too late.

Picking up the pieces of our shattered lives took years. The practical parts were challenging but manageable. Jennifer, Danny, and I remained in the house in Westport that Stuart had built and into which we had moved less than a year before his death. With effort and sadness, we had left our cherished Fairfield home, schools, neighbors, the networks we knew and where we were known, and had begun adapting to the very different adjacent community we had moved into when Stuart and I married.

After Stuart's death, I wanted Danny to have the continuity of remaining in his nearby private school and returning to his beloved Camp Robin Hood in New Hampshire during the summers. Jennifer decided to attend Columbia College, perhaps in part so that she could remain close enough to help us out if we needed her. When Stuart died, I immediately canceled our golf club membership, returned his BMW to his employer, and moved my office into the house, knowing the next years could prove challenging financially. I expanded my practice, accepted Yale's invitation to teach again, and gradually wobbled back onto my feet as my heart began to heal.

Time passed. When I was alone on Thanksgivings, I went to London; when I totaled the Mercedes convertible that Stuart had left to me, I bought a reliable Honda. I made it to Danny's soccer, lacrosse, baseball, and basketball games and to New York to have lunch with my daughter.

Two years later, love came to me again in a different form. The three-room cottage in Tenants Harbor, Maine, offered silence; salt air from the ocean that lapped against the rocks at the end of the dirt path; and a sanctuary where I could peel away roles, return to the quiet of my own thoughts and feelings, and attend to them. There, I practiced identifying what genuinely attracted me and what made me move away. I had no business buying the cottage, but a bank was willing to give me a mortgage, a man who lived in an adjacent village was willing to keep an eye on it during storms and to do seasonal maintenance, and the realtor who had found it was willing to help locate vacation tenants so that I could actually pay for the property with help from rental income. I needed something to absorb the love that I had unleashed in loving Stuart. The cottage, like my home in Fairfield, offered a symbiotic relationship: I took care of it, and it took care of me. I was determined not to ask my children to fill a void that was not their responsibility. Just as the house in Fairfield had become my "good mother," the one in Maine became my dollhouse, taking care of the aching little girl inside while the adult worked and parented. A home can be far more than shelter.

More time passed—years. The children grew up and launched adult lives. I grew stronger, more resilient, and even able to provide a few bells and whistles—trips for and with the kids; some paint and new furniture that made the house look and feel more like me; serviceable, classic suits; and massage therapy. I knew how much I needed to be touched.

Eventually there were men in my life. One long relationship became a third marriage. Once it was over, I wondered if I had somehow needed to punish myself for losing Stuart. But probably I had merely deluded myself into thinking I was more self-sufficient, needing nothing, than I really was. I had sealed off the parts of myself that had known the joy of being cared for, taken care of. And I was seduced by the idea that a man eight years my junior might be attracted to me, as well as by his charisma. After he helped me deplete my emotional and financial reserves, the relationship saw its painful end.

My girlfriends tried to help relieve the distress. They gave me indulgent gifts—a certificate for a facial, a ticket to the ballet, even a surprise party for my fiftieth birthday. In the winter of 1994, the hardest one, a friend handed me a set of keys to her office. On Sundays throughout the cold season that year, I bought a *pain aux raisins* at the new French bakery across the street, then unlocked the door to her quiet space in the building where I had rented my first office. After savoring my pastry, I lay down on the floor of that back room in the building on Bay Street. Meditating. Observing. The week I had spent in silence at an ashram in the Catskills helped me breathe through the most painful of the memories and moments.

And then, just as suddenly and perfectly—just as had happened when I had most needed to be able to love and felt I'd done as much as I could, just as Danny had dropped into my life, then Stuart, then the cottage in Maine—Luke appeared. In January 1995, when I arrived at my Pilates studio for an early-morning workout, I saw an empty crate sitting by the wall. I asked about it, and an instructor explained that the owner, a friend, was resting in the massage room with a dog; the crate belonged to him. I learned that my friend and her fiancé had bought the three-month-old bichon as a Christmas gift for his mother. At seventy-five, she doubted her ability to care for a puppy, and so Luke was sentenced to return to the breeder the following weekend. I asked if I could take him home overnight. He remained by my side from that day on—an angel, a miracle, a place to put loose, nurturing love after my children had grown up, the key to healing yet again. I was convinced that Stuart, who himself loved dogs, sent this small mass of white fluffiness with big black eyes to help heal my heart.

One year later, Luke and I were muddling through our second January together, roaming around our big, empty house, shoveling lots of snow, and greeting patients as they made their way around to the entrance at the back, the one that led directly into the family room turned waiting room adjacent to my pretty office. Luke sat patiently outside the closed office door while I met with clients, except for the one woman who found the puppy such a comfort that he joined us during our sessions. At night, he slept above my head. The fall before I adopted him, for the first time in five decades of living in cold climates, I had wanted a fur coat. When I analyzed the desire, I realized I had wanted strong, hairy arms surrounding me. Luke was the perfect solution to the real need, far more satisfying and long-lasting than any clothing might have been.

Then, one January morning, I uncovered the *New York Times*, buried in its blue plastic wrapping, while shoveling snow to clear the driveway for an early patient. Inside was an Air France ad: $279 round-trip to Paris. I heard a younger version of myself saying, *You will come back to Paris—but not until you can return with a man you love.* And then I heard an internal voice answer, *Yeah, sure. You're fifty-two years old. It's not going to happen. You cannot spend the rest of your life waiting. You need to get on a plane and go back there.*

I picked up the phone and, finding the Air France flights full, booked a seat on TWA flight 800 to Paris on March 27, 1996, the last weekend the winter fare was available. It was also the twelfth anniversary of Stuart's death.

For a fee, Luke's groomer was willing to board him in her home, where he played well with her own seven small dogs and where I knew he would be safe and cared for over a long weekend. And I had two of those hotel coupons that used to accompany frequent-flier awards— pay for one night, get the second one free. My only excuse for not going to Paris any longer was money. Because of my best efforts to stop the financial and emotional hemorrhage that had resulted from my last relationship, I no longer enjoyed the little luxuries that I had provided for myself for years. But I made mortgage payments on time; credit cards, my car, and the kids' college bills were paid in full; and I was working to cut back on the expenses of the house through a radical change in lifestyle as soon as possible. I even considered relying on my research to generate an academic position, an additional career path with simpler emotional demands.

I shared very few of these details with David that first weekend, remembering my yoga teacher's warning: "Yesterday is history, tomorrow a mystery, today a gift, which is why we call it the present." The moments we shared that first evening were what counted, and I was delighted to be doing something I did well: listening.

Paris had also enchanted David. He had spent 1960-61, his junior year, there in a study-abroad program from Princeton, and had returned to the United States determined to make France and the French way of life his own. After graduating in 1962, he had married a high school sweetheart and gone with her to Paris, where he attended the prestigious Insitut d'Études Politiques de Paris, commonly known as Sciences Po, graduating third or fourth in his class from his graduate program in international relations. David had been a twenty-two-year-old married man when I was a nineteen-year-old college senior learning to live on my own. Separate paths, both in Paris.

We soon learned that we shared more than the factual details of spending the summer of 1963 in Paris, marrying young, and having two grown children, the older ones both born in 1966. As we began to compare life histories, David was struck by the extent to which we had both walked out on a kind of visible professional success as our parents and peers, or those who had educated us, had defined it at that time. And we had both made our choices out of love. After earning my doctorate in clinical psychology at Yale, I interviewed for academic jobs but ultimately chose not to displace my children and move them far from their father and his extensive family by accepting a tenure-track offer from the University of North Carolina, UCLA, or Bryn Mawr. I refused to fight a potentially ugly court battle to gain geographical freedom, so, instead of becoming an academic, I opened a clinical practice in Westport, the town adjacent to our Fairfield. I loved my children fiercely and wanted to cause them as little pain as possible. Loving well came first. Meanwhile, I could do meaningful work that suited me and earn enough money to support us. I became a lecturer at Yale, initially full-time, replacing a professor on sabbatical, and then, following Stuart's death, teaching one course per semester for some years.

David, on the other hand, treasured his freedom. What he wanted from his career was support for living in the gentle and respectful manner he had discovered in France during his junior year of college and those two years of graduate study. Proudly holding his degree from Sciences Po, he inquired about jobs. Prospective French employers advised him to go back to the United States and earn a Harvard law degree.

So David and his wife returned to the United States. They spent three years in Cambridge, where Scott was born the summer before David's final year of law school. David managed to juggle parenthood, social life, moot court (his team won the final-year competition), Legal Aid Society, and classwork. He remembers three trips to Boston in as many years. When he again looked to be hired in Paris, he was told to gain legal experience in New York. So he and his family moved to Forest Hills and he scrambled to do good work in the corporate department of Weil, Gotshal & Manges. In 1969, Adam was born in New York City, and the years passed. David was sent to Paris only once on assignment and realized he would have to jump off the partner track and create his own path if he wanted to follow his dream. And so, motivated by love for a city that encouraged him to become the person he liked being, he took his wife and two boys, then ages three and six, and moved back to Paris. The year was 1972.

At first, David worked in an office with ties to his firm in New York. Soon after, in 1975, he set up his own law firm with a French partner. David developed specialties within international law: pharmaceuticals, banking, and entertainment. As his reputation grew, he was consulted more and more on matters requiring cultural appreciation and understanding. First he worked with American companies doing business in France. Soon he began representing French companies and their interests, not only in the United States but around the world. Eventually he worked with French clients who did business "only" in France.

In 1977, he and his wife separated, and the following year, she and the boys moved to Fort Lee, New Jersey. Scott and Adam spent winter holidays and summer vacations with David in France. They saw him during his frequent business trips to the United States and on most school vacations. Indeed, only a week before that night when we sat in the restaurant on rue Surcouf, sharing our first meal together, David's sons, then twenty-nine and twenty-six, had been sleeping on the boat at the end of a ski trip with their father to Tignes–Val d'Isère, repeating an annual ritual they had shared for nearly twenty-five years. After that last night in Paris, the boys had returned to the United States and their respective adult lives, Scott to his new wife and Adam to graduate school.

Those were the outlines. I learned all that and more during our first dinner together. Both David and I were committed to education and to working as hard as we could to learn and to apply what we had learned well. Both of us had walked away from fast tracks to fame and fortune. And both of us sat there, single, uncommitted, and very definitely *not* looking.

Eventually our conversation turned toward our romantic lives. I admitted the painful years I had just endured; David shared the story of a recent lesson he had learned from a relationship that was sexually exciting but had no meaningful substance and had threatened to leave him diminished, definitely not feeling good about or comfortable with himself. In other words, we had both been hurt. Were vulnerable. Not interested. And, underneath the conscious surface, completely available. I don't remember the details, but, as our initial phone conversation indicated, I do recall thinking that David was a man who was ready to shift perception, to see situations from new angles, to contemplate alternative ways of thinking and being. He was open to and capable of learning.

By the time Patrick returned to take our dessert orders, we had emptied the bottle of Bergerac and enjoyed each mouthful of food as much as each earful from each other. Suddenly, I could not find any reason to deny myself that *île flottante avec crème anglaise* that so tempted me. And I can still remember that first delicate, airy taste, as the spoonful of custard-coated meringue slipped into my mouth. Pure pleasure. That evening was so uncharacteristic of me: usually I drank very little alcohol, severely limited fats and sugars, and had trained myself to think of food solely in terms of calories and nutritional content. Desserts were not on my list of permitted luxuries. But discipline was melting away. Patrick brought us coffee. The restaurant began to empty out. He brought us "digestifs, *offerts*," after-dinner cordials, compliments of the owner.

As we sipped our drinks, David invited me to dinner on the following night.

"I have an opening tomorrow, an art exhibition outside Paris, but I can get back by late afternoon and would like to take you to dinner. I have something else I am supposed to do tomorrow night—a couple who are in Versailles; her 104-year-old grandmother just died—but I can postpone that a bit."

I smiled. With excitement, I added, "There is a concert at Sainte-Chapelle. I read about it in the *Officiel*. Vivaldi's *Four Seasons*. If I can get tickets, would you like to go to that first?" I had studied the *Officiel* well, crafting a weekend whose memories could weave a cashmere blanket to keep me warm the following winter.

"Sure," he said. "Give me a call late afternoon, and we can make plans."

We looked around and realized we were the last people in the restaurant. Rather than showing impatience, Patrick and Marie-Paule stood near the front counter with all those flowers, grinning at us with complicity. Remember, David was a regular.

3

Learning More

The next morning, I was up and out of my room like a shot. My list had barely a dent in it, and it was already Saturday. I must be organized, planful, efficient. I would go to the Marais first, getting off the metro at Hotel de Ville and walking down rue de Rivoli until it turned into rue St. Antoine, and then turn left until I wiggled through the neighborhood to the side street with the new Picasso Museum. From there to Beaubourg and then across to Île de la Cité and Sainte-Chapelle to see about tickets. I was becoming comfortable traveling around Paris, even though many of the routes and destinations still seemed only vaguely familiar.

As I approached the church Sainte-Marie on rue St. Antoine, I was swept into a stream of people headed toward it. Of course! This was Palm Sunday weekend. Mass would be said today all across the still heavily Catholic, if less practicing, city. I claimed a seat in a pew and closed my eyes. Meditating in a space consecrated to the spirit, the foreign languages that surrounded me only adding to the mystery, I said my constant prayer: *Please, God. Help me see thy will, and help me do it.*

After leaving the church, I made my way through the Marais to the mansion that had been renovated to hold Picasso's lifework. At that time, the art was arranged developmentally and I could follow the giant's evolution, learning style, and mistresses (and models) as he grew into and then evolved through adulthood, mastering technique after technique, later bringing them together, superimposing one skill set and internalized approach onto another. Would that I could do that with my life, I yearned. All the pieces, the chapters, seemed so disjointed, so muddled, at this moment. I was the Midwestern girl who had survived a childhood filled with polarity between her divorced parents and their lifestyles; who had been conditioned to fill the assigned role of expressing whatever my mother denied within herself. When I left Ohio, the relief of finding an adult inside me who could learn how to care for herself brought both astonishment and comfort. When I was seventeen, the childhood nurturing moments with my father were buried under the years of alienation that followed because of demands from his second wife. Thankfully, we were able to reconstruct and transform our relationship during his later years: the luxury of the fine restaurants and embroidered handkerchiefs he had once brought to me was replaced by the best meals I could create in my own kitchen and by his discovery of bargains at our local outlet stores. We came to love and appreciate each other and to cherish his visits to Westport in those years after his semiretirement and before his death.

When I was a child, my father introduced me to the world of art, and now, decades later, here I was, walking through room after room filled with treasures, moving through history with Picasso, from his childhood early in the twentieth century toward his later years during the 1960s and early '70s, when I had come of age. If there was a heaven, I knew my father was up there, smiling at me.

Amid the jumble of my moments in Paris, pieces of the puzzle that was me *were* coming together. My father's legacy of sensual pleasure, beauty, and adventure had always nourished the adult in me. He had taught me that the world beyond the one I had known in Akron, Ohio, could inspire, inform, comfort. But my mother's example of using seduction to exploit others as she gratified her needs for attention and admiration, or tried to satisfy her material wants, had been mirrored in my last relationship and had made me wary of being manipulated by charm, brilliance, all that glittered and glowed. Instead, I clung to meaning and gratitude in responsibility and opportunities to care for others. Coming to terms with the full range of my wants and needs still required some work; appreciation and exploration of my own sensuality had yet to occur. As when I had been young, Paris inevitably grounded me, opening my emotions in response to her beauty, her balance, her legacy of being loved; my legs and feet felt the connection to the cobblestones and to my own creativity as I walked.

I wandered across to Beaubourg, the Centre Pompidou, where François Mitterand had overseen the construction of a big box of a museum with dual purposes: it was designed to be both a home for the modern art owned by the French Republic and a gathering spot for the populace. The sloping plaza that led to its doors was to be filled with street artists, mimes, and musicians, each one attracting a crowd that would sit or stand in a cluster surrounding the magnetic performer. This museum, created with a commitment to democracy and transparency, made the building itself a metaphor: the entire infrastructure was color-coded to identify plumbing, wiring, transportation functions. An outside series of escalators made a diagonal climb to the top of the sixth floor, depositing passengers on a balcony with breathtaking views of Parisian rooftops and streets to the south, west, and north below and to vistas beyond them. Permanent collections on the fourth and fifth floors included a set of four bronze relief sculptures of a woman's back created by Matisse over more than two decades. Again, I was struck by an artist's development, changes in perception as he himself grew and evolved. The first piece, created by Matisse around his fortieth birthday, was fluid, representational, in progress. Gradually, across the twenty-two years during which he created the other three, clarity increased until his work eventually expressed an almost transcendent pure essence. I prayed that I could continue to grow over time, too. That one day I, too, could be clear and uncluttered.

Notions of development, transformation, and evolution floated in and out of my thoughts as I left Beaubourg, passed the bustling stalls and shops surrounding it, and headed down bd Sebastopol toward the river. I had a destination: the afternoon was passing quickly, and Sainte-Chapelle sat across a bridge, on the far side of Île de la Cité, opposite the Left Bank.

"*Bonjour, madame. S'il vous plaît, avez-vous deux billets pour* Les Quatre Saisons *ce soir?*" I asked the woman at the box office, proud of my halting French.

"*Mais, madame, ce n'est pas ce soir.*"

Here we go again, I thought. *Are my days still mixed up?*

I asked her to repeat, *s'il vous plaît.*

"*The Four Seasons* is for Sunday, tomorrow, not this evening," she replied, her English practiced and her patience in dealing with Americans evident.

Oops. Pleadingly, I asked her if she could make a telephone call for me and showed her a slightly used napkin with writing on it. She smiled, pleased to accommodate this flustered and obviously exhausted tourist. She dialed David's number and handed me the receiver. Luckily, he answered, back from his event earlier than I had expected.

"Hi. I'm at Sainte-Chapelle, and the concert isn't tonight; it's tomorrow night. Would you still like to go?"

"Sure. But I hope that doesn't mean we can't have dinner tonight also," he replied, unconsciously translating the omnipresent French double negatives into English.

"I would love it. Okay. I'll get tickets for tomorrow night. What time is good tonight?"

"Would you like to see the boat?"

"Sure."

"We could have an *aperitif* on the boat before dinner, or come back after dinner for a *digestif*, or both."

"Before." I was decisive. No way was I getting myself into any situation that could present confusion on my part or expectation on his. How well I understood that physical connection could lead me to

ignore inconvenient information that I might discover once I knew
a man better. Aware that I had a lot of love available to give and that
loving was not always safe, I needed to erect barriers to loving and
remove them slowly, carefully, only with full consent from both my
head and my heart—to say nothing of my body!

"Okay. I'll pick you up at seven, and we'll have a drink on the boat
before we go to dinner."

The woman at the box office clearly enjoyed the conversation that
David and I were having. Indeed, throughout our history together, the
French have always responded to and positively encouraged our love
story, acting as angels smiling down on us and easing our paths, no
matter where we were going. In this case, she sold me two tickets for
Sunday night's performance of the Vivaldi piece. She smiled know-
ingly (ah, what French women know and don't tell the men) as she
directed me toward the RER-C stop at Place St. Michel.

Again, David was right on time. Juggling the few pieces of clothing
I had with me, I had chosen the short black leather pencil skirt and
the cashmere sweater for Saturday night. A scarf probably added
some color. David did a double take when he saw me without the
shoulder pads and pristine white blouse, my grandmothers' pearl
circle pin centered at the collar. He led me to his car, and we again
began to follow the river. Only gradually did I grasp how the curves
in the Seine require shifting perceptions as the angles of the landscape
change along with the river's path. Just like a lifeline.

David drove over a bridge to the Right Bank, then turned onto
a ramp that led down to the river. He punched some numbers on a
keypad, signaling the gate at the entrance to slide open, and then drove
down the remaining driveway and along the cobblestone banks of the
Seine, under Pont de la Concorde, eventually parking his car against
the stone wall that separated the river from the streets and sidewalk
high above it. He helped me out of the car and guided me along a

plank onto a large white yacht, the *Christina*, and then across it to descend onto another boat, the converted barge that was the Berreti. I followed him onto a makeshift step, a wooden wine crate with the worn writing ROTHSCHILD still recognizable. He walked ahead of me and ushered me onto his houseboat. The sun had just set, and night was falling quickly. Lights came on, one by one, in the windows of the apartment buildings lining the Left Bank along the Seine. Street lamps added a soft glow to the river. Other lights began to blaze or blink. I took in the lit towers of Notre Dame to the left, the golden lights of the Eiffel Tower to my right. The framed facade of the Assemblée Nationale lay straight ahead on the other side of the river.

After unlocking the door and inviting me into the driving cabin, David led me down a short open staircase into his kitchen and then down another step into the living room. A fire glowed in the brick fireplace in the center of the back wall of the room. It formed a corner separating the area with a trunk containing his liquor from the corridor that led to the cabin where his children slept when visiting. Farther down the narrow hall were the master bedroom, then a utility room with a porcelain sink, decorated with hand-painted flowers, a tiny washing machine, and, of all things, a miniature freezer. The toilet and shower were at the opposite end of the long barge, behind the driving cabin.

An impressive stereo system filled the air with Chopin, the roses on the cocktail table with scent, the polished paneling and pure brass trimmings with authenticity and warmth. This was the real thing. A converted barge in the middle of the river in the middle of Paris where this man actually lived. Books were everywhere. End tables piled high with books, mostly novels, shelves double-stacked, a pile on the floor here and there. But on the coffee table were only the roses, a bowl with something exotic and crunchy in it, and Kodak envelopes, each carefully labeled. David poured me something delicious to drink in a crystal glass and then sat next to me on the sofa.

"Tell me the story," I said. "How did you come to be here?"

We had nearly an hour before we needed to leave for dinner. Just long enough for David to tell me about the boat and to show me photographs of trips that he and his boys had made on it, year after year, teenagers growing into men, as they cruised the rivers and canals of France during the summer, from 1982 until 1995. A counter separated the kitchen area from the living room, and only as I was leaving did I notice, sitting on the window ledge above the sink, several postcard-size photographs of beautiful women, some nude and provocative.

David had formally become a bachelor living in Paris in 1978, when his wife returned to the United States, taking the boys with her. A year before, he had begun renting a small apartment in the 7th arrondissement on rue Malar, just off rue St. Dominique, and he had remained there until he bought the boat in 1982. From his new quartier, he had created new patterns, walking to his office on bd. Malesherbes, frequenting a few favorite restaurants in his new neighborhood, ambling over to the Champs-Élysées for a movie with some regularity. He made new friends.

One new friend, originally a client, was Dan Rowan. He and his wife, Joanna, and David had begun spending more and more time together. Joanna loved to cook, and David loved to eat, and so she loved to cook for him. All this on the barge they had bought and converted when Dan had retired from making comedy with Dick Martin on *Laugh-In*.

One day, David's secretary suggested he pick up his office phone. The following conversation occurred in French, but I have translated it, for I heard the story in English.

"I hear you are looking for a boat," the voice announced.

"I'm not looking for a boat. What are you talking about?"

"Dan Rowan said you are looking to buy a boat. I have one that is going to be for sale."

"I am *not* looking to buy a boat," David repeated. "But where is it? Maybe I'll come look, just for fun."

The call came on a Friday. On Saturday David visited the boat. On Sunday he negotiated a price, and on Monday he went to his office and drew up a purchase contract. He had bought himself a *peniche*, one of the houseboats in the forty-eight-boat community nestled between Place de l'Alma and the footbridge, in line for reconstruction, that was then named Passerelle de Solferino, on the Right Bank of the Seine, in the center of Paris. He told no one except his secretary, who typed the contract and was most enthusiastic; he was determined to follow an impulse that came from his heart, his soul. He was not interested in arguing with anyone who might try to talk him out of it.

David did not know much about boats when he bought the Berreti. Indeed, he had become violently seasick during Atlantic crossings years before. But he knew that he was a good learner, could master driving it and earn his river pilot's license quickly, and would have fun discovering and maintaining all the quirky mechanical and other systems unique to homeowning when the home usually stands still in water but also moves at will.

Did David fall in love with the two-centuries-old polished pine paneling that had been salvaged from a dismantled Dutch church? Or with the *idea* of a barge that had been built in Utrecht in 1928 and later converted by a Dutch ship's carpenter? Did he fall in love with the light as it bounced off the river and danced in through the windows? Did he fall in love with a dream of floating through the waterways of France, his boys with him, as they discovered the countryside and each other? Did he fall in love with the community itself, only one other American and folks from all backgrounds, vocations, and perspectives? You could not have gotten farther from a golf club in Scarsdale than David's boat on the Seine. I reminded myself that people told me what they wanted me to know when they were ready for me to know it, and that I would have to let him tell his story in his own way and time. In addition, I must have understood intuitively David's fierce need to "drive the car," so I kept these questions to myself.

And so David had moved onto the Berreti. He earned his boating license in record time, cheerfully let his friend and client, renowned French chanteuse and showgirl Line Renaud, the real Mademoiselle from Armentières, buy him some rattan furniture, and carefully chose equipment for his kitchen: three bowls, three mugs, three plates, and three sets of silverware. Enough for himself and his boys. No more. Perfect.

Over the years he added planters for masses of impatiens on deck during the summer; a trunk full of *aperitifs*, *digestifs*, and Scotch; the perfect stereo system and a library of music, as well as of fiction; four crystal champagne glasses. He collected maps of the French waterways and drove on rivers and canals, through the locks, tying up at scenic spots along the way. He tended the engine room with required regularity, much as the Little Prince weeded his baobabs. On his boat David became master of his life, free to play and discover and invent. He sprayed special adhesive on jigsaw puzzles that he had assembled and then hung them on the walls; he taped posters bought from the *bouquinistes*, some of them provocative, on walls and doors. One fairly erotic woodcut decorated the bathroom. He vacuumed the carpeting and polished the brass and wood and washed his windows. In the summer he swabbed his decks and sat in his bathing suit in the sun, reading his books, smiling at tourists who crossed the Pont de la Concorde and looked down at him.

Initially, David did not tell the boys about the boat. During the winter trip when they discovered that their father had moved, he picked them up as usual at the airport. But this time he had oars in the backseat.

"What are those?" they asked.

"Oars," he answered.

In a typical fashion that I later came to know, they nodded and, knowing their dad, asked no further questions. Then David parked the car in a new location, on the "other" side of the river.

The Seine had risen and flooded onto its banks. Parking alongside the *Christina* was no longer possible. They needed to cross to the barge in a rowboat tied up at the foot of a ladder attached to the stone wall. After they climbed down, David lowered the luggage into the rowboat, put his confused sons inside along with it, and handed them the oars. He climbed in, and they officially began a new chapter together.

Now, fourteen years later, he was introducing me to his home and, through the photographs, to his other most precious attachment: his boys. Packet after packet, we looked at pictures together. I watched Scott and Adam grow over time. The winter when Scott could not ski because of a cast the length of his leg (a soccer injury) and they all spent Christmas vacation with Dan and Joanna at their beach house on the west coast of Florida. The summer when David, with Scott and his girlfriend (soon to be wife), Stefanie, visited Leslie Caron at her country inn and restaurant in Villeneuve-sur-Yonne. They tied up alongside it, and she joined them on the boat for drinks before dinner. The summers with the boys handling the lines, misjudging the width of a lock, enthusiastically salvaging food offered by a tourist barge that would have gone to waste when its generator failed. Riding bicycles through villages, searching for the *boulangerie* with the best baguette, the *patisserie* with the best croissants and *pains au chocolat*, the *bistrot* with the best *sole meunière*, always a favorite of Adam's. Somewhere between Sens and Joigny, as we sat next to each other on the sofa in the center of the living room of the Berreti, music playing, fire blazing, our thighs casually touched. Electricity shot through me. We both pretended not to notice.

The picture packets slowly stacked into a "seen" pile, the fire burned down, whatever delicious thing I was drinking disappeared, and David escorted me back across the *Christina*, back to the car, back to a more familiar world.

He had made a reservation at La Boule d'Or, another nearby restaurant that was a notch quieter, a smidgeon more romantic, definitely more expensive, and notably more suited to an actual "date." From the glass of champagne before dinner to the lemon soufflé that ended the meal, we talked. Paris. His life. My life. His dreams. My dreams. My closeness to my children, along with a determination that I not cling too tightly to them. His pleasure in the world he had created, the life he had created. Again, we closed the restaurant, oblivious to the tables around us or the staff serving us. After dinner he drove me all around the city, showing off the lights that lit her up at night, the monuments, the sometimes bustling but always orderly street life.

"What do you have planned for tomorrow? Other than *The Four Seasons* at Sainte-Chapelle in the evening, of course."

"I want to go to church; it's Palm Sunday."

"I thought you said you were Jewish."

"I am. But I love churches. Even more, I love church services. Wanna come?"

He was silent for a minute. He clearly did not normally include church services in his Sunday routine (or on his dates, even with Christian women).

"Sure. I'll pick you up at ten. That should be a good time."

The clocks changed that night. Spring ahead, fall back. By the time we reached the Hilton it was nearly three in the morning, daylight savings time, the beautifully named *heure d'été* in France.

On Sunday, David took me to the nondenominational American Church, mistakenly reasoning that I might want to understand the service (in English). I was not interested in understanding, only in being in the space, among the prayers, people who were praying, lost in my own gratitude. Again our thighs bumped against each other, this time as we slid over in the pew to make room for another worshipper. Another current of electricity. A beautiful service. A palm branch upon leaving—a symbol or a souvenir.

David guided me across the broad green expanse of the Esplanade des Invalides, explaining that Paris had put much of its parking underground some years back, permitting lawns and gardens to be groomed and transformed into welcoming spaces for lovers on a blanket, families with a picnic, a dog walker or strolling tourist or person looking for a pickup soccer game or a place to play *boules* or toss a Frisbee. At the far corner, we reached a small, gated garden and stopped to sit on a bench, observe the plantings, move backward in time.

"I grew up in the Midwest, and those roots run deep. I am not particularly sophisticated, although I've lived in the East most of my life," I said.

"And I grew up in the Catskills. At least, the part I remember. Until then, we moved a lot. When I applied to colleges, my mother helped me list the schools I had attended. There were fifteen of them before we landed in South Fallsburg for the eighth grade."

"Wow," I commented, trying to imagine a childhood with that level of geographic mobility.

"It was good for me. Made me adaptable. Good to discover new places, learn to live with different rules."

"Do you have siblings?"

"A sister. Younger. She lives in New York. She loves New York. She's in law school right now. When she turned fifty, after our parents had both died, she decided to go to law school."

"Are you close?"

"We're pretty different. But she gets to Paris often, and I get to New York."

"Is she married? Kids?"

"Never married. No kids. She made a career out of being on the cutting edge of fashion trends in the city. Then a career working in television—*What's My Line?*, *I've Got a Secret*, some others. She lives with a man she's been with for a while now."

We crossed the bd des Invalides to rue de Varenne, and David steered me into the Rodin Museum.

"This is probably my favorite museum in Paris. I love sculpture. Took lessons in it for a while." Another one of those discreet, unpretentious throwaway lines of his. But, in fact, I had noticed some small, smooth, sensual pieces on tables in his living room.

He continued, "This is the first museum I insisted the boys visit with me. They were reluctant, and when we left Scott announced, 'Well, I didn't like *everything*.' In fact, he loved *Le Cri*. I'll show it to you."

We entered the mansion where Auguste Rodin had lived, loved, and worked. Room after room of carved fireplaces and moldings, carefully arranged parquet or marble floors, tall windows that opened to views of gardens. A few paintings. And oh, the sculpture! When we reached a certain room, David pointed out the work of Camille Claudel, a student and then mistress of Rodin, her work compelling in its own right. He told me the story of her eventual decompensation and how her brother, the well-connected author Paul Claudel, engineered a campaign to lock her up in an asylum. We studied *The Gates of Hell*, the *Monument aux Bourgeois de Calais*, the cases illustrating Rodin's commitment to Michelangelo's belief that the stone held its message within and the task of the sculptor was to expose the essence. I felt as if I were peeling away layers obstructing my own essence as we walked along.

After a stroll through the garden, David led me to a brasserie on the opposite side of the Invalides. We ordered coffee, and I asked if he could request some bread. Having skipped both breakfast and lunch, I was beginning to feel the hunger. Indeed, having skipped a part of my self for so long, I sensed weakening walls of the sequestered part warning of eventual collapse. David asked for *une tartine, s'il vous plaît*, and the waiter brought two huge slices of baguette slathered with an obscenely thick layer of that delicious butter. No silverware. I looked at it and did not know what to do. So I began to eat it. Bite by bite, licking the sweet grease off my lips as I chewed the crusty treasure that transported it. Unobtrusively and with that great impish grin, David silently reached across the table, picked up the second slice, and scraped the bulk of the butter off with the back of his coffee spoon. Equally silently, I handed him the one I had already begun eating.

David guided me back to his car. He was wearing a woven patchwork vest that matched his Irish knit hat: blues and purples and dark greens and just perfect against his ruddy skin, deep brown eyes, sandy hair. No jacket. Eventually he admitted that the air had turned cool. I was grateful for my coat. One of our biggest differences emerged: David preferred the brisk restraint of fall and winter, the oranges and golds and reds giving way to whites and grays and browns, while I liked the heat, spring and summer bringing their bright blues, pinks, purples, yellows, and greens, along with an invitation to shed layers of the self, as well as clothing. David was a fan of French "discretion," leaving questions unanswered and facts ambiguous, while I believed in transparency, self-disclosure, that it was always better to know than not to know.

We drove along the river, then parked a mile or so farther along the Left Bank, on a side street near the beginning of Île de la Cité. He guided me through the winding streets with their charming shops and colorful clientele. The arcade with one restaurant after another. Down to Place St. Michel, where I recognized the bookstores from my student days. We crossed the bridge onto the island. Casually, David pointed out the Palais de Justice and commented that he would be returning the following Thursday for some hearings at the law courts.

We made our way into Sainte-Chapelle, a gem of a thirteenth-century Gothic chapel, built to glorify precious relics. Up the narrow staircase, into the main chapel, to unassigned seats with perfect perspectives. Because of the time change, we were able to watch the light shift, as the sun set soon after the first movement began. Again David and I sat next to each other. Again our thighs touched. This time they remained connected, though again we pretended not to notice. I wondered whether my dizziness came from the bliss of the baroque music, the biology of too little food that day, or something other, something mysterious and progressive and unstoppable.

After the concert, David took me to dinner at a romantic, rustic restaurant on Place Dauphine, behind Sainte-Chapelle. He explained that Bistro du Palais was named with typical Gallic wordplay: *Palais* for the Palais de Justice on the north, and *palais*, also French for "palate," where the taste buds taste. Two Irish setters, along with their mistress, greeted guests. Our candlelit plank table was near the flaming fireplace, warming the chilly late March night, and we sat opposite each other, ready for more moments of pure being. We shared a bit more history. Somehow we got around to my sadness upon burying my second and third babies, and David told me that his first child, a daughter, had been stillborn at term. Tears trickled across my cheeks when we spoke of that chapter in our lives, but when I looked up, I saw

David smiling. He handed me two thin, silky-smooth business cards. Later I learned that Benneton the engraver was located on the ground floor of David's previous office building. It fulfilled all his stationery needs, and he had become friends with the owner.

"Take one and write down your numbers on the other," he instructed. I just looked at him. Phone. Address. But here we were and this was Paris and I lived an ocean away in Westport, Connecticut, and my plane would leave the next morning and I would never be in the presence of this compelling man again. More and more, I began to believe I had met le Petit Prince in person. And he would return to his planet, untamed. At least not tamed by me. I wrote down my numbers and tucked the second card into my wallet.

We dutifully returned to the Hilton. David drew me to him, the closest we had been, and gave me a big hug. His strong arms brought so much heat that I could feel the ice inside melting, the walls crumbling, the armor that I had put in place to protect my heart disintegrating. "Take care of Roni Beth," he said. And as his arms encircled me for the first and only time that weekend, I felt something deep inside collapse, curves begin to resurface, warmth to surge. I stepped into the elevator and waved goodbye as two tiny tears dropped beneath those damned progressive lenses. Maybe if I had taken them off, he would have kissed me? The doors of the elevator closed. *Good thing I'm not going to see him again*, I thought. And went upstairs. Alone.

David called the next morning before I left the hotel. He said that his phones were acting up and asked me to call him at the office when I reached the airport. Feeling competent with my phone card, I agreed. The call from the airport was rushed, awkward, thank you for everything, I can't tell you how much I enjoyed the weekend.

I boarded the plane, stowed my red calico case in the overhead compartment, fastened my seat belt, and began repeating the mantra *just breathe*. I did not know what had happened to me. My heart was literally pounding, thumping inside my chest, announcing that it was alive and well and insisting that it would make its presence known. I felt filled with the magic that was David, the way he smiled and tilted his head and, like in the song, "the way he wore his hat." The way he treated me, talked to me, listened and commented intelligently. His irreverence and curious combination of near-rude directness, relentless avoidance of that which he did not want to address, and clear command of himself. I thought, *Here is a man who knows what makes him happy and does it.* He had taken my breath away.

My yoga teachers used to say, "When the student is ready, the teacher appears." The universe energetically arranges these things. Of course, a person needs to "show up," to do his or her part. Can't happen if instincts are ignored, no matter how impractical they may appear to be. That's where the leap of faith comes in. And only repeated tests over time can teach you how to hear and trust it. It's a paradox. As long as you think you are planning, trying to make dreams come true, you are spinning wheels. Destiny unrolls when you let go and hear it calling, relax into it, and yield to those scary choices. Which sometimes includes a lot of doing nothing, waiting, so that other important pieces can fall into place—especially important when another person is involved, one who necessarily digests information in his or her own way.

4

What Now?

The TWA jet landed at JFK midafternoon that Monday. I returned to a New York pace, hurrying to the off-site lot where I had left the Honda Civic. While waiting for the attendant to retrieve my car, I called the answering machine for messages. The sixth one stopped me cold.

"Hello, this is David Griff, the famous international lawyer. I am calling to welcome you home and, again, to thank you for a delightful weekend." He went on a bit longer, rambling over details of moments we had shared, but it was the voice that thrilled me, far more than the teasing words. His twinkle was in the tone. Later I copied his message onto a blank tape that I could listen to again and again. Having gotten somewhat used to his offbeat sense of humor, I caught the joke of the man who lived on a boat and rarely wore anything but jeans being a "famous international lawyer"—only to learn two years later that his "joke" was not totally fabricated.

David's message gave me the excuse to write a letter thanking him for three days of magic. He had called it *hors du temps*, outside of time. His office felt like an inappropriate destination for what I hoped would be a warm invitation to "continue our conversation," so I wrote "M. David P. Griff, Bateau Berreti, Paris, France," on the envelope, added postage, and, with unconscious trust that some invisible force would guide my written words to him, dropped it into the mailbox. A few days later, I could not resist and sent a follow-up note, thanking him again and attempting to describe details of my daily Connecticut life vividly enough that he might imagine the sparklies on the lake, the softness of my bichon puppy's fluffy white hair, the pride in moving a manuscript toward publication.

My orderly life just then was uncharacteristically chaotic. Applications for teaching jobs submitted. A journal article in final stages of preparation. My house was on the market but had not sold, and so my home was about to become a lucrative rental property for two years. The apartment I was moving into needed a closet, window shades, electrical work. While I had been in Paris, I had left the keys to the house with the divorced attorney who was to rent it. He wanted to show his older daughter her future home when she visited that weekend. The teen, perhaps still reacting to the recent sudden death of her mother, was not as ecstatic about the lake in the backyard, the grill on the deck, and the pool table in the family room as her father had thought she would be. When I called him yet again to ask for signed contracts, he quoted her as having announced dismally, "It needs a lot of work." The landlord of my future apartment had hired a friend and rented a van to help move some furniture the Friday following my return. And that Sunday, Renee and Matt, special friends since my San Francisco days in the '60s, were arriving with their truck to help move more personal belongings, like plants, clothes, and food, so that I would not need to pack them.

I did not want to abandon my house to a tenant without legal protection. The contracts had been due while I was in Paris. We had signed faxed copies, but I felt insecure without the originals properly executed. The house was by far my most important asset, and I was renting it, mostly furnished, to a stranger. These realities and a history of being too trusting had led me to seek legal advice, and my lawyer agreed I should have original documents. The contracts finally arrived that Friday morning inside an envelope left on the front stoop. They included multiple changes, handwritten across my lawyer's carefully prepared and agreed-to wording—the worst change being from a term of two years to one. There was no way I could let a man who believed such behavior acceptable live in my house. How could I ever trust him to water the plants? Pay the electric bills? Shovel the snow? Monitor teenagers' parties for drinking? Not spill coffee on the green leather sofas or red wine on the white flokati rug? Close the flue after a fire in one of the fireplaces, to prevent bats from nesting in the chimney?

Furious, I called the presumptuous man to tell him he had shocked and potentially hurt me and that the deal was off. Then I phoned a realtor. She came right over so that I could sign an agreement allowing her to negotiate a summer rental. April was late in the season but not impossible—Westport was a desirable summer destination.

I moved some furniture to the sublet apartment as planned that Friday, not knowing what lay ahead. The bulk of it came from my spacious downstairs office and, perhaps because of the Oriental rug, created a warm and cozy living room. My own king-size bed was too big to cart up the narrow stairwell, so I took Jennifer's queen mattress, along with a trundle so that the kids could stay over. The rest was improvised from camp trunks, folding tables, and shelving from the cellar. I added just enough equipment to render the kitchen and bathroom serviceable and brought some of the smaller plants for their company and oxygen. The apartment's dining area was transformed into a combined office–eating space. I stayed in the big house, however, because there was no good reason to leave it. My bed and clothes remained, along with other necessities, while Luke and I lingered, waiting for the lucrative summer rental contract to materialize and be signed.

The Saturday morning following our Monday farewells, the day after my furniture went to Fairfield, at precisely four in the afternoon his time and ten in the morning in Connecticut, the phone rang.

"David!" I squealed, unable to mask the utter glee I felt at hearing his unmistakable voice again.

"Hi. I thought I'd check up on you, see how you're doing."

We chatted casually, bringing each other up to date as though we had been sharing our daily lives forever. He described the Thursday hearings at which he had testified at the Palais de Justice two days before, along with the MGM film executives who had come from Los Angeles. As I listened, I again became aware that his world was a large and expansive one, filled with sophisticated opportunities and discriminating choices. In contrast, that same Thursday I had celebrated Passover with a friend, her small grandchildren raising the level of background noise in a dining room filled with foldout tables and portable chairs arranged to welcome close friends and family.

I shared with David the triumphs of receiving galley proofs for one manuscript and an acceptance letter for another, described moving some furniture and cartons of books into my six-month sublet the day before, and commented that my mailing address had changed. I had rented a post office box in Southport. The following Monday, I would begin seeing my patients in the sublet office space of a psychiatrist friend. David told me that he had received a note I had written, addressed to him simply at "Bateau Berreti, Paris, France." I didn't think to be surprised it had arrived—one of many instances in which everything and everyone in France seemed to conspire to help our romance flourish—and instead asked him if he had received *both* notes. He was confused; he had received only the second of the two thank-you letters I had written when I returned home.

David laughed and told me to include "Port des Champs-Élysées," what passed for his address, after the boat's name when I next wrote, and to specify "Paris 75008" (on the Right Bank), not "Paris 75007" (on the Left).

I did *not* tell him that visions of his smile had flashed across my mental screen with regularity throughout the week or that I played the tape of his phone message with embarrassing frequency. David described the Saturday afternoon view from his boat and his plans to see a movie that night. I did not ask with whom.

Nor did I tell him that I had awoken at five that morning and written him seven pages of a longhand letter that I never intended to mail. But after the phone call, late in the day, just before the post office was to close, I added a short psychology joke to the pages, along with a photograph of Luke, "this is the male I sleep with" written on the back, and then did indeed mail the overstuffed envelope. I managed to continue to keep my more private thoughts to myself. David received the letter ten days later.

Life went on. I struggled through the first date I had after Paris. He was a nice, well-educated, generous, and interesting man with whom I had gone out a few times before. My body announced that I did not want to be at the concert at Carnegie Hall. Then. In New York. With him. Our second date post-Paris was impossible. Sitting in a favorite Indian restaurant, trying to enjoy dinner, was a violation of my integrity and beyond my capacity to pretend or be polite. Not fair to either of us. I was distracted. My heart was with David. My thoughts were with David. My body yearned to be with David. With Sagittarian directness, I explained my situation as tactfully as I could, suggested splitting the check, and knew that I was sending away an attractive, smart, articulate, self-sustaining man who had been a pleasant companion until my circuits got blown by three days of contact with a mystery man I might never see again. A man who probably had women in his life on the other side of the ocean. Choices again, decisions. But when something feels wrong, deceitful, it is time to move toward honesty, even though the future is unknown and doors can close.

A version of the same scenario repeated with another man, and my social life ground to a halt. Teaching offers failed to come in. Reviewers wanted another revision of the manuscript. Managed-care companies continued to redefine "good clinical practice" into a kind of work that ignored the unique relationship I had with each patient. But I had a taped answering-machine message, memories from a weekend, and a Saturday-morning phone call to sustain me. I kept reminding myself how glad I was to be single, how much I treasured my solitude and independence, and how utterly in control of my life I fancied myself to be. In the back of my mind, a small voice kept reminding me once again that "man plans and God laughs." Fear can make listening difficult.

David called again, on one of those Saturday mornings when I was watering plants at the house on Signal Lane. I gave him new phone numbers for the apartment and for the Southport office. And then he called again. And again. My first letter finally reached him, well after the third had. We described details of our very different daily lives. I taped some favorite songs for him, Luke accompanying the music, and he sent me a cassette of Julee Cruise songs, an album titled *Floating*. A psychic told me that I would meet a man and have a great deal of fun with him. She saw water. We would go on a boat. My life would change. I had not said a word about the Berreti.

I began writing frequent letters to David. During the first month after my trip to Paris, he called two or three times a week and sent letters in response to each of mine. One day a package arrived: Paulo Coelho's *The Alchemist*. I read it overnight, and the next evening we discussed the phenomenon of discovering meaning where it had been evident all along. I told him that I loved female vocalists, Barbra Streisand was my favorite, and that "Ordinary Miracles" made me think of us. Especially the "just by giving and receiving comes belonging and believing" part. David immediately bought her new album, and the cut became a reference point, "our song."

My body went haywire when I heard from him, thought of him, dreamed about him, talked about him. First my breathing quickened and my stomach began to flutter. I could feel the adrenaline rush as my heart picked up the pace. It was addictive; I kept replaying memories of sitting across from him, breathing next to him, his hand holding mine as he walked me across the street, our thighs touching on the couch in his boat, in the church, in the concert hall, and that smile. Oh, that smile, the one that came with the "wicked sense of humor" I referred to in my early letters. That danced across his face, making the deep crevices in his cheeks lighten up and all seriousness disappear. Here was, indeed, a man who knew what made him happy and did it. And it seemed like I might become one of those ingredients; I needed to trust him to find a way.

I sent lengthy letters full of elaborate descriptions, hoping that he could visualize the new office in a converted mill straddling the inlet in Southport Harbor, the apartment above the Italian specialty-foods store in a converted house on a flat street in a recently upgraded working-class neighborhood in Fairfield. Or the intimate way in which the needs of Luke and my patients structured my time.

I began to worry about the "seeing again" part. As much as I knew that I had to leave it to David to figure out, I wondered what he was thinking, whether or not he really did want—or intend—to see me again. What, exactly, did, might, would, could more than three thousand miles of geographical distance represent? I kept reminding myself that his behavior said he was interested. Letters. A tape. A novel. All those phone calls. But at about this time, a book of advice to single women was published and zoomed to the best-seller lists. *The Rules* advised us not to be too available, to seduce a man by remaining a challenge. According to the authors, I had done it all wrong, was continuing to do it all wrong, and, indeed, was incapable of doing it right. After I read the book, I told David about it, confessing my utter failure at subtlety. He only laughed. And called again. But still he did not come up with a plan. At one point he offhandedly referred to a May weekend in Italy he was planning, but, just as quickly, he discarded the notion of my joining him there.

And so our early courtship acquired its bumpy rhythm necessitated by living six time zones apart in an era when e-mail was just beginning (and David did not yet use a computer) and cell phones, for us at least, were fantasy. I would think of David first thing when I awoke, and then, on weekdays, imagine him, six hours later in Paris, contemplating lunch and then his daily one o'clock nap in his office. Of course, I had no idea what his office looked like or what he might be doing in it. On weekends, I agonized with curiosity concerning his whereabouts. I knew that we had exploded into each other's lives in the midst of ongoing stories, and I assumed that there must be women he saw in one context or another with some level of regularity—or maybe not. By the evening, when I had completed my workday, David was usually asleep.

Early on we joked about his need to "drive the car," both because his own testosterone demanded it and because I needed to be able to rely on someone taking care of me. So I knew I must wait for him to act, to write, to call. But I could write letters. And because the conversations in my head were so elaborate and constant, because my need to give to someone who gave so much back was so great, write I did. Often. Nearly every day, sometimes twice. David received my letters, nearly one a day and sometimes two. His attitude toward the mailboxes that stood sentinel at the entrance to his boat community shifted; they became containers of surprises he looked forward to discovering. He saved nearly all of them. When my worries that he might misunderstand me became too great, I described them:

Dear David,

It's a long clinical day in a light clinical week. I want to write of so many things—the swans on the river, the sparkle in the office now that I've cleaned it, walking with Hope this morning and encountering an arrangement of buoys and moorings in the harbor that looked like a misarranged bowling alley, a Richard Estes painting, or an obstacle course for seagoing tricycles. Or listing my house for sale, which I also did today. And checking at the apartment twice for your letters, which still have not appeared.

But I guess the most urgent thing to write about (again) is process. I find that speaking truths keeps things clean, and since I have been starting to feel a little muddy, it's probably a good idea.

As discussed, I believe that we both need you to be driving the car—for different reasons, I am sure—and while I know mine, I can only guess at yours. No matter. You will share what you choose in time. Or not. And, yes, I know that I am responsible for deciding if I can tolerate how you do it, where you choose to go, whether you choose to use maps or not, etc. I don't totally trust you yet. Thank God. (Thank God I do trust me!)

I just need to say how hard it is sometimes to sit back and let you do it, even though that's what we both need. I've been orga-nizing and managing and making things happen for so long that I have to bite my tongue and not ask questions that would invade your process or your desire to surprise and delight. And I so need reassurance that you understand that my feelings for you just are: they do not carry expectations of you or demands. I just need to know that you exist on this planet exactly as you are. That makes me happy.

That said, back to my conflict. It's so hard for me not to initiate contact, and I just want you to know that. When many things arrive in your mailbox at once, I fear you'll feel flooded, rather than cherished. When you say little of wanting to see me, I fear that you do not. When I made my reservations for Canada in August, I felt awful that I couldn't discuss them with you. Biting my tongue.

After I hung up the phone last week and you had brought up Italy, I got angry at myself for perhaps missing a cue. I remem-bered how you'd invited me to the photography exhibit outside of Paris and then censored the invitation, deciding that I had other, "more important" things to do. And I thought of how quick I had been to see and agree with your reasoning (about Italy). After I hung up, I thought of how we can wait forever to make something perfect, and how much better it would be to make what is—to allow what is—to be perfect. In other words, maybe it couldn't have been ideal—but a terrific opportunity nonetheless. Maybe it still is; I don't know the dates. And I haven't been invited.

I'm not denying the transcendence, David. One of the most amazing things about this for me is being connected beyond time and space. But I don't know how to understand no talk of seeing one another. Often I feel I'm being tested—can I keep my mouth shut? Will I have expectations after all, therefore permitting you to potentially fail and evoke criticism? I refuse to play that game. Am I going to be overwhelming? It feels like fear of boundary violation to me, and I need guidance in what yours are so that I bump up against them rarely and unwittingly, if at all. Is it fear the magic won't be the same? That I (or you) will have unfulfilled expectations—or be pressured or manipulated into something that doesn't feel right? Are you giving me space to sort out my housing problems but not telling me? Intuitively knowing that I cannot begin a new relationship in a house that has held so much pain? Wanting to just savor the miracle of the past and not risk changing it—in either direction? Afraid of something that hasn't been talked about? Simply waiting to see how long it takes me to break down and ask my million questions?

These are the things going through my mind and occasionally bumping up against my heart. Then I pick up the book. And want to believe that you did not send it casually.

Roni Beth

That weekend, Renee and Matt and I took our older children and their spouses to a Lake Michigan resort town for a weekend celebration of their thirtieth birthdays. Its isolation made communication with David impossible. We were flying home from Detroit. Automatically, as soon as we reached the airport, I phoned home to collect messages from my answering machine. In addition to the predictable calls from friends and patients and a dental appointment reminder, I heard a surprise message from David.

"When you get home, there will be a fax waiting for you. You are to read it, and then you are to call me. Just as soon as you calm down. No matter what time it is, call me."

That was about all he said in that message. But his phone calls had become more frequent, we had been sharing dreams and fantasies, and David had finally made it clear that he would like to see me again. I knew that he had not yet conceptualized a reasonable way to do it and that the distance had been a gift. Over the weeks, I had been getting to know him slowly, through time—his thoughts, his style, his attitudes, what I could glean of values reflected through them. I liked what I was learning. He had mailed me wildflowers gathered in Sologne, called every time he had said that he would (and on time, too), and patiently followed the saga of my housing fiasco. Then there was that electricity that ran through me each time I heard his voice. It is so easy to fill a new relationship with fantasies, to make the other person into projections of some kind of ideal or to set them up to repeat relationship patterns that feel familiar, for better or worse. Time and space force information to be collected more mindfully, the red flags of omissions or possible commissions rudely popping onto gray psychic tabulation sheets with relentless insistence. A lack of physical contact tempers the ability of hormonal sweeps to blur messages, and the reality of daily life introduces a window of observation: How does this person respond to x, y, or z over time? Patience becomes an ally.

We faced two and a half hours of flying time from Detroit, and then I had the drive back to Connecticut. It felt like forever. When I finally got home, I raced to the fax machine.

On Sunday, April 28, 1996, at six in the evening Paris time, a day short of a month since we had met, David had written the first fax of the hundreds that shaped our courtship. In a cover letter, he apologized, and then, with a reference to Rosanne Cash's song from her album *The Wheel*, instructed:

> *Noon in Connecticut* [when he wrote] *but closer to midnight when you see this.*
>
> *Sorry to keep you up so late after a long trip and drive, but soon we'll be sleeping in Paris and the angels will watch over you (or something like that).*
>
> *First: listen to the message.*
>
> *Second: read this (to the end) if you can.*
>
> *Third: call me (I'm at home and soon to get up or already up if your plane was late or if you read slowly).*
>
> *And do calm down—you are a professional, aren't you?*

The five pages with tiny handwriting that followed mapped out his process and a plan. He was inviting me back to Paris, in time to join him for the Harvard Law School Association of Europe weekend in Turin, followed by two more days in Paris. While I had been climbing sand dunes in Michigan, he had gone to the Normandy coast, where the salt air and an Air France reservation agent had helped him come up with a plan. That night, sitting on the terrace of his hotel, knowing how much I appreciate understanding someone's thought processes, he began his letter.

Dear Roni Beth,

I wondered why it was so hard for you to let me drive . . . and I got it! You worry I'm not gonna drive in the right direction (yours) or worry I'm goin' there too slow or too indirectly—too many detours and side trips (yeah, but an occasional shortcut). I'll never get there. . . . You are right in letting me drive (unless I am also wrong about me), for the reasons you think. Don't push—I resist. And yes, I do like to "surprise and delight." I'm less impulsive, more cerebral and "calculating" (not in the pejorative sense). All in good time. But all that time "wasted" (it's not) or "lost" (uh-uh)? I like things slow—courting, for example (and there are others). Anticipation is nice. So is getting ready. And here, yeah, use your imagination, go ahead and fantasize a bit. . . .

So! Thinkin' all that, walking on the beach, thinking, "Was I wrong about the photo exhibit" on that magic Saturday? No, I wasn't. You did need to sort things out, there was more important stuff. And there was no rush. "Was I wrong about Italy?" No, not for my reasons. (Altho, yes, you're right, I do seek "the perfect setting"—when I know perfection is not attainable.) On the other hand, there was/is (oh, surprise) a solution. (Logistics.)

You see, we have so much to discover, and I wanted you all to myself for hours and hours. Solution? Easy. Come to Paris

*two days before, and we'll have "our time"—and then what a
wonderful three days in Turin. And then another day or two
just us in Paris.*

*I am still driving the car. I did not yield to your hints/
requests, or decide, "Oh, OK, I'll make Roni Beth happy." Nope.
As I enjoyed walking alone on the beach—my quiet time with
me—I thought about telling you about it, then thought it would
be easier (and much nicer) to be walking with you, then going
back to the château with you, having dinner with you, spending
evening and night with you, breakfast with you, maybe some
other stuff in between.*

*Shift to weekend in Turin (Friday, May 17, to Sunday, May
19). . . . So, how to combine sharing (taking advantage of)
that weekend and spending time with you? Thursday 16th is
Ascension (holiday). So, if you could arrive, say, on Wednesday
15th (leaving New York on Tuesday eve the 14th), we could
have Wednesday evening (or maybe I can take off the whole
day) and all day Thursday, before leaving on early flight (7:30
a.m.) Friday for Turin (then return Sunday 6:45 p.m. to Paris),
and then (depending on how much time you can take off)
return to US Mon. 20th or Tues. 21st.*

*Can you get away? Take a whole week? Do you want to? Are
you scared? Even if it doesn't "work" (covers lots of territory)
we will both, each of us and together, have a very nice weekend
in Turin (I'll fax the schedule, events, dress, etc.) and then stay
pen pals or something. See how easily I can come to terms with
things?*

*OK, enuf—rest a second, catch your breath, calm your beat-
ing heart, and call me (it's gonna be almost time for me to get
up anyway), and then you can go to sleep.*

Do I always have to express everything in words?

David

The above is extracted from what was, with many side-margin notes, parentheticals, stream-of-consciousness ramblings, and tiny, hard-to-read handwriting, David's first fax to me. I read and reread it, trying to digest the invitation. The background and further details came out in the phone conversation that followed. He had been walking on the beach in dense fog, trying to imagine the logistics, and then, as if an apparition, a phone booth had appeared in front of him. One lone red phone booth in the middle of an isolated stretch of the Normandy coast, out by the landing beaches. And the telephone in it actually worked. He had called Air France, given his member reference, and spent over half an hour on the phone with the special-service reservation agent, telling her our story, discussing his concerns, and working with her first to hold a reservation for me on his already booked Paris–Milan–Paris flights and then to sort out good New York–Paris–New York options to get me over and back. She was holding a transatlantic round-trip reservation in my name. I will be forever grateful for her patience, enthusiasm, kindness, and completely unsubtle Gallic encouragement to "get this woman to Paris."

The weekend in Turin referred to the annual Harvard Law School Association of Europe "meeting." Its three purposes were to decide on a site for the following year's gathering, to allocate scholarship funds donated by the members, and to elect officers for the following year. The event was always on Ascension weekend in May, and David had attended many times over the years. From cocktails on Friday through brunch and a river cruise on Sunday, it would be forty-eight hours or so of fine food and wine, lovely lodging, discovering local sites hosted by an HLS alumnus—in this instance, the deputy mayor of Turin— and conversation with interesting people who converged from across Europe for the party. He would fax the itinerary for the weekend. But because we had not spent a great deal of time together (a euphemism for the fact that we had never even kissed each other), why not come to Paris for a few days first, arriving on Wednesday, and we would go to Italy together on Friday, then spend Sunday and Monday nights back in Paris? There was a second sleeping cabin on the boat if I wanted it, and I could have my own room in Italy if I chose.

The detail of the fax was meticulous—dates and flights; choices of departure times, of airports, of alternatives to the basic plan. I was dumbstruck. Whose life was I in? Was this really happening to dreary, responsible me? Could I actually do such an outrageous thing? Then again, how could I not?

It was after midnight. David would indeed be waking up soon to begin his Monday. Trembling with excitement, I pulled out the card with his number written on it and, for the first time, dialed it.

"*Oui, allô?*" he answered, sounding very sleepy.

"*Bonjour,*" I managed to squeak out.

"Roni Beth! It's you. You got my messages, the fax. What time is it?"

"A little after midnight here. Sun coming up there?"

"Soon. You got my messages?"

"Uh-huh."

"So, what do you think?"

"Think? I can't think. I'm overwhelmed."

"Well, are you happy about it?"

"Happy? Yes, happy."

"You don't sound very bubbly."

"Oh. I guess you don't know that about me yet. When I get overwhelmed by deep emotion, I get silent. My heart jumps into my throat and closes it off or something. No words."

"Oh, I see. . . . So, do you want to come?"

"Want to come? Yes, I want to come. But I have to think about it for a minute. I don't even know what to think. Can I call you back in the morning?" I knew I was babbling.

A little confused and obviously disappointed, David nonetheless reassured me, "You can call me when you get up. Now go to sleep."

Early the next morning when I returned home from walking Luke, I found another fax, a follow-up to our conversation the night before. It included:

Not every decision is dramatic (or most of us would never decide anything), and here nothing terrible can happen. Very worst is disappointment, and certainly the bigger disappointment would be not even having the chance to try. Sure, I could talk you out of it—logically and intelligently—as I did last time . . . but you don't want me to, and this time it would be a mistake. And if the trip is a mistake—but it won't be—that will be my fault and my responsibility, and at least we'll find out (instead of allowing expectations and anticipation to continue to develop, with an even bigger risk of a bigger deception as we keep stalling).

When I had agreed that I would come, I had asked him, "What should I do with my credit card?"

"I don't know. What do you usually do with it?"

"I mean, who should I give the numbers to for the flights?"

"Roni Beth, this is an invitation. You just have to go to New York to pick up the tickets because Air France won't issue a transatlantic ticket in a different name without seeing the person face-to-face. Put your credit card in your wallet."

I was going back to Paris. And to Italy. But all I really cared about was that I was going to see David again.

A week was a long time to leave my practice, even though I could move as many clients as possible to the Monday and Tuesday before I left and the Wednesday through Friday after the return. One friend invited Luke to stay with her and her mother, and another agreed to cover my practice should an emergency arise. David had faxed the complete, decadent agenda, and I began to think about wardrobe.

The consuming pain and stresses of the previous seven years began to float away. My father's sudden death. Unexpected flights to San Francisco for hospital vigils or to facilitate residence changes for my sick-then-dying mother. Unresolved conflicts with my first husband that resurfaced when our daughter prepared to marry. The raw truth of a foolish third marriage. Disappointments. Lost resources—time, money, energy—that go into attempts to repair, to move along. The depletion that comes from trying to stay constantly in your rational-adult and best problem-solving mode. Attempts to offset strain with exercise, healthy diet, keeping the house, car, calendar in running order. Burying needy parts of yourself deeper and deeper, until they are nearly disconnected from consciousness. Almost forgetting you have a soul.

Soon after David invited me back to Paris, he brought me another step further into his life when, during a phone call, he described a challenge he had faced the night before with a woman he had been seeing. A married woman. Of course, he *did* live in Paris. And the woman *was* French. And details like multiple relationships had never bothered her—or presumably him—very much. During that conversation, David told me about the movie he had gone to see with her and described how, after the film, she had become insistent about walking home with him. He said he had to practically throw her off the boat. I silently wondered why he had let her return to it with him in the first place.

We had dropped into each other's lives midstream. I knew what mine looked like: I went to bed early, got up early, and worked late, usually until it was time to stop working and go to bed. On weekends I treated myself to a yoga class and occasionally went to dinner with a friend. Four times in the winter and again in the spring, a girlfriend from my college days picked me up and we drove to Manhattan to see matinee performances of the New York City Ballet—my greatest indulgence for the past several years. I had stopped my occasional dating soon after my return from Paris. I had my car serviced seasonally, my teeth cleaned every six months, annual physicals, and semiannual checkups of my house's heating and air-conditioning systems. Not tending to something (or someone) I felt responsible for made me nuts. Aging made more and more of my life feel like essential maintenance: without it, things broke down—cars, houses, relationships, certainly bodies—and repairs were almost always more costly, in both time and money, than doing the maintenance.

Now here I was, preparing to go to Europe for a week to stay with a man whom I feared I barely knew and to immerse myself temporarily in the very world and lifestyle that seemed so different from mine. His work dealt with great big, broad issues, like international film distribution rights; research, development, and distribution of pharmaceuticals; subtleties of intellectual properties as they crossed national borders. David negotiated for and with huge corporations, taking into account the culture in Europe or Japan or China or the United States or wherever else an issue arose. I addressed issues of individual consciousness, of pain and suffering, of struggling toward well-being, one breath at a time. David lived in the most visited city in the world, on a boat, in a location where he could walk nearly everywhere he might need or want to go. I lived in a town of fewer than thirty thousand people in a nearly four-thousand-square-foot house (I lived upstairs, worked downstairs, and was trying hard to sell it) and depended upon my Honda Civic to get me where I needed to go—whether the destination was a relatively nearby beach for a walk, New Haven for scientific collaboration, or Maine. I had two grown children who still considered our house "home," and he had two sons, one recently married, who had not lived with him, except for vacation visits, since before they had reached puberty. I had countless relationships with people I had known from one venue or another within the confines of Fairfield County, and many of them had become friends. David was a loner. He did admit to a brief period of service on the board of directors of the boat community, but he was quick to protest that he preferred dining alone with his book, keeping his calendar clear of social engagements, and visiting museums with concern only for his own reactions. One exception was when he joined a couple for dinner every Sunday, at the same time and in the same restaurant where they had originally met as customers at adjacent tables. Over the years, this couple had become part of David's French "family."

To me, his life was filled with glamour and intrigue and flexibility, mine simple and direct and loaded with commitments. David's daily reality felt mysterious and familiar at the same time. In some ways, it reminded me of my father's long and exotic bachelor years and the five weeks we had shared during our European trip together in 1960, the trip that had awakened me to the joys of sensory pleasures and that had planted the seeds of my unrequited desire for adventure. By now I was pretty sure that David had more depth and insight than my dad, perhaps also more imagination, and he was definitely more romantic and expressive. Visiting his world was going to be thrilling, but definitely only a visit. The possibility that I was on the threshold of a life with more caring and sharing and discovery than I had ever known excited, intrigued, and terrified me.

And I was going to go back to France and to Italy to be with him. The day after the fax invitation arrived, I woke up to find another one with details: reservations confirmed and paid for, but I must pick up my ticket in person at the Air France office in New York or at the airport. Departing from JFK on Air France flight 007 on Tuesday, May 14, arriving in Paris on Wednesday morning, and returning on Air France flight 006 the following Tuesday. It was now Monday. I would plan to go into the city on Thursday. Maybe Danny, my young adult son, would be able to have lunch with me; I had not seen him in a month or so. That day, every patient I saw commented on how I appeared different somehow. A few of them wondered if I was "okay."

No, I was not okay.

The phone calls and faxes between us began flying. Given the six-hour time difference, David would go to the office and send me a fax that greeted me when I awoke. I began setting the alarm so that I had extra time to write back immediately, ushering in his afternoon. He almost always wrote one last fax before leaving the office, which I then received early or midafternoon, and then I wrote one at night before bed, assuring that he would have a note awaiting him when he arrived at the office the next morning. That was the minimum. Often one of us added a cartoon, a short newspaper article, a xeroxed joke. We strove for a combination of lightness and seriousness, for there was much that was serious to discuss before we saw each other again.

In the mere two weeks between the invitation and the trip, I needed to tell David that I was afraid he would not find me attractive because of my chubby thighs. He had to admit concerns about how we might come together in reality. I wanted him to get an HIV test, and so, fair is fair, I had to get one myself so that I could legitimately ask him to suffer this inconvenience. Just in case. He had to select a welcome gift for me, and I needed to find an "appropriate" thank-you gift to bring to him. I also needed to celebrate Mother's Day with my kids, plant a dozen flats of annuals, and open the Maine cottage so that it would be ready to greet my favorite annual tenants when they arrived while I was in France. Given that the trip to Tenants Harbor required a minimum of six and a half hours of driving time, I was grateful that it would also give me a chance to buy "special" hats for David—a crusher from L.L.Bean and an Australian "ultimate hat" from the specialty store in Camden.

David and I each got a clean bill of health. I purchased some underwear when the Fairfield Store announced its going-out-of-business sale. David went over tickets and timing and details and worked hard to clear his desk so that he could spend four and a half weekdays with me, plus the weekend. I delayed moving into the apartment, which was by then approaching the third month of the six-month lease I had negotiated. The construction of closets and repairs of range and refrigerator had been completed. Nonetheless, I wanted to depart for Paris from my nice house with the walk-in closets, familiar bathroom, and full selection of luggage.

Packing was a bit of a challenge. My one remaining dressy dress, which I had bought for Jennifer's wedding four years before, was perfect for the formal dinner on Saturday night. My other dress was just too summery for May. Luckily, my best suit, black silk with a straight skirt and white piqué trim on the cuffs and the V-neck, would work for Friday night's dinner. But my wardrobe included very few choices beyond basic work wear—nondescript suits and silk blouses—or jeans and cotton shirts.

Finally, I decided to travel in my purple suit, the least dowdy among the choices, and to fill in with black slacks and a few tops. I knew how to dress for Yale meetings, but weekend wine tasting in the Piedmont was not quite the same. Somehow, what I owned needed to be sufficient. Besides, even with events to attend and a man to help with my luggage, I still wanted to travel light. Portability had become a badge of honor.

And then, before I knew it, I found myself sitting in an aisle seat with extra legroom on an Air France jet, smiling as I gave David credit for the seat assignment and noted that he had thought of everything. He was right: on Air France, the visit begins as soon as one boards the plane. The flight attendants dress beautifully and behave in a gracious manner to match. The menu redefines what airplane food can be. The pilot provides frequent, chatty updates in both French and English. I felt near heaven, and then, in less than seven hours, we landed. The double doors leading from baggage claim, past the unobtrusive customs clearance area, and out into the hallway at Charles de Gaulle Airport, Terminal 2C (the new terminal this time—an omen?), opened. I stepped through them.

5

Courtship

avid was waiting opposite the customs doors. The increasingly frequent and fiery (and sexy verging on erotic) phone calls and faxes had prepared us both for the reunion. I fell into his arms as if I had always belonged there, snuggled against his chest. We stayed that way, embracing each other in the central corridor at Charles de Gaulle Airport, Terminal 2C, for a very long time. The first kiss fried synapses in my brain; I felt foggy, fluttery, transported into some alternate reality as I felt his clean-shaven cheek against mine, the soft confidence of his touch and firm assurance of his hug, the chemistry, electricity, sheer magic of being together again. He later reminded me that he had begun to "court" me.

He led me to his car and turned on the ignition, and we drove onto the Autoroute with "Ordinary Miracles" playing on the stereo. David "did" details. Even though I was still "only" fifty-two, jet lag was real and I could feel the fuzziness of all that adrenaline and too little sleep. The early-morning ride into Paris was a jumble. Again, I was intrigued by the outside—the boat-shaped Sheraton Hotel, the windscreens and the billboards, the signs above us that announced each BOUCHON, and the time it would take us to get to various destinations, given the delays due to traffic—and by the inside: the somersaults in my stomach, the smell of this man seated next to me, the feel of my slightly chubby legs tucked together as discreetly as I could possibly tuck them. We passed in front of the Stade de France, which showed visible progress since my trip two months before. Soon we had switched highways onto the bd Périphérique. David turned off at Port de Champeret and drove down city streets abundant with May flowers, grand architecture, and people moving smoothly through their Wednesday activities. He pointed out the imposing Banque de France, and I realized we were on bd Malesherbes, the street listed on his business card. We passed a gorgeous stone building he identified as the site of his office, then turned onto a side street, where he double-parked and ran into a bakery. He returned quickly with a bag that held croissants, *pains au chocolat, pains aux raisins*, baguettes. I asked about the lack of skyscrapers. David explained that Paris had laws against buildings being built too high, a lesson learned after the regretted construction of the Tour Montparnasse on the Left Bank, visible even at our distance from it. With its magnificent architecture, vigilant maintenance, massive underground parking, and vast expanses of green, Paris seemed more a playground than a major urban center.

We continued toward the Madeleine but turned down another side street before we reached it. Past the American embassy, through Place de la Concorde, and across the bottom of the Champs-Élysées. David turned right along the river and then left and then left again, an extended U-turn, and then through a gate and onto the quai to park alongside the Berreti. He guided me across the *Christina* and onto his boat, handling my suitcase as though it were an empty paper bag, offhandedly telling me that he had spent college summers working as a bellhop at a resort near his home in the Catskills.

We inched across the plank to the wine crate that served as a step to his "front" door and entered. David had arranged a huge bouquet of irises, daffodils, and mysterious white flowers on the cocktail table and perched a crystal vase holding a single long-stemmed red rose on the counter at which we would share our first breakfast.

Then he handed me a meticulously and beautifully wrapped box. A little embarrassed, fleetingly wondering what I was getting myself into, I opened it. I was dumfounded. Inside the elaborate Casoar wrappings lay a pair of the most dramatic and elegant earrings I had ever seen. Long, kite-shaped drops of rust-colored carnelian hung from a marcasite button base studded with a small pearl. I caught my breath; these were a quantum leap from the practical and nearly invisible accessories I bought for myself.

"David, these are magnificent. I don't know what to say. . . . I own only two dresses."

"What are you trying to tell me?"

"They're gorgeous. Just not like anything I've ever bought for my quiet life!"

"Maybe they are for a new life, one with places yet to be discovered."

I just smiled at him, vaguely remembering facets of myself that had once existed. The earrings were to wear with sophisticated, feminine clothes. Luckily, I had brought my dressiest suit for the Friday-night dinner in Turin. The earrings would look perfect with it.

That was the morning I learned about croissants with Normandy butter and blueberry jam, a uniquely sensuous combination. As though we had always known each other, David suggested I might want a nap, although, always the one to take things slow and to savor anticipation, he insisted we eat breakfast first. Sex had never felt more inevitable or more thrilling.

After we had made love for the first time, with that twinkle in his eyes, still not totally convinced I was Jewish, he recited the prayer "*Baruch atah adonai, eloheinu melech ha'olam, shehechianu, viki-amanu, vihigiyanu, lazman hazeh.* Thank you, God, for bringing us to this day. If I die, tell Scott I had a wonderful time; it was worth it." Laughter after lovemaking became part of the lightness that became us. We giggled and snuggled together in a hazy reverie, rocked by the waves.

Although that morning I truly began to learn about David, it was a long time before I could put it all together—there were so many sides to him, so many contradictions, so many curiosities, so many cultural differences born of twenty-four years of living in a foreign land. For starters, that morning I learned that I could trust him to take good care of me. Sex says so much in so many ways. We lay in each other's arms in the high, firm double bed that nestled exactly into its corner of the master cabin, sun shining behind those velvet curtains and brass gleaming in rays that slipped through, the boat rocking gently most of the time and more rhythmically when a *bateau mouche* passed by as I slept off the jet lag. When I awoke, David suggested we walk over to his office so that he could sign some documents his secretary had typed up before the Thursday holiday and its long "bridge" weekend began. He helped me climb up the fire escape ladder, scurry across the busy Cours de la Reine, and navigate a shortcut through Place de la Concorde.

When we reached 97 bd Malesherbes, David punched a code into a keypad and I heard a click that released the lock in the heavy, carved wooden doors. He pushed them open. The concierge's small private apartment was on the left, a door to a stairway on the right. We passed them both and entered a courtyard, then walked across its cobblestone pavement, balconies in front of ten-foot French windows looking down on us. David took us through a door that serviced the quieter half of the building at the end of the courtyard. A glass and wrought-iron elevator sat in the center of the scarlet-carpeted stairwell, steps winding around it, and we ascended, one floor after another, to the third floor of the elegant six-story building.

David's white-carpeted office suite included five rooms that each featured a molded plaster ceiling, floor-to-ceiling windows opening onto tiny balconies with intricate iron railings, and a marble fire-place with a hand-carved mantle and ceiling-high gilt mirror above it. All different in each room, of course. In the conference room, an eighteen-foot oval table made from a single piece of rosewood was surrounded by twelve of the most comfortable leather chairs I had ever sat in. No diplomas. Much later, he told me that he had misplaced them, along with his Phi Beta Kappa key and his award for graduating third or fourth in his program at Sciences Po. The daily *Wall Street Journal* sat on his desk—at least something we shared, even though his international edition was slimmer than my American daily. Down a long corridor, after a bathroom, another reception area, a room with filing cabinets and office equipment, a secretarial office, and then a room he used for storage. His bike was against the wall. A kitchenette at the end of the hall. His secretary, Mme. H., greeted me, glad to turn the source of all those faxes and phone calls, and her boss's new preoccupation, into a reality. She and David had worked together for a very long time. She was superb in her skills, devoted to cats, and formal, though direct, in her interactions. She was not always easy for him to deal with, and she knew it. She and I got along beautifully.

I don't know what I had been expecting, but it wasn't this. One man and his secretary occupied over 170 square meters, 1,700 square feet of prime real estate in the middle of Paris. I understood large Park Avenue or Wall Street law firms, sometimes with luxurious corner offices for the partners. And I understood private practitioners, sometimes with a small suite to accommodate support staff and storage. But I did not yet appreciate what David had created, who he was in his professional life, or how unique it was. To recap my confusion, none of this made any sense to me: This huge expanse of elegant, impeccably furnished space in the middle of a major European capitol, and he was the only lawyer who worked in it. A single secretary as "support staff." He drove a Ford Escort, a fairly modest car in the United States at that time. And he lived on a boat. A boat with an often-broken toilet pump. Clearly, David had two sides to his personality: the urbane, accomplished professional who flew either business or first class (and sometimes even Concorde), and who understood fine wine and food (indeed, he had incorporated Foods and Wines of France in the United States, as well as Cuisinart in France). And the man who went to work in jeans, kept his own appointment book (keeping it as clear of social commitments as possible), and loved a Whopper with cheese and *frites* at Burger King, especially after a Friday-night movie on the Champs-Élysées. David loved to call himself "a sophisticated hillbilly," a description coined by a former college roommate.

That first night of this first day, after we had become lovers, David took me to dinner at an intimate romantic hideaway, Nuits St. Jean, again on rue Surcouf, where I tasted *girolles* and *cèpes*, wild French mushrooms, for the first time. The chef combined them with garlic to create an *entrée* (appetizer in English) that remains a taste I still imagine, yearn for, and try to replicate. The *saumon grillé à l'unilateral* was also a first, along with the *crème brûlée au gingembre*. A Russian samovar gleamed on the shelf by my shoulder, mildly erotic paintings decorated the red velour walls, and the chef and his glamorous wife welcomed us warmly. We finished our meal with a cordial that was new to me, something made from apricot pits, then walked back to the boat across the Pont Alexandre III, partially dismantled for its centennial restoration. In the middle of this incredible bridge with the Eiffel Tower on one side and the spires of Notre Dame on the other, David stopped to give me a hug and a passionate kiss, the first of countless kisses on bridges that have followed. My dreams could not have come more true: I was in Paris—in the very middle of Paris—in the arms of a man whom I had come to love.

The next day was a delicious blur. We walked and walked and walked. And ate. And made love. Lying in each other's arms felt like a homecoming. Friday we rose early; the morning plane to Turin required braving the rush-hour traffic in and around Paris. I learned that David, like I did, preferred arriving early for plane departures. That, like I did, he became a little anxious until he was checked in at the airport. David was excited about the weekend. The annual HLSAE junkets were one highlight of his year—convenient excuses to visit European cities and see lawyers who came from all over the continent, several who had become friends over the years. Doors normally closed were opened by influential lawyers who lived there and had the power to open them. Only once before had he taken a woman with him. He said that was long, long ago.

I felt like I was a walk-on in a film from my childhood, maybe one of those European extravaganzas starring Cary Grant and Audrey Hepburn. The first night a bus drove us up winding, hilly roads to a villa seductively peeking out along the curves of the mountains high above Turin. Our local host and hostess welcomed us to their villa for cocktails and dinner. We strolled through lush gardens, sipping exotic aperitifs, before sitting at round tables for six in the portico of what were once the wine caves of Cinzano. The next day, during a quiet moment, we ignored the espresso that was too strong to drink as we sat underneath the colonnades that surround the central square of the city and watched the world stroll by. Then another bus trip, this time to vineyards set high in more distant Piedmont hills, complete with Barolo and Barbaresco to "taste" and a castle walkway to climb. Visits to palazzos and piazzas, walks through the exquisitely rational yet decorative streets of this baroque city, the capitol of Savoy. A formal dinner Saturday night, with David in his tuxedo, so elegant, so perfect, the silver strands in his still-dark hair looking like they had been colored to accentuate the shimmer in the satin lapels. The Sunday-brunch boat trip, chatting with people we'd spent time with throughout the weekend as though they were old friends.

I remember that the other women, almost all married, looked at me strangely when I answered (honestly) a question about how or how long I had known David. That David thought I looked beautiful in the black suit I wore to the Friday-night dinner. That the size 6 navy silk sheath with the puffy white lace sleeves still fit well enough to make me feel pretty. And that when David put on his comfortable tuxedo, he was underscoring that other side of himself, his life, different from the one that I had seen on the boat. I remember chatting with his friends from Dublin, Copenhagen, Stockholm, Prague, and, of course, Paris. That he got his first glimpses of how easily people tell me their stories and of how inevitably and routinely, being an introvert with social skills, I need quiet time to settle my own energy and stay centered following a lot of social interaction. And the fun we had selecting bottles of Barolo and Barbaresco that I could bring back to America for Scott and his new wife, Stefanie.

I don't remember Sunday night or Monday, either, although Monday night I asked David to let me treat him to dinner and he brought us to Chez Gildas, a gem of a warm, informal traditional French restaurant on rue Surcouf near the quai. During dinner, he asked, "What do you think your parents would say about the weekend?"

"I don't know."

"Let me guess. Your father would ask you what you ate, and your mother would ask what you wore." I fell just a notch more deeply in love with this insightful man.

And I remember saying goodbye on Tuesday. Somehow, David put my suitcase and me in the car and drove us through Paris, onto the Périphérique, and then onto the A-1. Somehow, we parked the car and walked into Charles de Gaulle Airport, Terminal 2C. Somehow, he checked me in, onto the Air France flight. A final embrace. Then, somehow, I must have passed through the immigration booth, sent my luggage through security, and walked onto the small escalator that would take me to the gates and out of David's view. As I looked back one last time, I could not see his face clearly through my tears.

II

Getting to Know You; Who Is This Man?

6

Home Again

On Air France flight 006, crossing back over the Atlantic after those magical days with David, I tried to digest my feelings on paper:

What makes this return from Paris so different from that of 1 April, less than two months ago? Why have I eaten and drunk too much, been unable to get comfortable, refused to try to read? On that trip, I sat in astonishment, heart throbbing, all my being vibrating with what had begun. On this one, I sit in denial, afraid to let the force of the feelings be known. A glimpse breaks through here and there—the notion of rolling over, unable to say, "Good morning, David, I love you," because he is not there; the pull of the lengthening connection as I walked toward the boarding gate and he stood still, rooted behind the passport barrier, watching me walk away. Before I had felt the fullness, the yearning, the delicious anticipation of wanting to be with David. Now I feel the cold, the emptiness, the shadows passing through my being as the current is withdrawn. That's how it feels—life source of electricity shut down, plug pulled, flow interrupted. Mentally, I know that he is there, that I will hear from him, that we will be together again—and again—and

that the time between will not be infinite. But then there's this
feeling—hollow heart. How much of my reaction is simply the
return? Long lists of responsibilities, none unmanageable but
all annoying: patients, data analyses, moving, dealing with
leases and air-conditioning, flowers and electricians—living a
new life in a new space with a new configuration of activities—
and all I want is to be with David.

The professional in me knew that when an experience lights up parts of the brain, of the body, the paths that connect them and reach into the soul—especially when those parts of the self have never been known or have been carefully shut down, placed in shadow—that light can be brilliant. That light can also be blinding in its seduction. I am reminded of Buber's *I and Thou*—the return to "I-It" is inevitable and essential. Fighting for full consciousness, balance, becomes a physical, psychic, and spiritual demand. Practice required.

The next day, I returned to life as I had known it Before David. Disciplined. Busy. Purposeful. Filled with relationships with people who were important to me. And involving a final move into the apartment at the end of the week. When I returned from the second Paris trip, I knew far more about David than I had before. That the feelings I had had when I had been with him in April had intensified. That we could share imagination, conversation, silence. That he did seem to have an effective adult work life. That he wanted to—and would—take care of me. Making love is communication and a metaphor for so much else. But I still had questions. In contrast, David insisted (then, and still insists) that we knew everything we needed to know about each other the first weekend we had met, perhaps that first shared dinner.

Home that May meant massive movement. Although I had been working in the Southport office since earlier in the month, I had yet to sleep at the apartment. My six-month lease had nearly half passed. I had been paying rent while doing repairs and constructing closets and was still living in Westport, waiting for a signed lease and verified deposit from a recently committed summer tenant. A Manhattan family had scooped up the opportunity. Problem was, once again, neither lease nor deposit appeared. Finally, the Friday following the week with David and the day that I was to move the fax machine and the rest of my essentials to the apartment, I decided not to rent to the people who had said they wanted my house for the summer but whose behavior was unreliable, in spite of the lucrative rental payments I had hoped to collect.

So there we were at the end of May, life going on around me with professional activities in Southport and New Haven, research analyses in Westport, many of my home essentials in the Fairfield apartment, and Danny coming up for the weekend to help me complete the move and hang his gold record, a trophy from his years of working for BMG, in the new apartment. A symbol of a shift for us. He brought Stefani, the first woman he seemed to be serious about, with him, and, since there was no urgency, we continued to sleep in Westport.

After they left that Sunday, I went to New York to deliver the Italian wine to Scott and his Stefanie (the one whose name is spelled with an "e"), whom I had invited to brunch. Stefanie had just announced her pregnancy—in fact, she and Scott had phoned David with the news while I had been with him in Paris—and they were bubbling brightly with anticipation of parenthood. The baby was due in February. We had a lovely visit and a delicious meal, and Scott later reported to David (who then reported to me) his enthusiasm about meeting me. It sounded like he hoped perhaps this time his father's "affair" (in French, *aventure*) might last for a while. Scott knew and understood his dad well: "But she lives in Connecticut and you live in Paris. How are you going to do that?"

"I don't know, Scott. We'll work it out."

"Oh—I get it! You see her when you want, and then don't have to when you don't want to. Sounds perfect!"

When David told me of this conversation, I made a mental note of it, what the psychologist in me labeled a "flag." David was close to Scott, who had watched him maneuver his way through eighteen years of single life since David had separated from Scott's mother. I generated a few professional hypotheses: Did David prize freedom? Was he afraid of commitment? Was that related to his earlier marriage? Did he get bored easily? Was he a particularly private person? Did he just like to have things his way? Or, worse, to have his cake and eat it, too? It all boiled down to: *What can I trust about him, and how much can I trust it?*

By the following Friday, ushering in Memorial Day weekend, I had moved into the apartment. Danny stayed there with me the first two nights. David called and sent faxes to the new location, reporting on a movie he had seen, a book he was reading, a matter he was working on, a Tibetan wedding ceremony he attended, Sogyal Rinpoche officiating and Taittinger champagne flowing and foie gras abundant. I listened, snuggled on the sofa underneath the dangling chandelier made more unsafe by poor electrical wiring.

We both began operating on two time zones, calculating when phone conversations were feasible and setting aside chunks of our day to "be with" each other. We feasted on voice infusions, ignoring practicality and restraint, struggled with the vagaries of mechanical failures that cut off a fax transmission prematurely, and tolerated frustration from the apartment's frequent power outages, which invariably disrupted delivery. As David said, *Well, ups and downs, highs and lows, some days two letters plus a new/old letter (or an old/new one), and some days half a letter (better than none). Some days there's magic, sometimes the electronics screw up and phone lines have temper tantrums. And sometimes . . . sometimes there's music!* Confronting the minutia of daily living helps keep the continuum between divine and mundane in perspective.

We discussed his coming to Connecticut. June looked busy. I had planned a weekend at the Maine cottage with Renee and Matt and a daylong yoga workshop the following weekend. In between, I had offered to puppy-sit Luke's Maltese girlfriend, Bridget. David decided he could slip in a quick trip on the third weekend in June, before I went to Hastings-on-Hudson in Westchester, where I had volunteered to assume responsibility for a close friend's twelve-year-old daughter while my friend and her husband belatedly celebrated her fortieth birthday with a week in Paris. David and I kept discussing dates. I kept repeating, "Just give me enough notice that I can reschedule patients in order to get to the airport." While I juggled unusually heavy work demands and commitments that I had made before I had met him, David arranged his first trip into my world. I scrambled to install air-conditioning units in the apartment, a baby gate to contain Luke so that I could leave the doors open, and window shades.

Meanwhile, and even as we planned the June trip, we began to talk about the summer. Again, we had been forced to confront that there was no "perfect" time. When he asked me, "What are you doing in August?" I stuttered. I had agreed to present papers at conferences in Banff and then Toronto. Bought airline tickets and made reservations for lodging. He thought he'd like to join me. And hang around for his midmonth birthday. Perhaps we could go to Maine? Of course! Even though the sacred eighteen August days together that we began to plan would be constrained by the talks I had to prepare and deliver, we would be able to share them and through their diversity get to know each other better.

Early on, I had realized that David was far more discriminating than I and more insistent upon excellence. I got picky only when it came to my work and relationships. I hoped that I might benefit from his evaluative nature. And early on he had learned that I would not let an emotionally loaded conversation go by until its origins and implications had been understood. We would need to negotiate some resolution between his style—intuitive, impulsive, attentive to details, and often avoidant—and mine, which was, to his obvious but often unstated annoyance, more insistent on "processing" (that is to say, discussing with intent to bring into awareness that which might have been unconscious or just unnoticed) information that he was perfectly happy to ignore. And then there was my insistence on honesty.

From Maine, I wrote:

Morning now, early Sunday. Foghorns in the distance, rain gentle on the roof. The flowers I delayed planting yesterday are being watered by God, their new homes softened by nature's bounty. I need to tweak the front beds and prepare the barrels on the deck, but the hardy cultivated geraniums, snapdragons, marigolds, petunias, and lobelia should thrive through the season, taking their places among the glorious wildflowers of this northern region. . . .

These last two days have been a series of imaginings [of you being here with me]*—everything from messy, giggly dismantling of lobsters as we sit together on the dock at Miller's to reaching the vista at the top of Mount Megunticook. Soon you, too, will be a part of this place—absorbing its mystery, hearing its music and other messages, smiling at the starched curtains I stenciled impulsively (and with errors), as well as the eight sets of Hunter Douglas Duettes that I agonized over for eighteen months before committing to purchase and installation costs. We will walk on the rocks, eat tiny wild blueberries and plump mussels, and listen to the silence. We will hold each other and love each other and yet give each other space—you reading your books, me reading mine; consultation about the music.*

David, reliably centered, reminded me to stay in the present. He had yet to visit me in Connecticut! The next day, back in Fairfield, I wrote:

I awoke with a start, your voice, your words, your presence radiating throughout my being. I shall indeed be more mindful—of where I may chase you (only places we wish to go), of images yearning to become realities, of the necessary constraints of living in "real" time in the "real" world. And when intention and/or behavior threaten to undermine these promises, I will simply ask the angels who watch over us for a little guidance and protection. You are right: ultimately the complexities are

*intrinsically simple; the prism is one. This morning my heart
feels full and whole. Your carefully chosen words are both a
velvet cloak keeping me warm when fear threatens to make me
cold and a tuning fork to my soul. Your request that I replay
them* [your words] *was a wise one. I woke up full of language
particularly and communication more generally, enjoying
having an expanded time/space/dimension. Yes, you do teach/
are teaching me. Yes, you are good for me. . . .*

I was living the lesson that balancing past realities and future possibilities with precious present moments is the key to allowing love's transcendence to respectfully reach across individual destinies and bring each other along in awareness.

We were definitely not in August yet. First we needed to finalize details for David's June visit. He delegated the task of arranging dinner with Scott and Stefanie the evening of his arrival to me. His sister and her longtime boyfriend, neither of whom I had met, were to join us. I promised to collect David at Newark International Airport on Thursday afternoon. We would drive through the Holland Tunnel to the West Village, to the Archives Building, where Scott and Stefanie lived, and all gather at their apartment. Because I knew nothing about restaurants in lower Manhattan (and barely anything about restaurants anywhere else in New York), Scott took charge. He made reservations at Capsouto Frères, a gracious space with high ceilings in the dining area and a long bar to the side, conveniently located so that David could retreat with a cigarette when he felt overwhelmed by emotional intensity (or anything else). I bought tickets for a late-Friday-afternoon Bach concert at Caramoor the day after his arrival; afterward, we were to join the couple who had initially given me David's name at their favorite restaurant. Saturday, my children were coming to the house in Westport, where they could meet David and we could eat dinner together. Sunday, David and I could take a deep breath and just be together, and then Monday he would leave. The first of our many crazy four-day visits across the Atlantic promised to be full and intense.

David somehow managed to keep up with an accelerating amount of work, to make plans with me, and to provide support and encouragement for my own juggling.

> *Delighted with your busy day yesterday and busy day today. That's what I want to hear. Do your things. Accomplish. Fulfill. Have fun. Enjoy your life. Be happy. Smile. Laugh. See friends. Eat dinner in those restaurants. None of that makes me less present, it makes you more of a present to me and the sharing makes me more present for you. And do get irritated about the light/electricity—a salmon dinner in the fridge* [left by the landlord as an apology for avoidable power failures] *is nice, but only an apology and doesn't fix the problem.*

He was so lucid, so grounding for me, so unfailingly understanding and sane. And I knew that if I were to see him again, the way I had forced my body to shut down when I had left him would need to be addressed. I made an appointment for a massage. And then a second one. I kept readying the apartment—liquor in one camp trunk, linens in a second, office supplies in a third. Finally, my heart pounding, I drove to Newark.

We maneuvered our way through the tunnel under the Hudson and then into the Village. Found parking on the street, shared one more reunion kiss, left the car, and announced ourselves to the receptionist in Scott's building. We were given the key so that we could wait in their apartment for him and Stefanie to return from work. A few passionate hugs, and then we left David's bag inside to take a walk around the neighborhood, still a bit overwhelmed with the chemical rush of being together in material reality.

Eventually Scott and Stefanie came home, and, soon after, David's sister and her boyfriend arrived.

His sister greeted me warmly. "I'm so glad to see you. I was up half the night wondering what you might look like." I began wondering what her comment meant. What had she been expecting?

What about me was reassuring? Was it that I was anything but hip? Or some pounds above New York fitness levels? Or nonthreatening in my dowdiness? Or too quiet and suburban to endanger the bonds between her and her brother? Or simply not sexy enough to be taken seriously?

Soon we had flagged down two taxis and headed farther downtown, where we could order three-course meals in a trendy French restaurant during the wee hours on David's biological clock. Wouldn't he have enjoyed something he did not get at home? I wondered. He retreated four times to the bar area to smoke cigarettes. I couldn't identify what was triggering his absences. Was he uncomfortable with some interactions I was not tuning into? Was he anxious about sharing our relationship with his family? Was he worried about what was going to follow? Or was he simply still nicotine-deprived from the long flight?

Finally, we retrieved my car and David drove us to Connecticut. We stopped in Westport to pick up Luke, who had spent the afternoon and evening at Bridget's house, and drove two more miles to Fairfield. We climbed the narrow staircase to the apartment and were "home." I tried to get David to talk about the dinner, hoping to better understand what had been going on with him, but he would have none of it, denying that anything had made him uncomfortable and just insisting he wanted to get home and into bed. I knew that meant get into bed with me.

The visit was not a smooth one. Neither of us was aware at that time just how unfamiliar David was with life in an American suburban town. Through his then-twenty-four continuous years of living and working in Paris, he had traveled to the United States with regularity. Easter vacations he would collect his boys and travel with them; business trips brought him to Los Angeles, New York, Washington, Philadelphia; he went to Southern California to visit his parents. But nothing—not our conversations or my descriptions or even books he had read—had prepared him for my life. The collision between his beliefs about Life in America and the realities of my specific life in

Connecticut would require him to assimilate much that was new and
to change many perceptions and expectations—not an easy task for
someone used to being very smart and knowledgeable. Clearly, angels
would need to guide us as we came to recognize and then appreciate the differences in the contexts of our respective lives—what my
mentor had labeled the "ambient stimuli" in our worlds—and how
those differences affected us and influenced our relationship quality and dynamics. Intuitively, David had even brought me an angel
as a gift, a Baccarat crystal figurine appropriately named *Reverie*
(*Dreamer*), who forever after reminded me of him and of our guard-
ian angels and who could act as a concrete, silent go-between when I
needed one. Thank you, Rosanne Cash.

We walked Luke around the neighborhood with the regularity he
required. That alone could have irritated David if he and Luke had not
bonded as strongly as they did, with surprising rapidity. Especially given
that generally, according to information I thought I had received, David
did not much care for dogs. And now he needed to share a bed with
one. But Luke, with his quick and playful manner and enchanting white
fuzziness, won him over. There was the baroque concert at Caramoor,
in an open-air country theater, an event that David had not imagined
in his city-oriented mindscape of America, followed by a long dinner
with Spanish delicacies with the couple responsible for introducing us.
Whether it was from jet lag, the intensity of his work combined with
travel, reconnecting with me, the load of two large meals two nights in
a row, or even just all those stairs up to the apartment, David felt sick
that night. As he struggled to find a position he could sleep in and complained of shortness of breath, I begged him to let me call the EMTs.
Images of Stuart dying before my eyes in the space of twenty minutes
kept flashing across my mental screen. I struggled to respect what David
was telling me—that this was a reaction he had experienced several
times before, that it was from jet lag, combined with too much eating
and drinking and active lovemaking, and that he would be fine in the
morning. I tossed and turned, slept fitfully, traumatic memories returning, as they tend to do. He awoke the next day feeling just fine.

Then there was the matter of housing. On one of our early walks with Luke, I was forewarned. David had announced, "I *never* want to live in a house. Never have. Too much work and responsibility." That was before we stopped at my office in the mill on Southport Harbor. Or spent an hour in Super Stop & Shop, gathering supplies for dinner that evening. Or crossed the town line into manicured Westport. Or finally, laden with groceries for an informal barbecue, reached the house on Signal Lane.

From the street, the house looked like a simple ranch, on the smaller side, with a two-car garage in the front that hid the depth of the structure. Only upon entering did one recognize its size or architecture or efficient functioning. Or its beauty, its setting on a lake, or its warmth, resulting from natural materials and carefully selected colors. I gave David a guided tour, explaining where the furniture that was now in the apartment had been placed when it had been in the house, interesting if only because the house appeared to remain nearly fully furnished. I described how well the house had served us after Stuart's death. At that time, Danny had moved upstairs and, three months later, when my office building changed hands, I had transformed downstairs into working spaces, complete with a separate path around the side of the house to the sliders on the patio facing the lake. They became entries into the family room–waiting room and my clinical office. I still have the photograph of the setting that one of my patients, a professional photographer, asked permission to take one brilliant fall morning.

David and I returned to the car to gather the rest of the groceries. He was agitated.

"Roni Beth, I am intimidated."

"By what?"

"By this. I never imagined."

"What are you talking about?"

"Your house. I can't give this to you."

"David, what are you talking about?"

"It's so big. So comfortable. So luxurious."

"David, this is just my house. The home where my kids and I live. The house is on the market. The flyer is on the marble table in the front hall. Look at it. Besides, you give me Paris. You don't need to give me a house. I have one. In fact, I have two."

He picked up the sales brochure describing the house, its features, its price. I could see he was calculating, translating the dollars on the listing into francs. The lines in his face went away; he broke into a big grin.

"Oh. I guess I *could* give you a house like this," he announced. He relaxed a bit.

The moment passed, but I was again confused. David's offices seemed almost as large as my house, and they were far more elegant. Not only that, they were located in the heart of a major city, Paris, France. What had he thought I had been talking about the last three months? Where did he think people in America lived? The house was indeed warm and lovely and welcoming and highly functional. It was also more than I needed now that the children were grown. But it was far more modest than the majority of homes in Westport. It was anything but pretentious. David had left the United States during the very beginning stages of his career, still young, with a young wife and two very small children, leading the simple lifestyle of someone just getting started. Now he was well established, but in France, and more than two decades had intervened.

Gradually I came to see that his perceptions and concepts evolved out of a relatively structured and deprived adolescence in a small town in the Catskills, combined with exposure to his sister's cutting-edge Manhattan style. His own years at Princeton and Harvard Law School, and then living in Forest Hills, had been so focused on working hard and "succeeding" that lessons he might have learned from peers and the settings themselves were largely lost.

We went to work in the kitchen I loved. I had brought the marinating meat from the apartment, and we began threading our supplies onto skewers so that they were ready for the grill. David was taking a strangely long time with his job of skewering lamb, mushrooms, peppers, and tomatoes.

"What are you doing?"

"I'm counting them."

"Counting what?"

"The pieces of meat. The mushrooms."

I laughed. "Why would you do that?"

"I don't want anyone to get screwed."

I looked at him, uncomprehending. "David, there is plenty of meat. There is plenty of everything. Anyone can have as much of anything to eat as they want or need. We don't count black jelly beans in my home."

"What do you mean, count black jelly beans?"

"It's a phrase, a gift from one of my patients. She described her childhood as one in which she and her siblings and parents were eternally competitive, afraid that one might receive more resources than another. She referred to the phenomenon as 'always counting the black jelly beans.' I never operated that way. Whoever needs, gets. And what they might need could be very different. But we have always worked as a group to see that everyone has what they need as best we can."

He thought about what I had just said.

Jennifer and Steve and Danny arrived later that afternoon, ready to sleep over in the house because there was no compelling reason not to. Of course, Jennifer and Steve had to sleep in my bed because theirs was at the apartment. And we all missed the music in the living room. But other than that, it was business as usual on Signal Lane and we had a marvelous evening. David had brought two bottles of "the good stuff," wine given to him by the client-friend who belonged to the Rothschild family, and, in spite of my protesting that the kids did not often like wine and might prefer beer, we downed it like it was liquid gold. Intuitively, the younger generation knew the difference between what David had brought and my under-$10 specials. We discussed books and movies, politics and work aspirations. Jennifer pronounced him "very good to talk to. He's interested in so many things. Not so interested in people though, is he? Except he really does seem to care a lot about his boys." And even Dan, nervous about my relationship with a man who lived across an ocean, had to admit that he enjoyed David, his humor, his energy. *Welcome to my world, dear David; my children are central within it.*

Our first real crisis came the following morning. I left David at the apartment to attend the christening of the firstborn of a longtime patient whom I loved deeply. Sitting in the serene space of the church, feeling the blanket of affection and family all around me, I became frightened. This was my world. It was a modest one, a world filled with important relationships and simple rituals, with God and significant life events, with the daily struggles that lead to triumphs as people fight adversities one day at a time and strive toward honor and integrity. It was a world of commitment and courage and meaning, low on glamour and high on heartfelt connections. I felt the tears hot behind my eyes and my determination to hold them back. I was alone here, in my world, and could see no possible way I could manage an ongoing relationship across an ocean, even though I had been doing it for more than a month. My life was here, and his was there. By the time I got back to the apartment, I knew what I needed to do.

"David, I'm sorry, but I just can't do this," I announced.

"What are you talking about? Do what?"

"Manage this relationship. It's too scary. It can't last. It can't go anywhere. And the longer and deeper I am in it, the more it is going to hurt when it falls apart. I've had so much pain and loss in my life already, I can't open myself up to more."

"I can't believe I'm hearing this," he answered.

"We have had a wonderful time. We should just stop it right here. Call it quits. I know you are planning on coming in August for eighteen days. And I guess that's okay. We can play together. But we should sign off on anything more significant."

"Roni Beth, what are you reacting to? I don't understand." Now it was his turn to be confused.

I was sobbing. He wrapped his arms around me and held me, rocking me until the deep remnants of all the other lingering, unresolved pains from losses melted away in the heat of my tears, and then he just stroked my hair. Somehow he understood that silence and presence were the way through the pain. Not argument, not trying to cheer me up, not anger. Just holding me and letting the terror run its course. Gradually, the primitive fear of the little girl raw from abandonment subsided and the woman returned. With her came the courage to continue. As two adults, we made love.

On Monday, adults still in control, we drove to New Haven before we needed to head back to the airport for David's return flight. I wanted him to meet one more person in my life, Stan Kasl, my colleague in the Department of Epidemiology and Public Health of Yale Medical School. And I wanted Stan to meet David. Stan was a key person to me at that time—teaching, collaborating, guiding my scientific self. He had also become a friend. In the brief hour in which we were all together, these two important men in my life developed respect for each other and a better understanding of what motivated me. Then David and I doubled back and headed to the airport so that he could return to his life in Paris.

7

Rethinking

avid's June trip had been a difficult one, in part because it was so short and our agenda was long and in part because we faced separation for another six weeks. But we had survived, and the phone calls and faxes promised to continue. David even signed up for a Kallback account, one of those early electronic services that bypassed the expensive phone lines, that guaranteed serious savings, and that his sons and I, all on the other side of the Atlantic, could use. We could take advantage of the coming six weeks to get to know each other better, as we continued to share stories of and reflections on our daily lives. August would come quickly. But first we had to finish the unfinished business of the weekend. Later that week I wrote to David:

> *I am beginning to digest bits and pieces of the weekend—the extent to which Luke took to you (you should see him tilt his head when he hears your messages); the exquisite and unique perfection of my gifts (I've actually taken to having discussions with Reverie; with her crystal transparency, she is the ultimate object for projection!); the reality that, in spite of history and language, you are far more French than American; my fears, their provocation and resolution—or not, and so on. . . .*

Uneasiness over my Sunday meltdown lingered, and I continued to feel a need to apologize, explain myself:

David, I can't promise to be/feel what you may want—only honestly to be how I am. Maybe there's not enough (a) control or (b) balance sheet, bottom line, the way you want them in there, for you. If not, tell me and I'll go away—my emotional integrity is not negotiable. I happen to be a very positive person who generally loves the moment, or can find something to enjoy in it—just not always, especially under triggers. Do remember that I watched (literally) a most beloved husband die in front of me in the middle of the night—with only minimal previous symptoms, even in retrospect. Yes, I got scared. Danny had to be hospitalized five times for ear tubes before I got over the association between death of a child and hospitals, but I did get over it—I can learn. Or maybe I just come with too much history for you. In any event, it is what it is. And there has been a lot of challenge, pain, and growth in it—all of which have helped me become who I am, most of which I like a lot. And I probably won't get substantially lighter till a few of my major current responsibilities are out of the way. There's a lot on my plate. I'm sorry that Connecticut—and the trip to the USA—wasn't more fun, but not sure I like the "shape up or I'm outta here" implication either.

My dear, level-headed, rock-solid David wisely responded:

Now what do I do about the rest? Ignore? Give you time to process? Or jump right in? I'll try to navigate a middle course. You should try to see the positive in what I write (or say)—my happiness at seeing/feeling you happier. I did not say you could never be sad or worried or anxious or fearful, nor did I say I didn't understand—or that I wanted to run away (please stop that). I did say you were worth waiting for and being patient

with, 'cause you can and do work it out and then you smile and
I'm fine. Maybe I am more optimistic. But I am not trying to
interfere with your emotional integrity. I am, sometimes, trying
to help you work through the anxieties and fears. Is that so bad?
Am I lacking in understanding? Or compassion? Or support? In
short, and being totally honest (my integrity), I had expected a
much brighter reaction to my long letter followed by my bright
and bouncy phone message.

Quit picking fights with me. I am not going away that easy.
I'm gonna keep up the courting and the seduction 'cause I want
you in my life and I want to make you happy and I think I can.
I do not want to cause you sadness.

I apologized:

David, you are so truly wonder-full. Not only are your mes-
sages like cashmere wraps on a cool summer night, warm and
fuzzy and elegant and comforting and indulgent, but they have
permitted me to begin to reshape my perspective. As I told you,
the Sunday morning conversation permitted me to realize that
my real (at least current) fear is of being part of a "couple," the
possibility of my deepest dreams coming true—sharing, part-
nering, building—fused with vivid knowledge of how painful it
has been to give up those dreams (again and again), to accept
a life in which I rely solely and totally on myself for my own
happiness. Thus, letting you in on that feels incredibly vulner-
able—that is, unless I take a leap of faith and decide to believe
that you really mean what you say. . . .

Again, he had helped calm my incipient panic. His words reminded
me that the best way to deal with fear, pain, and disappointment can
be acknowledging the emotions, remembering all the times that you
have coped with them, and reassuring yourself that they, too, can be
temporary. Most things are. Add that faith and patience fight fear. I

had to remind myself that I can be charging along in one direction, fueled by adrenaline and perhaps applause of peers and sheer satisfaction of "progress" toward some goal, and then the universe will come along and turn me in a new direction. I chastised myself: *Can you slow down, be still enough, to know it, feel it, follow it, in spite of the fears? Stop thinking you are running the show.*

The pace of our relationship had a life of its own. We had met less than three months before, and already we had reached some agreements concerning decision making (David drove the car) and curiosity (we were going to let the relationship take us wherever it needed to go). We had begun to explore what was fun (being together) and what was not (sometimes accommodating others), as well as our different approaches to honesty ("discretion" versus disclosure). We were clear we were going to continue seeing each other.

Lacking opportunities to be together in physical reality, we continued to plan. Our July faxes were filled with proposals for the upcoming trip and examination of details. Even though much had been blocked out—the biannual meeting of the International Society for the Study of Personal Relationships (ISSPR), being held at the Banff Conference Center in western Canada, followed by several days in Toronto for the annual convention of the American Psychological Association and then a final week at the cottage in Maine—we needed to discuss when and where to spend time with Scott and Stefanie, with his sister and her boyfriend, with my friends who were eager to "entertain" David, hoping to make him feel welcome. We discussed flights and weather, wardrobes and restaurants, and the inside information that someone I trusted knew a romantic lodge for dinner near Lake Louise. We were going to be in Maine over his birthday. On his first visit, I had longed to introduce David to Stan and to my New Haven world, far more central to my identity than the context that surrounded me in Fairfield County, even with its sparklies on Long Island Sound. Now I wanted him to meet my precious Maine, the St. George River and Penobscot Bay, the sweep of Route 1 as it crosses over the bridge in Bath, the magnetism of Monhegan Island.

The distance and our forced separations permitted us to get to know each other's rhythms and relationships to our own lives and others who populated them. Fears, reflections, and coping mechanisms continued to surface. The sharing helped us to identify misunderstandings and resolve them. I could tell David, *You are good for me; indeed, I'm better for you being in my life, which merges into I need you in order to be the best I can be, which, of course, is frightening to a woman committed to self-reliance—although I* am *beginning to believe that that part (helping me be better than I can be on my own) is okay with you. And now, being conscious of it, I'll work on it being okay with me. . . .*

In the bigger picture, I feel so much is an invention. The distance fosters nontraditional relating on both ends—when we are together, an intensity and escalation and almost minimum of processing (it's a waste when compared with an opportunity to be "in the moments" together). And when we are apart, there is all that time for reflection, variety, revealing multiple facets of self, ensuring that concerns are heard, addressed.

David teased me about my appreciation of the images he created in his faxes. *Are you getting bored? You're gonna tell me you love all these details, learning about and hearing my life. Good. There will be a quiz next week.* And he asked me, again and again, to be mindful of how much energy I devoted to meeting the needs of others and ignoring my own.

In one beautiful love letter, he insisted that we were good for each other because we were different yet both independent and self-reliant.

That's the base we build on, that's the infrastructure, that's what also impresses each of us in the other, and what each of us then gets is in addition (and a discovery) and takes nothing away from the self-sufficiency we retain. . . . My understanding of you as disconcerting? No, just more of my overwhelming you in every possible way and on every possible level, and again anything I add takes nothing away from what you are (and what you must remain—the marvelous woman I fell in love with). I love disconcerting you—it's (mostly) intentional, and part of the courtship and the seduction. I want to impress you. I want you to be impressed. I love when you are speechless or flabbergasted. It means I have surprised you again—as we keep surprising (and discovering) each other. Constant newness! Perpetual renewal! More and more wonder. Living in and with the present. The excitement and intensity of it. No need for (or time for) processing. I love the nonquestioning aspect of my feelings for you—and am learning about the added value of some of your processing at some times (having—quickly— gotten over the instinctive/immediate rejection of having to "analyze" everything). And you get your positions from the processing, while learning with and from me about the delights of just being and feeling and living in the moment, the gift, the ordinary miracle, unquestioned and with no need of or for analysis (until—maybe—later, reliving moments and memories and words and gestures . . . and silences). Prettier now in French, but oh so appropriate from your first writing it to me in English: "le passé c'est de l'histoire, le futur mystère, le présent un cadeau."

My yoga teacher's quotation—"the past is history, the future a mystery; today is a gift, which is why they call it the present"—had crossed the ocean in a more eloquent form, appearing on a huge billboard opposite the Pont de la Concorde (or was it the Pont Alexandre III?).

8

August in (North) America

Our eighteen August days together played out like a musical composition. They began with a burst of intensity and joy, slid into tension, then conflict, recovered with resolution, moved into bliss in the middle, slid back into more tension and more conflict as we approached the final days, but then ended with another burst of joy and good feeling. This pattern repeated whenever we were together long enough—and sometimes even when it *wasn't* long enough. Then, left with frustration, we needed to resolve whatever had surfaced during our moments together, flooding the phone calls and faxes that followed the separation with a heaviness that could weigh us both down.

Long-distance relationships bring both curses and blessings. They require a couple to cherish the precious real-time shared minutes but also to create a reliable relationship dynamic, one with opportunities for reflection, flexibility, problem solving, and change.

We began David's vacation visit brightly enough, with dinner at a restaurant that Scott and Stefanie had selected, a gem named Provence, around the corner on Macdougal Street. They had reserved a table for a reasonable hour, given that David's internal clock was striking well past midnight. We shared warm conversation and delicious food and soaked up the ambience, all of us in good cheer.

Later that evening, after driving up to Connecticut, we collected Luke from his extended visit with Bridget. After pretending that he did not recognize David, Luke rejoiced in having his buddy around again. Because the house had not sold and I had decided to move back into it as soon as the listing expired, I had carted sufficient clothing, food, and wine back to Signal Lane so that we could sleep, eat, and dress there in comfort. All three of us were delighted.

We had dinner at a charming country restaurant on Saturday night, David's sister and her boyfriend joining us in Westport. Sunday we packed and prepared for our travels all day long. We had to be ready to leave—complete with all my presentation paraphernalia—early the next morning. A quiet evening was not in the plan: three of my closest girlfriends, the ones with whom I had had breakfast the morning I was given David's name, had decided they would make a dinner party in our honor. And what a party it was! We all dressed up and sat in the hostess's gorgeous home, drinking and eating one impressive offering after another, each served with exquisite appointments in a gracious manner by a uniformed helper.

As the evening progressed, David's mood shifted from mildly to acutely uncomfortable. He seemed to become more and more critical, less and less willing to joke, imagine, flirt. Finally, he grew quieter and quieter. I didn't understand. These were my girlfriends; I had known them and their spouses for many years; we had shared births and deaths, personal triumphs and tragedies, the pleasures and worries of watching our children grow into adulthood. We had helped and supported each other through family festivities and funerals, osteopenia and menopause, hurricanes and floods, effective and less effective government administrations, shifts in Fairfield County town priorities, the openings and closings of local schools, enterprises, restaurants.

Although he was clearly a little edgy that night, I tried to explain away his increasing emotional distance by invoking lingering jet lag, no smoking allowed on airplanes, and probably some anxiety about making the early flight toward western Canada the next morning. Or perhaps he was reacting to the unknowns in the situation. Neither of us had been to Banff before, and I had presented at meetings of this particular scientific-professional group only once, two years earlier, when they had convened in Grönigen, on the northern coast of the Netherlands, so I could not reliably orient David to the event in advance. Add that he had never attended a convention of academics intent on learning from one another. Generally, novelty arouses interest, but when the situation is too new or too complex, fear can result. Fear of the unknown creates anxiety. Was he anxious? Was I? Always the psychologist, always generating possible hypotheses, I needed to wait until answers to my questions revealed themselves.

The next day, when the plane passed Pittsburgh, David admitted that the previous evening had felt a bit "excessive" to him. By the time we reached Chicago, he described having been "uncomfortable" with the elegance, the many courses, the presentation of the fine wines. I explained that our hostess had been eager to reciprocate, to show her appreciation for the times she and her husband had enjoyed his own hospitality in Paris, including "the most orgasmic pâté" they could ever remember having tasted. To celebrate how well her introducing us appeared to have worked out. And to help me in my romance by demonstrating that, in her words, "the best thing about you is your friends." By Minneapolis, David was voicing anger at the formality of the previous evening. And, finally, as we approached our landing in Calgary, he blurted out, "It felt like a goddamn engagement party, for Chrissake!"

I had been trying to hear, to listen carefully, to grasp what bothered him most. And there it was, or at least—once again—I *thought* I understood. Perhaps David was feeling shoved toward an involvement that he did not want. About the last thing either of us was up for was marriage. And yet now he was feeling pressure to conform to what he had seen as a suburban standard for and interpretation of coupled relationships. Marriage. Formality. Unbridled elegance. Socializing. I got it.

And then *I* got angry. How dare he think I was setting him up for something neither of us wanted? How *could* he see me as responsible for the behavior of my friends? What *did* he expect from people who invited him to a party in their home? It was still too early in our relationship; I did not yet grasp the cultural basis of our respective reactions. Only later did I learn how rarely Parisians entertain friends, especially *new* friends, in their homes. To do so is considered a tribute to deep and binding friendship, an offering of great honor, requiring serious thought, expense, and effort. And four of the six hosts of our dinner had never even met him before!

David was appalled because of his own misinterpretation of the evening. He had been out of the world of his American peers for a very long time. In many ways, he still saw himself as a hillbilly from South Fallsburg. My friends were only doing what they did often, with generosity, ease, and pleasure, just as I had hosted bridal and then baby showers for their children or opened my home for their charity benefit parties.

The road from Calgary to Banff, David driving our rented car on the well-maintained, deserted highways, was picture-perfect, and gradually our irritations dissipated. Talking had definitely helped. By the time we arrived at the conference center, we were both ready to switch gears. The dormitory-style living was a far cry from the opulence of the hotel in Turin. The meals at the dining hall were simple and self-service. The lectures, symposia, and poster sessions were first-rate. David's intellectual curiosity got the best of him, and he had a wonderful time, absorbing new ideas, asking lucid questions, bringing intelligent and naive eyes, his own point of view, and a lawyer's logic and perspective to discussions of complex relationship puzzles.

After the Banff conference with a few hundred participants, sequestered away in a self-contained conference center, we flew to Toronto for the annual meetings of the American Psychological Association. More than ten thousand participants were housed in rooms all over downtown; a friend had helped us reserve one in the sought-after SkyDome. Organized sessions spilled out beyond the huge convention center next door into ballrooms and meeting rooms at nearby hotels. My talk was well received. I knew my way around

APA meetings and was in control. To my surprise and pleasure, I kept bumping into people I knew from all phases of my professional life, from graduate school onward, colleagues whose lives and careers brought stories I loved hearing, the friend whose cousin I had called my first night in Paris. David got a kick out of meeting them, learning about their work. A quick study, he picked up an enormous amount of lingo and spoke to these people in their own language.

We flew home, changed clothes, did laundry, repacked, collected Luke, and drove the 344 miles to Haskell's Point Road, Tenants Harbor, site of my cottage in midcoast Maine. My spirit grew lighter and my smile broader as we crossed the borders that took us deeper and deeper into northern New England.

I had been nervous about David's reaction to the cottage. Sure, he lived on a boat—just about the same size in square footage—but this was a near-isolated, three-room dwelling down a deeply rutted dirt road. Overgrown foliage claimed the expanse behind it, threatening to one day obscure the views of the ocean lapping or crashing against the boulders, now a stunning real-life painting seen through the glass doors that ran the length of the front of the cottage. Wildlife lived alongside the humans. At twilight the peepers and crickets sang to us, at night we went to sleep to the sounds of foghorns and nocturnal creatures, and in the morning the sun woke us as it streamed in through the eastern-facing sliders, the birds serenading us. We built fires in the kerosene stove, bundled up for the ferry ride to Monhegan Island, and, sitting on Miller's dock, ate lobsters with our hands, gently prying the sweet flesh from its shell with a primitive pleasure. Fantasy became reality.

At sunset one afternoon we sat on the deck, drinks in hand, and watched the colors shift on the sky and in the water.

"Beautiful, don't you think?" I asked.

"Gorgeous."

"I always feel so perfect myself here," I added.

"I can understand that. I could even see myself living here. Except what would I *do*?"

Something in the tone of David's voice—plaintive but also a bit defensive—told me to drop the topic. This was not the time to open a discussion about the distance to Boston. Besides, I was assuming that David needed a city, not only to do what he did but also to keep his curious mind and aesthetic sensibilities sufficiently stimulated.

On his fifty-seventh birthday, I presented him with two V-neck sweaters and shirts to go under them.

"They are beautiful, Roni Beth."

"I was hoping you would like them. I couldn't decide whether the navy or khaki green would look better on you, so I had to buy them both."

"I've never owned a cashmere sweater before."

"Then it's time."

"I won't be able to wear them in Paris, though. I'll get too hot."

"What?"

"I get hot. And they don't go with my life."

"But I thought you wear jeans a lot. And these can also go with a sport coat. Do you like the shirts that go with them?"

"I can probably wear the shirts. The one is a little loose, though. I like my clothes more fitted."

"Oh. Sorry. I tried. Maybe if you visit me in the winter, you could wear one here."

"I guess. I don't usually pack much when I travel, though."

By this point, I was near tears. I had tried so hard to hit the right note with his gifts. I had thought that a classic, high-quality cashmere V-neck would bring his skin pleasure, his wardrobe a new elegant but understated (like David) note, and enough practicality that the luxury could be acceptably rationalized. Now here he was, reminding me how well I did *not* know him.

I remembered early on in our courtship, before I had gone back to Europe for the Italy weekend, when I had painstakingly created a tape of some of my favorite songs for him. Luke had insisted on occasionally accompanying the music. When David received the tape, he called to say he couldn't play it on his sound system. The quality of my recording was so poor, and the background noise (Luke) so annoying, that he was afraid he would damage his speakers. That was just how I felt when he basically didn't want the sweaters. I became a little girl slapped on the wrist for not doing something well enough. My open and eager heart said, *Be careful—he may not want what you have to give.*

Later that night, I took him to Jessica's for his birthday dinner. Jessica's was my favorite restaurant in the entire Camden-Rockport-Rockland area, famous for its seafood risotto. Situated in a Victorian house in Rockland, across the street from the ocean, each room had a fireplace and a different type of New England decor. The menu, developed and executed by a Swedish couple who had migrated to midcoast Maine, was inventive and made use of local delicacies like fiddleheads and sea creatures. David did not like Jessica's, not the decor or the food or the service. He retreated into his critical self and seemed ready to complain about everything. The risotto was too "heavy," the waitress was overweight, the individual dining rooms in the converted house too cramped, the table too small, the fabrics too uncoordinated. I was not sure what had happened, only that I felt "not good enough." Again, I was misunderstanding the source of his reaction and had to wait for it to reveal itself.

The following day we drove up US Route 1 beyond Camden. After climbing Mount Megunticook and breathing in the vast views of August-blue Penobscot Bay and the islands that dotted it, we returned to the picturesque village where *Peyton Place* had been filmed many years before and headed for lunch at Cappy's Chowder House. David reluctantly admitted that the clam chowder tasted superb, and he seemed to relax a little. Nonetheless, his uneasiness escalated visibly when, after lunch, we wandered through some of the shops and galleries in the scenic seaside town. Finally he told me he was having a panic attack. We returned to the car, and I navigated us away from the bustling, tourist-filled village; past the farm with the "Oreo cows" (black on front and rear, white in the middle) grazing opposite the Atlantic; toward the breakwater in Rockland, adjacent to the Samoset

Resort. It was one of the few times in our relationship when I drove the car. After walking in silence across most of the mile-long stretch of boulders that formed a jetty connecting the shore to the lighthouse, we sat down on the rocks and began to talk.

David started. "All the fancy little shops. And people buying things like crazy, not just looking. Hats. Leather goods. Ceramics. Art. Jewelry. They are all buying. And eating. Eating all the time. Even fudge. Or walking down the street with ice cream cones. Or carrying a drink. It's overwhelming. All too much. This is out of my league."

"David, I don't understand. Every day you walk past Hermès and Baccarat on the way to work. You eat lunch or dinner with celebrities. You get seated next to the guest of honor at business and social events. You go to these amazing weddings. Sogyal Rinpoche officiated at one of the recent ones and the Taittinger flowed. Camden is a small resort town in midcoast Maine—that's all. It's very sedate as resort towns go. What are you reacting to?"

"It's the materialism, the lifestyle. All those souvenir and craft shops. People consuming. And Jessica's—too heavy, no subtlety. And I don't like it."

I guessed that he might still be unconsciously reacting to what he had experienced as the over-the-top dinner our first weekend in Westport. Again, he felt intimidated. Or to my indulging him with his birthday gift, even as he showered me with beautiful things. The village of Camden was only the trigger. He was forced into recognizing that the feelings and behavior he was expressing were hallmarks of anxiety. I understood that the forced revision of his view of "life in the United States" had flung him into fear born of insecurity. Apparently, realizing he did not know what he thought he knew catapulted conflict—and, with it, fear of not being in control—into consciousness.

We sat and talked, breathed in and out, and let the salt air bring its healing power. David became settled again, safe. Reassured that he could be imperfect and that this American woman, still with her mysterious sides, would continue to love him, he became more loving. He had yet to learn that the more I could understand him, the more real he could be with me, the more I *could* love him. We reconnected in spirit and body. As on every trip, then and later, lovemaking inevitably brought us together. This communication with touch and energy said more than language crafted from words ever could.

So David's extended August visit ended sweetly, along with the sad farewells that always bracketed our separations. But this time we had a concrete plan: David wanted me to come to Paris for the Jewish holy days, the entire ten-day period, arriving the morning of Rosh Hashanah Eve on Friday, September 13 (I would leave the night of the twelfth), and staying until Tuesday, September 24, the day after Yom Kippur. I had not taken more than a week away from my patients since 1986, when I had gone to India, but this invitation was irresistible. I agreed to consider it. If I said yes, we would be apart slightly less than four weeks until the next trip.

On Sunday, August 18, David boarded Air France flight 007 from JFK to return to his boat, his clients, his life. He arrived Monday morning to a secretary who had collected and organized all the legal matters that needed tending, to phone calls from visitors about to arrive in Paris, and to the bustle of the annual fall *rentrée*, when Paris emerges from its sleepy, monthlong *grandes vacances* and children go back to school, the arts begin new seasons, fashion turns to a different palette, and a revived populace digs into its work and play with renewed enthusiasm and energy. The following day, he scrawled his next fax to me on a piece of graph paper:

Formal Invitation:

David Griff
requests the pleasure of
a visit by Roni Beth Tower
to share his bed
onboard the Berreti
at any time *(mid-September, for example)*
and for extended periods
whenever the schedule of
Roni Beth Tower (realistically) permits
This invitation is valid for multiple visits
Minimum 24 hours' notice to guarantee
Clean sheets—no guaranty of bathroom facilities
Wishful thinking → *(spare key still on order)*
Paris, 20 August 1996

9

Culture Clash

*L*uke took David's departure badly. To the extent to which a bichon can become depressed, he became an exemplar. Too many changes, shifts in energies, unknowns. He stared out the window, waiting in vain for his buddy to return. He approached his meals without enthusiasm and his walks with less curiosity. I knew that I needed to get out of the rented apartment, back into our house, and stabilized as quickly as possible. My landlord and a friend of his located a truck somewhere and moved the furniture back, while I dealt with smaller things: clothes, plants, perishables.

Meanwhile, back in Paris, David kept a close eye on my efforts to reclaim the rhythms of the nourishing life I had lived before I had met him. Just three days after his return, he wrote:

> *Caught up on almost all bits and pieces, current pending, most correspondence and administrative and personal stuff. Hence, time to write to my girlfriend, who just barely has time to sleep and rest and dream. I know how much you have to do—and the physical and emotional burden it all represents. But it does keep you occupied and soon it will be done and part of the past, and your trip to Paris in September will be part of the nearer (and always mysterious) future. . . .*

With this encouragement, I studied dates and finally called Air France to book flights, beginning a mere three weeks in the future. As David had proposed, I would arrive in Paris on the Friday morning of Rosh Hashanah Eve and leave on the Tuesday morning following Yom Kippur.

Over the next three weeks, David made countless supportive phone calls, left messages when I was out or working, sent faxes, and wrote an occasional letter. With customary synchronicity, crises that needed to arise so that we could create solutions together dropped into our laps. In an unexpected complication of our September plans, my daughter's mother-in-law called to say that she and her husband were going to Paris and they would like to meet my new boyfriend. Same time as I would be there. She was (still is) a beautiful and accomplished woman, interesting, an attorney who could share David's background in intellectual property law. Indeed, she was coming to France to work face-to-face with her new French client. Even though she had been remarried for less than five years and her husband would be with her, I began to worry. When I was a teen, my boyfriends were routinely seduced away by another female (my own mother) whom I saw as prettier, smarter, more interesting and savvy.

Luckily, I was sufficiently aware of both my reaction and its origin to try to explain it to David. Again he reassured me, and then he made reservations for us to take them for dinner at a classical Parisian brasserie, La Coupole, that was guaranteed to have fine food and ambience that offered historical authenticity and charm, but was not one of the sexier hideaways. He confronted my neurotic fears head-on but with sensitivity and imagination. No denial here. I was grateful. Trying to argue someone out of an irrational concern rarely works. Treating it as important to the person, whether "legitimate" or not, is a far more effective response.

David had been invited to a cocktail party one night before my arrival. He told me about the woman seated next to him, who had invited him to a benefit gala, a concert, and an art opening. That was of minimal concern to me. But the next day, he received a call from a woman he had met during her trip to Paris the previous fall. She wanted him to take her out to dinner. He explained to me that he had turned down her request to join her in Vienna during the previous Christmas holidays. On the other hand, he could conveniently have dinner with her in Paris after I had left. They had set a date. And then yet another woman, the longtime lover whom he had "thrown off" the boat in June, called him to announce that her divorce was final and she would like to see him. Yes, she did know that he was seeing another woman, an American.

My insecurities exploded, concerning both David's potential resistance to a woman's seduction *and* my doubts about his own ability to stop a determined woman's pursuit, in light of how adept he was at charming females. He had to be vulnerable to the flattery to his ego, coupled with his desire "not to hurt"—read: disappoint—any woman whom he had enchanted. I had grown up with a needy mother, been privy to story after story of seduction in my own consulting room, and could attest firsthand to sexually based manipulation. And this was France, where affairs were an integral part of the social fabric, the easy solution to remaining in problematic couplings. David kept trying to reassure me that my fears were groundless and that he was dedicated to his relationship with me. I wrote:

> *David, do what makes you happy. That was one of the things I initially fell in love with and something I am learning from you: do what makes you happy. Decisions I have made about other men have had to do with me, not you. I admit I love the flattery. And there's a measure of safety in knowing that an attractive man will still follow me onto a train and . . . But, in a word, I want you to do whatever makes you happy—including collecting whatever additional information you may need about other women, yourself, or yourself with other women. Does it affect me? Sure. I feel lots of things. Less safe is one of them. But we have to live our lives.*

I knew that I could not tolerate a nonmonogamous love affair. He reported that he had told the visitor-to-be that he was "seeing" a woman, and that he turned down invitations from the woman at the party who had kept calling him. He tried to further reassure me:

> *Net, net, net—I'm looking forward to seeing you, to being with you, to holding you and making love with you and eating with you and sleeping with you and wandering Paris with you and seeing Lone Star with you and going to antiques shows with you and the Calder exhibit with you and taking you to the Orangerie and sharing the wonderful Monet Nymphéas with you—and not anyone else.*

Many long phone calls later, my heart had been reassured and the tension melted. But the question remained: Could David's acceptance of my idiosyncratic needs transcend the impact of all those years of living as a Frenchman and loving it? My longer visit over the Jewish holidays would bring an opportunity to learn more.

⸙

I arrived at Charles de Gaulle Airport, Terminal 2C, on Air France flight 007 early on Friday, September 13. On that blustery fall morning, David guided me into the gleaming Ford Escort, and once again its sound system was programmed to "Ordinary Miracles." We drove slowly, stop and go, the rest of the way into the center of Paris, as I tried to peek into boutique windows on rue Boissy d'Anglas and smiled at the gardens that abut Place de la Concorde. We finally turned down the ramp and moved past the barricade onto the quai. The smell of the warm croissants we had picked up on the way promised infinite moments of pleasure to share while we were together.

David had polished the boat, brass to mahogany and pine paneling, and he had even managed to convince his plumber to come repair both the hot-water heater and the pump for the toilet. Finally, the

sink and shower ran forcefully and hot and the toilet flushed without
a bucket of water drawn from the Seine. Grapefruit juice and exotic
jams half-filled the tiny refrigerator, colorful linens straight from the
laundry adorned the freshly made bed with the extrafirm mattress,
and fresh flowers decorated the living quarters. I felt welcomed.

When David was on his home turf, he could more than "drive the
car": he could decide which metaphorical vehicle he wanted at any
given point in time, where he would like it to go, and what sort of
route he wanted to take in getting there. This promised to be eleven
days and nights bracketed by High Holy Day services on the first night
and the last. Which it was. But so much more.

Until then, David had attended only Paris's Orthodox synagogues,
where men and women were seated separately. Raised as a Reform
Jew, I considered myself an open-minded woman who had strong
opinions, influenced partially by my religion major at Barnard, about
what of Judaism I accepted and wanted to follow and what dogma I
rejected as unrelated to my beliefs and identity. Separate seating was
unacceptable. David located the Union Libérale Israélite de France,
headquartered at 24 rue Copernic, and then arranged to buy us tickets
that permitted access to adjacent seats. We could share participation
in services throughout the entire High Holy Days period.

After picking up our tickets during the day, we returned for the
first service that evening. To our surprise, neither the rabbi nor the
cantor was in the nameless building with the small and understated
white-and-gold sanctuary. We took our assigned seats on the wooden
pews and recited the prayers, which, when in Hebrew, were so familiar to us both. David marveled at being able to sit next to me, someone
he loved, during a service, just as he had sat next to his father throughout his childhood. Hearing me reel off the familiar Hebrew chants, he
finally began to believe that I really *was* Jewish, in spite of my affection
for churches and interest in all religions. I fought back tears of joy at
being able to share all this, for the first time since Stuart had died, with
a man who actually cared about this Jewish holiday.

The bliss of reunion and of our shared discovery of Reform Judaism in Paris carried us through the first weekend with feelings of increasing intimacy, transcending cultural differences between us. When we realized that the bulk of the nearly four-thousand-member congregation was worshiping at the immense Palais des Congrès with the rabbi and the cantor, we blithely congratulated each other on our shared contentment with the less prestigious but equally formal services we were enjoying. We had not known that there was a broader presence of Reform Judaism in Paris. Intuitively, we both somehow realized that the sanctuary services, peopled with mostly aging French Jews, more closely matched David's experiences and expectations of his religion, forged primarily in the tiny synagogue in South Fallsburg, New York, where he and his adolescent friends were often pulled in off the street to form the daily minyan (quorum for a service), and his later attendance at services in the august Orthodox synagogues of Paris. Had his first experience of Reform Judaism been in the larger and more "normal" venue, High Holy Days services in a huge auditorium, he might have run screaming from a brand of religion that was unfamiliar to him in spite of two languages in which he was fluent.

Heady from having worshiped together that evening and rested from our long morning nap after our passionate reconnection, we walked over to Carré Kléber, a sophisticated dining room in a hotel a few blocks toward Trocadero. We sat opposite each other, sheltered by branches from flowering trees set in stately vases and placed discreetly around the sleekly modern but romantic restaurant. David ordered glasses of champagne.

"Welcome to Paris, my love."

I responded with a broad smile. He continued, "I propose a toast. To all the love and celebrations that we are going to share throughout our lives."

I was stunned into my characteristic silence as tears of joy began tumbling down my cheeks. They said it all. These were the words with future implication that I had longed to hear. We were crossing a new threshold. We now had an acknowledged future, as well as our treasured present moments. David did indeed intend us to be a "couple."

As a bonus, during this dinner, David introduced me to *magret de canard*, destined to compete with *confit de canard* and *carré d'agneau* as my favorite classic French dish.

We returned to Copernic the next day for Saturday morning services and then spent the afternoon exploring the booths at the Biennale des Antiquaries, a gathering of fine-arts and antique dealers from all over France (and perhaps Europe) that convenes every other year. That evening, David drove us to Au Vieux Paris, a candlelit, stone-walled restaurant with a beamed ceiling located on a side street near the Panthéon. He wanted to introduce me to *pousse rapière*, an aperitif from the southwest of France, basically Armagnac and champagne, along with foie gras and an excellent *confit de canard*.

Sunday following services (David being a "two-day Jew"), we drove through the wealthy 16th arrondissement and into the Bois de Boulogne, the enormous park that sits along the western boundary of Paris. Past the lake with the parasol pines, Le Pré Catelan, the bike paths and horse trails, the families spending a sunny Sunday with a picnic or game of *boules*, we turned into the parking area for Bagatelle, a square enclave of gardens with paths winding through its broad expanse. There we examined roses of more varieties than I had imagined existed, laughed at children playing in the grotto, snuggled on inconspicuously placed park benches. My life in Westport seemed very far away; the woman who monitored her lists and prayed not to skip a responsibility was vanishing with the geographical and cultural distance. In her place, I was again in the moment, softer, more feminine, more aware of the world around me and especially of the world that was David. That evening when we joined his Sunday-night-dinner French friends, Jacques and Corrine, at Du Côté 7ème, I almost forgot that I didn't really speak the language very well and chattered away as though my fractured French were actually comprehensible.

The next day, with David's declared intent to nurture our relationship over time established, we faced a challenge: being together in his daily Parisian work world. I had brought both the data for and the beginning drafts of my current manuscript. We were going to spend a "normal" workweek together in Paris, folding me into David's routines. Could we move beyond "vacation" to daily life?

He had asked the concierge to clean the empty office adjacent to his, and it awaited my laptop and me, complete with its fireplace, tall mirror, French doors that opened onto the balcony to invite in fresh air, and off-white grasscloth that papered the walls with softness. Even the ring of the telephone sounded like music. I was swaddled in beauty. I settled in on Monday morning, plugged the keyboard into the computer and the computer into the wall, and began staring at the data I had brought with me, contemplating their implications, considering ways to present them in tables, and imagining narratives that could bring their story to life most effectively.

No doubt about it: in these 305 older couples, one type of marriage—described through the data they had provided—was strongly associated with longer life for men, and also for their wives if the women had ever had or raised children. This happened when the wife named her husband as her primary emotional support or confidant *and* he was a bit of a rock, not claiming that he turned to her for support or as a confidant. These results were dramatic and occurred even after we allowed for age, education, race, financial strain, chronic illness, disability, cognitive impairment, depressive symptoms, overweight or underweight, alcohol use, current or former smoking, their self-perception of health, and even widowhood. None of these other risk factors could explain the findings. Something truly intriguing was going on.

For an entire week, I was going to be able to examine other data in my massive files for possible explanations, explore theories that might predict or explain the findings, and be fully absorbed by my research project, with no patients awaiting consultation, no dog needing a walk, no mail or phone messages requiring responses (although I did check for messages a few times each day), and no checks to write or clothes to launder or office supplies to order. David was in the next room, available for a hug at any moment and most certainly for lunch. A sandwich of chicken on *pain de campagne*, eaten at a desk or in Parc

Monceau and washed down with Badoit, was going to taste delicious. Even Mme. H. was cheerful.

Then, just as it had after our reunion the month before, uneasiness simmered and soon erupted into a rolling boil. This time, I was the one who was upset.

Monday began innocently enough, although with a bit of a jolt, as we jumped into the workday routine. Rather than a leisurely cuddle and lingering breakfast with croissants, baguettes, and fresh-ground Grandmère coffee, we awoke to an alarm clock, ate slices of Wasa bread, and hurried as we began the walk to the office. We climbed up the ladder on the wall of the quai, took the shortcut across Place de la Concorde, detoured around the Crillon, and headed up rue Boissy d'Anglas. Partway up bd Malesherbes, David pointed out the whimsical windows of a tea shop. Casually, he commented on the worldwide range of teas sold inside. The hour was early, the shop was closed, and I reacted with my customary open mouth and wide eyes. Perhaps added an "oh, wow!" for extra enthusiasm.

Soon we reached his office. I worked all morning, happy to be absorbed in my manuscript with no interruptions. None, that is, excepting David. He kept checking in, reassuring himself that I was indeed in the room next door and cheerfully typing away. He had yet to learn that I don't switch gears easily; I tried to ignore the interruptions.

The crisis came after lunch. We walked down the street to buy our sandwiches, and on the way back he steered me into the tea shop, where a beautiful woman in chic, sexy clothes greeted him with three kisses on both cheeks. By then I understood that a demonstration of familiarity—or intimacy?—was taking place. He and the woman became engaged in an animated conversation, loaded with smiles and locked gazes, that excluded me. When they finally made their way to a sufficient pause, I reminded him that I was still with him. A little startled, he introduced me again and tried to describe the range of teas and teapots in the shop. Both came from all over the world, in dozens of varieties. The woman's assistant served us samples of

Autumn Blend. The gorgeous shop owner offered us English biscuits. I shrank deeper and deeper into my rounding shoulders, as I felt more and more invisible (or was that wishful thinking, a desire to run from my rage and shame?).

After we finally left the shop, which had become airless to me, I looked at David and announced, "I can't ever be like that."

"Be like what?"

"I can't ever be like her. Stylish. Chic. Gorgeous. So sure of myself."

"What are you talking about?"

"That woman. The one in the tea shop. You clearly have a relationship with her. I can never be French. I'm too old. Too pudgy. Too Midwestern. I could never even *sound* like that, with the melody in words making music. And besides, I can't imagine taking the time to put myself together like that. To take care of my body like that. Or do the shopping."

"Roni Beth," he began, "you can be anything you want to be."

With that comment, our conversation turned away from my jealousy of the beautiful French woman and distrust of her seductive attitude toward David, combined with his absorbed response to her. We moved into a huge fight about differences in our motivations, perceptions, and values. I was crying by the time we reached Église Saint-Augustin, half a block away. David tried leading me into the church to sit down and calm down, and I refused. He steered me to a bench in a small adjacent park, and there we sat. Just as we had on the flight from New York to Calgary, we confronted our differences, identified them, aired them, argued about them, defined feelings they evoked, and, finally, reached a (temporary) resolution. This process took more than an hour. He insisted I could be or do anything I wanted. I claimed the right to find joy in being what I am, a B or B+, the A's reserved for relationships and work. We had different styles on this one, as well as genuinely different values.

We forged a truce. David would not expect me to become the stylish, elegant woman who seemed (to me) beyond my reach, and I would not ask him to refrain from judging what lacked perfection.

His pride in his superb command of the French language reflected years of working on and mastering accent, grammar, vocabulary, and idiom; I could respect and admire it yet insist on not holding myself to the same standards. On the other hand, he remained free to correct me. The enduring lesson of the High Holy Days of 1996 was to maintain my own integrity, even when it meant permitting conflict, while simultaneously keeping clear on what aspects of myself and my values were open to change and those that compromised the core of my being.

Stability recovered, we returned to the office. I happily typed away on my laptop while David fielded phone calls and faxes and made dinner reservations. I failed to become unhinged when, toward the end of the week, I feared I had "lost" my data. We steered clear of tourism almost all week during "working hours," limiting our feast on beauty to daily walks to and from the office. We did not go back into the tea shop. We strolled along the river, through the gardens on either side of Place de la Concorde, along the Champs-Élysées, and into the Tuileries. As a special treat one afternoon, when we were nearly home, David steered me into the Orangerie. I gasped at Monet's *Nymphéas* and discovered David's affection for Soutine, an artist whose work I had not known. In addition to our weekday indulgence in Paris's soul-feeding beauty, during our second weekend we visited the markets at Avenue d'Iéna, then ambled up the street to see the Calder exhibit and the Dufy room at the Musée d'Art Moderne de la Ville de Paris (not to be confused with Centre Pompidou, the national modern art museum). I was delighted to compare works with those on display at the Whitney in New York.

We walked nearly everywhere that week, taking the car only twice, to the Panthéon and to bd Montparnasse, for specific restaurants. From the boat we could easily meander through the 6th and into the Latin Quarter in one direction, to the Eiffel Tower in another, along the Champs-Élysées or toward the Grands Magasins, or down the rue de Rivoli toward the Marais. The Tuilleries, the Invalides, and the Jardin des Champs-Élysées were our neighborhood parks, along with Parc Monceau, so close to the office. We studied the wares of the *bouquinistes* as we walked east, the shop windows to the north or south, the people strolling to the west. Always, everywhere, the architecture, the green-suited municipal employees who keep the lamps lit and garbage collected, the smells that enticed from bistros or brasseries—all brought us pleasure.

Evenings were a different matter. David carefully selected restaurants for variety in menus and mood. He rotated rhythms by punctuating our romantic evenings with social ones. The delicious dinner in the legendary art deco brasserie with my daughter's mother-in-law and her husband passed pleasantly. Another, with David C. (a friend and colleague with whom he worked on MGM-UA matters) and his wife, introduced me to a British perspective on being expats. Sunday with Jacques and Corinne brought me into their tradition. On Friday, we even went to see *Lone Star* in VO (*version originale*, i.e., in English), a film our children had loved, on the Champs-Élysées.

All our activities reflected David's sense of balance and pacing, coupled with his determination to surprise me as he introduced me to "his" Paris. He created a sense of daily life in which I was constantly encountering novelty yet never overwhelmed by what was unfamiliar. A moderate amount of novelty allows one to stay in the present, not needing to rummage through the past to graft a discovery onto what is already known or to radically modify an expectation for the future based on new information. We sailed through those nights solidly situated, as always, in whatever moments presented themselves.

For Saturday night, David had selected his favorite restaurant for haute cuisine so that he might introduce me to dinner in the grand style. By the time we arrived at Carré des Feuillants for our multi-course culinary climax to the week, I was ready to step carefully across cobblestones in my high heels and best outfit, even lace underwear and real silk stockings, and sit coquettishly and appreciatively like the indulged girlfriend I was being, soaking up the pleasure for all the senses. From the stained-glass Tiffany chandeliers to the fine linens, *amuse-bouches* to *migniardises*, David and I sat like king and queen, attended to by a full staff who presented dish after dish, two waiters simultaneously lifting silver domes to reveal art on a platter while other servers looked on, ready to provide a sauce here or garnish there. The chef's creations included complex combinations of the freshest seasonal ingredients with presentations that made me feel guilty as I disturbed their balance of color and form, their utter delight to the eye. We walked back to the boat slowly, both satiety and sadness lingering beneath our measured footsteps. Awareness that our time together would soon be ending lurked just under consciousness.

Sunday night was Kol Nidre, the evening service that marks the beginning of the Yom Kippur day of fasting and repentance. Before services, while we ate omelets at a brasserie at Place de l'Alma, a man spotted us through the window. He came inside to introduce himself. David, always polite, performed the formalities in French, announced that I spoke very little of the language, avoided acknowledging the fact that his former law partner was fluent in English, and insisted that we were in a hurry to move on to our synagogue. Again, his ongoing life in Paris, which long predated me and most of which did not include me, had become present. And a little baffling. Again, I silently spun possibilities but said nothing.

David's insistence on the rules of observance of Yom Kippur with which he had grown up—not only fasting, but spending all day in temple, plus no napping and definitely no sex—well, those were okay by me. But when many people left the synagogue for the Monday afternoon memorial service, instead of flooding into it, as had been the case in congregations I had known, he "explained" that only people who had lost a parent—and preferably *both* parents—should stay for the service. Thus began a long fight that threatened to bracket our visit on its other end with serious disconnection.

We left the small synagogue at 24 rue Copernic that evening after the final shofar had sounded. David pulled me into a bar on the corner so that he could order a *café crème* and a croissant and smoke a cigarette, splicing together his own tradition from a French one (coffee and croissant) and one he had watched his father repeat (the cigarette) throughout his childhood. I patiently waited for him and then sat silently as we drove back to the boat.

David grew more and more angry and insistent.

"It's how it is. You can't stay for the memorial service unless your parents are dead."

"That's ridiculous. I buried a daughter, a son, and my husband well before my father or mother died and would never have considered not staying for Yizkor, standing for Kaddish."

"Well, you aren't supposed to. Not until your parents have died, anyway."

"You can't tell me how to practice my Judaism. I've always stood for my children. For Stuart."

"You're just wrong. You don't know. That's tempting the angel of death. What kind of Judaism did you grow up with, anyway?"

"Mine is just as valid as yours. And this is a deal-breaker. A boundary thing. It's about my identity. I'm every bit as much a "good Jew" as anyone else, the way I practice it, and you can't say I'm not."

At some point, as we became increasingly polarized and sounded more and more like three-year-olds, I realized that this fight had nothing to do with its ostensible content. It had to do with differences and needing to manage them and, even more, with our impending separation. Anger, with its righteous illusion of control, can be an easier emotion to handle than the sadness of loss. We parked on the quai alongside the boat and walked over to Chez Gildas on rue Surcouf for the meal that would break our fast. As we began to put food into our growling bellies, the adults in us acknowledged that the deprivation of physical contact was not permanent, that we would be together again soon, that any lingering conflict could be negotiated at a distance, and that neither of us wanted to waste our remaining hours together fighting. By the time our crème brûlée arrived, we had tacitly agreed to put aside our attempts to convert each other and to bask in the blessings of those differences. We crossed Pont Alexandre III, ornamentation now restored to its original splendor, and stopped in the middle to embrace. David held me tightly, giving me my guaranteed hug on the prettiest or at least most elaborate bridge in Paris. We resolved to be gentle with each other during the year we had just begun and to handle the precious gift that was our love with tenderness, gratitude, and awe.

The next day, David took me to Charles de Gaulle Airport, Terminal 2C, so that I could board Air France 006, leaving Paris at one that Tuesday afternoon to fly to JFK, and then he returned to his office and all the work that had come in while we were in the synagogue on Monday. I arrived home in time to pick up Luke at Carmella's, where, in addition to playing with her five Yorkies and two bichons, he had managed to jump up onto her kitchen counter and eat most of her home-baked apricot pie. My puppy and I went back to our pretty house on Signal Lane. I brought with me a check for $1,000, David's first monthly contribution to stateside household expenses. He had insisted that if he was going to visit me in the United States and stay in my home, he wanted to help with its upkeep. This would be a very new year indeed.

10

Negotiating Differences

Once again, onboard an Air France flight to New York, I thought about what I had learned and wondered about what I did not yet know. Eleven days in Paris with David had filled in some context: I knew that, with the exception of the day when he went to meetings in Gennevilliers, he had gone to work wearing jeans. He dove into matters as soon as they came in, often muttering complaints about others' drafting, inconsistencies, or stupidities. He prided himself on working quickly. He considered himself *un marchand de tapis* (a rug merchant), but the morning when he defined the term for me, I watched his face change shape and character. Deep lines formed gorges the entire length of his cheeks and across his forehead. The distortion was so severe that his normally square jaw broadened to create angles that made his whole face form a sharp rectangle. His eyes remained clear, but the sparkle receded. When he was working, his language was forceful, his words carefully chosen, deliberate. I had already noticed that his voice had many tones, and that the authoritative ring, the calculated tantrums, the seductive softness, could all be invoked at will. While he could explode into a rage, he could also restrain his reactions if the situation called for more modulated behavior. When he wanted something, he adapted his telephone communications so that they hit the bull's eye on their target.

I had learned that Mme. H. managed much of the administrative detail of the office but that David kept his own calendar and decided whom he would see, when, and usually where. And that when meetings involved participation in group conferences with his clients, rather than complaining about negotiating with an opposing party, he was often annoyed with those he represented. That he almost always walked to work but occasionally needed to stop and sit on a bench for a few moments, acknowledging intermittent pain in his right ankle that dated from 1992. And that he preferred to push through the pain, pretending it was not there.

I learned that he ate and drank with joy and gratitude and that he had introduced me to some of his closest friends with pride, both in them and in me. That after living and working in Paris for twenty-four years, he was more French than American. I had witnessed repeatedly that he was noticeably more at home with the slower tempo and rule-bending or -breaking style of Paris than that of New York. He knew how to get his needs met in Paris, how to treat others with respect and genuine interest, how to explode when that was the behavior that would get him what he wanted. He seemed to know his way around all corners, nooks, and crannies of the city, and to have a sixth sense about what activities were worth doing and when and how to do them. In Paris he was supremely confident and on top of his game. The panic attack I had witnessed in Camden seemed unfathomable.

I also glimpsed the richness of his years in France before I had dropped into his life. Although David described himself as a "loner" and told of taking books, rather than dates, to dinner, he knew people—along the streets, along the quai, in a brasserie, and even in the synagogue he'd never attended before—throughout Paris. He had stories involving his boys, such as the first time he took them to Flora Danica, when, on the walk home, they had to wait while he sat down on a curb, settling his alcohol-infused brain, before they could help him walk back to the boat—not drunk, no, just a bit fuzzy. Or those that included a celebrity, such as the reception at the Hotel de Ville for Perry Como's Christmas special when it was filmed in Paris. That one had movie stars and dignitaries, like Jacques Chirac, who later became president of France. Sometimes the stories reflected his intimate connection to the city. While we walked along the riverbanks, he pointed out the offices of the boat community, built into the supporting stone structure on the Right Bank side of Pont Alexandre III. He showed me the markers that measured the height of the Seine, talked of times when the banks had flooded, described driving his car to high ground for safety and making his way to and from the Berreti in his rowboat, using a jerry-rigged rope and pulley system. Offhandedly, he told me about the time Diane Sawyer and her crew asked if they could film an interview with Baryshnikov on his boat and he refused. Not wanting the disruption, he directed them to a neighbor's barge instead, watched the chaos, and then helped out when the boat ran out of gas in the middle of filming in the middle of the river.

I saw a man with ingenuity, perseverance, determination, and a huge appetite for biting into life. When David pointed out each Aubade lingerie ad—the current campaign was "for women who love men who love women"—or watched the curvy and well-dressed women saunter along the streets, I knew he had become a part of this culture in which sexuality and seduction are integrated into daily life, as basic as breathing and perhaps even more central than food. Bodies were not alien monsters to be tamed and mastered, as in the United States. Rather, they were precious resources to be nourished with natural activity, delicious offerings to all the senses, and a free energetic exchange with the world around. As David pointed out, *plaisir* was heralded in ads for everything from reading a book to sipping an espresso; it underscored a central commitment of the culture.

I returned to Westport not only more aware of who David was (and was not) but also with increasing awareness that my own sense of self was beginning, slowly, to unravel. The careful, organized, practical, efficient, clear-thinking scientist and the empathic clinician were both being pushed aside by parts of me that I began to nickname the Brat. A demanding, willful, childlike presence, she wanted what she wanted when she wanted it and was not interested in logic or reason or waiting. But whereas David's tantrums were predictable and sometimes felt almost staged, mine threatened to erupt when I was faced with any real or perceived impediment to my access to him and our relationship. The Brat needed the grown-up in me to patiently talk her through to appropriate problem-solving behavior.

On the plane, I wrote David a thank-you note, cataloging the blessings of the twelve days and eleven nights that we had spent together. And just two hours after my plane took off, David was in his office, writing a fax that arrived in Westport before my plane landed. *I miss you. There's an emptiness in the office, and an emptiness inside me—and I'll find an emptiness in the boat when I get home later.* We were both a little drunk with the intoxicating period we had spent together and facing withdrawal as we disentangled.

The week after my visit, David did indeed go out to dinner with the woman who had invited him to Vienna the previous Christmas. I felt my jealousy and our separation more vividly. We discussed the merits and possible consequences of honesty and finally agreed to respect my intolerance of deceit, and David's need to feel I trusted him—cornerstones of communication in the couple we were becoming.

Eight days after I had left, David reserved flights for a trip to see me on November 1. He was scheduled to arrive on a Friday and stay through the following week, so that he could join me in attending the wedding of a friend's daughter the evening of November 9, and then return to Paris the next day. With concrete plans in place, I settled down—and "got up and got going." My practice expanded again, the data I was analyzing fell into place, manuscripts got written, and I attended the annual meeting of the Connecticut Psychological Association, at which I was formally elected to the governing board.

On September 29, I wrote:

> *I realize that today marks six months since I met you. It seems so much longer—and shorter—truly "hors du temps." Maybe part of that is the "comfortable" quality from the beginning—as though we already knew one another. Maybe*

*combined with the anticipation of all the experiences we both
yearn yet to share. In either event, for whatever meaning, happy
anniversary. I could say "and thank you for dropping into my
life"—but the deep gratitude I feel seems better directed toward
the gods who arrange such things. Not that I don't "deserve" this
blessing—I do feel worthy—but I am so grateful that joy and
sharing (and the joys of sharing) are now part of my life. Thank
you, God, for bringing me to this day.*

The Hebrew prayer that David had recited to me on his boat that
Wednesday morning in May had been repeating again and again and
again. Still does.

David countered:

*I still take more credit (and responsibility) for the good
things (and the bad things) that happen to me, and believe you
and I made/created/were open to what we are now living, and
we both not only "deserve" but "earned." But if you want to toss
in "favorable circumstances" and divine intervention, maybe
it's only definitional.*

Whatever forces had conspired to bring us together, we were both
intent on sharing what we each could bring to the other, offering what
in ourselves or our lives might be of value to the other, and discovering new ways to be as we honored the "we" that was becoming its own
entity. In order to do that, we needed to ask what our couple needed,
as well as what David or I individually might need. Both deeply
entrenched in the kind of complex lives that middle-aged people tend
to have created, we had begun to identify what in those lives might
nurture and what might be toxic to our precious baby, our relationship. In creating agreements for how we would treat each other, we
forged a foundation for our future.

III

Family, Friends, and More Friends

11

Our Connected World Expands

*D*avid arrived at Newark at 12:35 that first Friday afternoon in November. Still in the parking lot, we steamed up the windows of the Honda with our hungry embraces, evidence of our gratitude over being together again and our eagerness to reconnect. Once we got home, Luke tried his best to pretend once again that he did not recognize David; his efforts lasted all of a few minutes. David quickly set up an "office" in Danny's room. There, he could work on documents, speak to his secretary and clients, send and receive faxes, and dictate memos and miscellany on his portable Dictaphone throughout the week.

Adam, David's younger son, who lived in Boulder, had come to New York to visit his mother, an aunt, and some friends for a few days. Conveniently, because he could drive up to Connecticut with Scott and Stefanie, and because Jen, Steve, and Danny were all available, we had an opportunity to introduce our four adult children, along with two spouses, to one another. We gathered them all in the dining room for Sunday brunch. Both of our older children were married, did not yet have children, had lived in Manhattan with their spouses, and were involved in careers they enjoyed. Adam had gone to college in the Lehigh Valley, as had Danny. He enjoyed the outdoors, as did Jen, Steve, and Dan, and all six of them were avid fans of music and

movies. All the men loved sports, both as participants and as specta-
tors. Jen and Dan had traveled in France, where Adam and Scott had
lived for five or six years when very young, and Stefanie had visited
France with Scott. Scott and Adam and Dan and Jen came from families in which parents had divorced when the oldest child was on the
threshold of adolescence. And they all loved to laugh.

In spite of external similarities, their perspectives and worldviews
were different. I was particularly aware of the contrast between the
ways in which Steve, Jen, and Dan saw me and how I appeared in the
eyes of Scott, Stefanie, and Adam. To my children, I was a mother with
a career and a deep attachment to her kids and her local community.
They appreciated the uncomplicated lifestyle in which they had grown
up. They were used to having their home filled with people of all ages;
interacting freely with my adult friends and their friends with me; a
proven history of sharing with and supporting each other through
divorce, death, trauma, and sickness; and always, always celebrating
the good stuff. We had developed a shared communication style, patterns that insisted on direct and open discussion of any discomfort.
Passive-aggressive behavior was quickly confronted and thus almost
always avoided.

In contrast, David and his sons filled their time together with
humor, adventures, and challenges but little, if any, processing of
emotions, observations, or conflict. Their annual trips on the boat
in summer and to ski in the Alps in winter had been supplemented
by travels within the United States when David could get there, but
they were travels nonetheless. Awareness of each other's daily lives
had been limited since the boys' return to the United States with their
mother in 1978. Now, as I saw them, the young men seemed sophisticated, cosmopolitan, and definitely not interested in learning more
about my kids or me. Jen and Dan and Steve tried to find natural ways
to make these strangers feel at home. The luncheon event seemed
pleasant enough, but awkward. On first meeting, the Brady Bunch we
were not.

The week flew by. David did have a good bit of work come in, so he labored away in his makeshift office while I saw patients in mine. He took Luke to Sherwood Island State Park again and again, letting him race around until exhausted. He learned how to find Super Stop & Shop for staples and my favorite gourmet store for treats, and he happily gathered miscellaneous supplies for us. We met Hope, my intrepid early-morning walking partner, and her husband for dinner and attended the wedding of another friend's daughter. Before I knew it, I was driving David back to JFK for his Air France 007 flight to Paris.

When David left on November 10, I knew that I needed to wait six weeks before we saw each other again. First there was the shock of his absence. I wrote to him:

> *I know you probably don't want to hear it, but Luke is pretty sad. I had this wonderful message waiting for me when I got home* [David always called from the Air France lounge at JFK after he had checked in and before I could get home]*—and he just listened to it longingly, wistfully. He's not crying constantly, but he does seem rather lost. Me too.*

Over time, we came to understand that that feeling, the one of being "lost," was the one we felt when real-time physical sharing was no longer possible. Because we had spent so much of our lives emotionally alone, the contact on all levels permitted an expansion of soul and a recognition of the mysterious sense of wholeness that came with it.

The next day, missing the rituals of saying, "Good morning, my love," and, "Good night, dear David," I ignored the hour and called him before I went to bed. I knew that it was five in the morning in Paris. In the fax that followed the phone call, I wrote:

> *Again, I apologize for waking you—but my need to say, "Good night, dear David" was very strong, and I imagined that you could probably collapse from exhaustion promptly after*

the phone call, and you didn't say not to call, so I indulged.
Hearing my sleepy David's voice (you know how strongly I react
to your voice) was comforting. Helped the ripping apart be ever
so slightly more gentle.

I had been very busy with patients, consultations in New Haven, traffic on the ride home, more patients, even a gorgeous morning walk with Hope and our dogs, but there was an undeniable hole in my heart and an emptiness in my household. My profession added to my sense of disconnection, rendering the bulk of my day-to-day experiences confidential and thus off-limits to any sharing. To shift gears and bring him closer, I suggested we have a party when he came for the holidays, one like the open house the kids and I had thrown just before I had met him. I sent him:

Draft of invitation:

We had so much fun that we
Decided to do it again
Please come to another
Potluck open house
This time we can celebrate
The winter solstice, the approaching new year
And, just generally, the gift of life
Bring your houseguests, children, and an hors d'oeuvre or dessert.
Please call and let us know how many you will be.

He enthusiastically approved, and we worked on a guest list together. I was eager to include any of his East Coast friends whom he might want to see again, as well as his family. Meanwhile, he jumped on the availability of cheap winter fares offered in the United States and proposed I fly over in January after his Christmas trip, eliminating yet another long separation before his grandchild was due in February:

Of course, if you can't for reasons of patient scheduling, professional or social commitments, that's different. But if the hesitation is "rationality," let's be irrational, irresponsible, decadent, and obscene—and enjoy ourselves. Let's give ourselves the gift of the present. And charge it to my Visa card.

The weeks passed with a string of radically different activities for each of us. My December birthday brought sweetness and sharing with my children and friends. I continued to plan David's holiday visit and our first joint party.

Suddenly, communication from David slowed down. Brief faxes, scanty updates, and no phone calls. Near silence. From a man who was rarely without words. I grew concerned, then alarmed. Finally, I left a message insisting he call me back. Reluctantly, he complied. He had become sick and did not want me to know the extent of it. He knew I would be able to hear it in his voice.

Finally, on Friday, December 20, 1996, I drove to JFK with blankets, a thermos of hot tea, and a tin of freshly baked Christmas cookies in the passenger seat. My lover stumbled off Air France flight 006 at 3:00 p.m. (9:00 p.m. on his biological clock), somehow made his way through immigration, collected his luggage, and hobbled through the double doors for international arrivals at Terminal 4. I wrapped him in my arms, took possession of his cabin luggage, and guided him to the waiting Honda. Because it was then after four o'clock on the Friday before Christmas, the ride from the airport to Westport took longer than usual, but he was here, he was with me, and I could care for him. Even wrapped in blankets, he shivered through the last leg of his voyage. I was astonished but grateful that the crew had let him board the plane.

David's December trip to the United States, seventeen nights and eighteen days, was the opposite of my long, lyrical visit to France the previous September, the one for the Jewish holidays, in which tensions rose and were resolved with rhythm and reason. In contrast with that trip's beautifully orchestrated balance of work and play, social and personal time, giving and receiving, celebrating and resting, this year-end visit felt almost bipolar. The first half was filled with illness and recovery, stresses and strains, triumphs and disappointments, and most of all radical shifts in focus and attention that left us a little confused about how to be together in the demanding context of my complicated work responsibilities and very social life. Luckily, the second half permitted time for reflection, time for a growing awareness of how much we still needed to learn about and appreciate in each other. In spite of David's repeated insistence that he knew "everything [he] needed to know" about me the first evening we met, *and* his ability to learn with lightning speed, *and* his pleasure in trying out alternate perspectives, he needed all of his adaptive abilities during that visit. He was going to return home with a deeper grasp of our differences, as well as with respect for our combined ability to honor and work with them.

Perhaps some of the confusion we faced during that visit came simply from David's perception that we were "on vacation," while I continued to see the time as filled with work—both literally, with my patients, and domestically, as I strove to create happy memories of shared moments with our respective children, his sister, and some of my friends, who I hoped might become "ours." But "playing house" in Westport was nothing like living together in France. The choppy nature of the transitions seemed natural to me. That was my life: all my attention in one direction, and then—boom!—turn to the east or west and move on, even though managing transitions was definitely not my strong suit. David, on the other hand, was terrific at switching gears, which made the jerkiness in my lifestyle all the more apparent to us both. Nonetheless, we were in love, determined to use our moments together to their fullest, and so we soldiered on. We tried to be conscious of our differences as they arose, and to use them as a springboard for expanding our individual repertoires, rather than as occasions to fight over who was right and who was wrong.

First of all, there were the differences in being with our children. My relationships with Jennifer and Steve and Dan were fluid, easy, anything but formal. We lived by the mantra that everyone was responsible for his or her own happiness, which included asking directly for whatever might be wanted or needed. A sense of safety results from that respect for autonomy and trust of directness, no fear of stepping on eggshells, just trying to come together and share whatever anyone might bring to the table that could be of interest or value or need. A genuine intention to help one another if and when that is requested and possible, but also respect for each person's right and ability to figure it out for him or herself. Yes, I did try to feed my children well—they were always my most important "guests"—but I never worried about disappointing them if a roast was overcooked or vegetables underdone. No crisis—there was always the pizza delivery guy. Mom did not pretend to do perfect.

Perhaps because we had shared our home through so many years, through so many events, even though they no longer technically lived there, the young people were comfortable using any resources that might be around in the service of their own comfort. They were at ease bringing anyone or anything they wanted into the house. I made sure there was a reliable supply of drinks and snacks, along with glasses or bowls to serve them in; clean towels in the closet; art materials, puzzles, and games in the storeroom. The microwave and burners, stereo and television, piano and pool table went in and out of use as desired when they and their friends were around. When they became adults, sharing replaced helping and caretaking as the core of our connection, and we were all fine with the substitution.

David's experience with his children, especially after they returned to America with their mother, was different. He lived on a relatively compact boat an ocean away from them. When Scott or Adam visited, separately or more often together, they did indeed have a dedicated space to sleep. And each had a plate, bowl, and cup; knife, fork, and spoon; towel and set of sheets. But they depended on their father to fetch each morning's breakfast and then return to serve it; to select restaurants for lunch and dinner; to somehow generate clean linens when necessary; and to supply the structure for days and activities for evenings when they were together. Although David "served" them devotedly, the services that he provided were different from those my kids associated with Mom or home. He was—at least in my imagination—a host; I was merely the stage manager for the dramas or comedies or improvisations in which my now-grown children might want to engage. David felt a need to organize and take charge of a visit with his children, while I simply allowed it to take place.

We quickly bumped into a second difference. A holiday American-style, and also *my* style, was an opportunity for celebration shared with other people, preparation of "special" foods, and the creation and maintenance of traditions that had been crafted and evolved over years. My "favorite" holiday was Thanksgiving, appealing both because of its emphasis on gratitude (to me, "to celebrate" was synonymous with "to say I am grateful") and because of its then relatively noncommercial trappings. The New England culture mandated a turkey—or some equivalent centerpiece for a meal—but gifts exchanged were of the spirit. Schools emphasized arts and crafts; our own family committed to an annual nature walk.

Christmas was different. In America, the holiday had become far more commercial and overloaded with social "rules" or expectations than the ways in which David experienced Noël in Paris, where his social engagements were relatively spontaneous. He loved the decorations, the windows, the whimsical presentations of seasonal foods, but he saw them more as artistic expressions of the miracles that underlie the messages of the season (whether Hanukkah *or* Christmas, the holiday *is* about miracles) than as attempts to stoke the unconscious to spend, spend, spend. From our phone conversations, he had understood (or picked up the message) that he might want to bring gifts for my adult children; I had not grasped that my generous David might never before have purchased a holiday gift during his whole life. Had I thought about it, I would have realized that the Christmas trip he took with this boys, skiing in the Alps, was itself a sufficient gift to them, and that an exchange of additional material presents was off his radar screen. Besides, he had told me he did not remember having received gifts *from* them, even on his birthday, although on a recent summer trip to France, Scott and Stefanie had treated him to a magnificent birthday dinner in a Michelin-starred country restaurant on the river.

David had no childhood memories of celebrating anything in December. No packages to open. No songs to sing. No rituals to repeat. He did not even remember having lit Hanukkah candles, although he reasoned he "must have" done so. He could not recall ever having decorated a Christmas tree, even with Christian friends, or having hung stockings. For David, gift-giving was unhooked from celebrations; it occurred when one person was inspired by an item that might bring pleasure to another person. Ah, again, *le plaisir*. Nothing here about obligation, or observance of what was "done" or might be "correct" or expected. Or even about giving a person something to remind him or her of you, a symbol of the experience of being together. Only acknowledging who the other was and providing a moment or more of pleasure, delight.

But December celebrations had been a major organizing force in my life. When the kids were little, we lit candles and exchanged gifts, often homemade, throughout the eight days of Hanukkah. We baked cookies for Santa, hung stockings, and read *The Night Before Christmas*. We made gifts for grandparents: baked goods or candy, but also candles, aprons, fudge sauce, framed artwork. Annual viewings of *Miracle on Thirty-Fourth Street* and *It's a Wonderful Life* replaced *Frosty the Snowman* and *How the Grinch Stole Christmas* as the children grew up. We never decorated the outside of the house, nor did we indulge in a tree until they were fully grown. But Christmas morning without *schnecken* (our homemade miniature yeast rolls, filled with cinnamon, raisins, and nuts), or December vacation without a cookie-baking day, was unthinkable.

When Jennifer was about eight, she asked me to stop celebrating Christmas alongside Hanukkah; it was "too confusing." So, for a period of years, we skipped the stockings and December 25 breakfast with carols on the stereo. But once the children grew up, I went back to Christmas Day traditions: festive breakfast, gift exchange, stockings, an annual holiday visit to the family who lived across the street from our Fairfield house. Later, home again, we completed a jigsaw puzzle in front of the fire, agreed on a late-afternoon movie in a theater, and stopped on the way home to pick up a Chinese feast. Why in the world did I ever imagine I could simply fold David into this agenda and expect him to find it natural, normal, acceptable?

We had different styles of interacting with our respective children, different memories and expectations concerning the Christmas holiday period, and then, perhaps most of all, radically different ways of being in and reacting to the larger social world. David had close relationships with his children, his sister and her boyfriend, and a limited number of people on either side of the Atlantic. What puzzled me was his seemingly constant socializing in Paris. His Sunday-night dinners with Jacques and Corinne. His regular lunches with some of his buddies. His honored placement at Harvard and other events. All the people who greeted him when we walked along the quai or through the streets of the city. And it seemed as if Americans and people from other places were always passing through Paris and requesting time to be with him.

What I failed to appreciate in the winter of 1996 was how much more orderly and regulated he kept his interactions, and how, in fact, he merely "tolerated" some of those people because of his view of himself as a "nice guy." How rarely he combined the people he knew with one another. And thus how strange the diversity in what he came to call *my* "two hundred best friends" must have seemed to him when I put so many of them in the same room for a party.

As it turned out, David got lucky. Several of my closest friends had travel plans over the holidays and were unavailable for the open house on that Sunday after Christmas. Up until then, he had been able to understand and accept the dinners-for-four that we scheduled so that he could gradually meet a few of them. Two more such dinners that we shared before our big party did not seem so strange: an evening with Madeline, a colleague turned friend, and her husband, before they went to California; another with Barry and Judy, a couple who had been essential supports since my earliest Fairfield days. They had deep ties to France and were leaving for the Caribbean on Christmas Eve. They had treated me to dinner when I passed my orals and held me tight during my darkest hours.

But in retrospect, what *was* I thinking when I arranged a casual December drop-in and invited people whom I or my children were fond of, spanning generations and all walks of life, friends of decades or acquaintances from recent encounters? I wanted David to know and feel a part of my world. I wanted people who had heard so much about my new boyfriend to translate the phantom Frenchman into concrete reality. I wanted to cohost with him, to "play house" in a way important to me. To me, home was a place to welcome not only the weary but also the wonderful relationships that people could forge with one another.

David's actual visit began with worry—my concerns about his illness and the toll of his long trip, and his concerns about feeling well enough to celebrate (euphemism) our being together again. When he got off the plane, I saw that he was really sick, and the long drive home did not help.

"I managed to get you an appointment with a good internist; we're going there straight from the airport."

"What are you talking about? I'll be fine. I just need to be with you. Maybe some sleep."

"You are going to see a doctor. It's Friday afternoon of a major holiday weekend, and I don't want to take you to the ER tomorrow, because no doctors are in their offices."

"Honestly, I'll be fine. I'm better than I was yesterday. It's going away."

His eyes were red and watery, nose running, and muscles so weak that he had trouble standing.

"Look at it this way: I refuse to let you have any contact with your very pregnant daughter-in-law without medical clearance."

He thought about that one.

"Okay. I guess you made your case."

David was examined and a proper course of treatment and precautions prescribed. We were both reassured that he was neither wildly contagious nor dangerous to himself. He needed only to avoid getting too close to Stefanie, who was scheduled to arrive with Scott the following day. Grateful, I bundled my honey back into the car and took him home for some makeshift nursing care. A surprise awaited him.

Earlier that day, my friend Madeline, even though she had not yet met David, had delivered a homemade ice cream cake as a welcome/holiday/get-well gift for him. Based on her husband's dynamics, she had reasoned that ice cream would be more curative than chicken soup. When David saw the ten-inch springform mold release its circle of ladyfingers hugging layers of mint chocolate chip, mocha espresso chip, and French vanilla ice creams, fudge sauce between the layers, he shook his head in wonder. This man who lived as a loner in a fairly formal culture was flabbergasted that a stranger to him, a friend of his American girlfriend, purely out of concern and the generosity and goodness of her heart, would have done this. Angels who walk the earth abound. Disguised as humans, like you and me, they bring light and support into our lives when our own resources have run too low or may not meet the challenge. Madeline was one of those angels.

I helped David settle onto the sofa opposite the fire, Luke by his side, and brought him something fiery to drink, along with cheese and crackers and the best pâté I could find. A long, quiet *dîner en amoureux* followed, just the two of us, so glad to be together again. My homemade gingerbread house made the dining room table look festive. After dinner, David presented me with a belated birthday gift, a pin with an outrageously large amethyst set in gold forming the body of a cat. He had emerald eyes and a sapphire on his tail. Exquisite. Unique. I cried. And then served us both that decadent frozen dessert.

We thank Madeline's ice cream cake for about 80 percent of David's impressive recovery. I will take credit for the remainder. By the next day, when we picked up Scott and Stefanie at the train station, David breathed clearly, moved easily and enthusiastically, was far less congested and uncomfortable, and behaved like his usual self. We gathered around Stefanie's five-weeks-to-go belly, able to see the baby kicking through her mother's clothes, perhaps an omen for our future soccer star. The overnight became the celebration it was meant to be: a special dinner, followed the next day by shopping for a glider for Stefanie and baby equipment for her baby, and climaxed by stopping for eggnog at Hope and Alvin's Christmas party. We drove Scott and Stephanie and their gifts back to the East Village later that Sunday, snowflakes providing appropriate seasonal atmosphere as night began to fall.

With David restored to acceptable health, we moved into the next two weeks.Tuesday, Christmas Eve, Danny made it home before traffic became unbearable. His Stefani remained with her family. After sharing the festive dinner I had put together, he left to spend time with friends who had come home for the holidays. Jennifer and Steve arrived early the next morning. With *schnecken* the centerpiece for our continental breakfast in the living room, we emptied stockings and opened gifts, carols playing on the stereo. I had, of course, added a stocking for David.

David had brought a tie printed with frogs for Steve, a watch for Dan, pins for Jennifer and Stefani. He gave me a red heart pendant and matching earrings that he had noticed in a Baccarat window as he walked home one day. I gave him silver cuff links and a blue French-cuff shirt that required them. A Save the Children tie, a Mini Maglite, a Bolling and Rampal CD, and chocolates filled his stocking. Jennifer and Steve gave him a book of Julian Barnes short stories. Danny brought him modern jazz and Rachmaninoff piano CDs. We all sprawled out on the living room floor to collaborate on a jigsaw puzzle, the outline always assembled first. Later, we drove to the home of former neighbors to share brunch with them, their children and grandchildren, the annual visit back to our Fairfield street. We went to see *Shine*, the movie about David Helfgott, then ordered Chinese takeout, including everyone's favorites. David, in spite of his unfamiliarity with these activities, cheerfully went along with them, hiding his perplexity as best he could. He went outside to smoke a cigarette or walked Luke whenever he became overwhelmed. Taking a break from the situation was his preferred coping style, his way, unconsciously, perhaps, of "breathing."

Then we got really busy. Cooking. Preparing. Making lists. Getting ready to open the house to a whole lot of people, most of whom were strangers to him. People streamed in for the party. Young adults (mostly the children's friends), middle-aged and older people, people with their own children of all ages, a sibling, a parent. David was surprised by my ease at entertaining, especially with no hired help, but even more so by all these relationships that I had with other people. Even though he did not know quite what to make of it, he was prepared to have a wonderful time.

His sister and her boyfriend came. His best friend's widow and her lover came. People he had met before—the parents of the November bride and groom, neighbors, Hope and Alvin—came. David did not feel completely out of place—perhaps a benefit of having moved so often as a child. Even though many other people who were essential to my life were still unknown to him (those who had gone to Florida, the Caribbean, Mexico, Arizona, London), David was gaining a sense of the diverse social world in which I lived. The house was full and alive, and the goodwill and good spirits were palpable. Coming from a culture where years of restaurant dinners might precede an invitation into a person's home, David found my social circle and all these relationships bewildering at best. In a funny way he acted as host; in another, he was the guest of honor, even though a few people had wrongly assumed that the tall guy wearing a beret must have been the mystery man from France.

The week that followed the party offered quieter moments. I had fewer patients to see, and finally we had nothing at all on the calendar that Monday night. On Tuesday, New Year's Eve, we wandered downtown wearing our First Night buttons, stopping in and out of local performances, demonstrations, entertainments. Shivering in the frigid weather, in spite of the new parka that David had bought me,

I took him to the bridge over the Saugatuck River. Watching the fire-works display, we ushered in 1997 together.

For more than two weeks, David and I played house, explored our differences, forged new routines, shared memories and meaningful bits of our histories, and began creating our own traditions. Luke loved it. And so did I. Then, on Monday, January 6, 1997, after yet another extended period of lying quietly in each other's arms, breathing deeply as we clung to each other and our last moments of being together, David and I closed his valises and left for JFK so that he could board Air France flight 007, headed for CDG, departing at 7:50 p.m. As I drove home, my tears blurred the lamplight as day melted into early winter evening. Knowing that I would fly to Paris eleven days later registered intellectually; my heart, however, felt the separation and screamed, *Tu me manques!* I was beginning to grasp that culture is embedded in language. The English "I miss you" failed to capture the poignancy of the French "you are missing from me."

12

Growing Inside and Out

David returned directly to the boat after his early arrival that January morning to discover the consequences of having turned off the heat for two weeks in winter. The Berreti was iced up. The water line from the outside had frozen, radiators and pipes inside were swollen and cracked, and the onboard reservoir soon emptied down to its dirty bottom. The new toilet pump and hot-water heater were broken, useless. All his attention for the next two days went into identifying problems, finding plumbers and artisans who could help him solve them, and restoring his space to habitable condition. He finally managed a shower and shave in cold water three days later. Crisis mode overpowered his jet lag.

By the end of the week, three larger, more efficient radiators had been installed, fresh water again ran from the quai, the shower operated, although still at a trickle, and a new toilet pump was on order. The reliable bucket lowered into the Seine on a rope still worked for flushing. Practical reality, balancing the demands of living on a boat against the cost of our efforts to be together as much as possible, had again intervened, monopolizing David's immediate attention. Even our romance had to recede into the background while he addressed more urgent matters. Away from his fax machine, David relied on the telephone to stay in touch. I felt his absence even more acutely as a result.

When he could finally turn his attention to the work, mail, and messages that had been waiting for him since his return, David skipped over more pressing professional matters to focus on the May 1997 HLSAE junket, taking place that year in Dijon, center of the Burgundy wine region. Yes, of course I would like to join him. He made hotel reservations. We would drive to Burgundy from Paris.

That urgent matter tended to, David learned that a client had set up meetings in Singapore with an Australian group the following Sunday night. David and in-house counsel had to be there. So, only five days after his return from the long winter holiday trip to the United States and to his frozen boat in Paris, he boarded yet another plane. He would be gone for almost a week, returning the same morning on which my previously ticketed flight would arrive from New York. We planned our reunion at CDG Airport—just another lesson in flexibility.

On Friday, January 17, 1997, at 6:20 in the morning, I landed at Terminal 2C, weekend luggage slung over my shoulder in that red calico bag, and took the shuttle bus to Terminal 1. David and his colleague straggled down the corridor following four days of tension-filled meetings and the fourteen-hour return flight from Singapore. They had crossed seven time zones; I had crossed six in the opposite direction. We had less than seventy-five hours to spend with each other. Being together was becoming a priority that pushed aside common sense and our need for sleep.

More quick and crazy trips followed. Only two weeks later, David returned to his boat from a Saturday-morning hike to discover multiple answering-machine messages from an American telephone operator. She was trying to place collect calls, apparently made from a hospital. Having no more information than that but correctly interpreting the clues, David booked an Air France flight for that evening. His American girlfriend then got through to the switchboard at St. Vincent's Hospital and, uncharacteristically, used her "doctor" title to confirm that Scott and Stefanie's baby had been born. She was thrilled to inform David that he had a granddaughter. David stopped at his office for his passport, bought a pink Baby Dior dress in a nearby boutique, then crossed the Atlantic, fell into my arms at JFK, chattered as we made our way through the Queens Midtown Tunnel and across Manhattan to the hospital. He was holding his first grandchild, Sofia, before she was twenty-four hours old. Back to Paris the following Monday. He returned to America ten days later on the weekend trip he had booked when the baby's due date had first been announced.

The disruption all this travel caused to my normally orderly life was taking a toll on me. So much shifting gears was destabilizing my core identity. In addition, the needs of the "we" had begun to take priority over the needs of the "me," and I knew I had to recalibrate. Reflecting on my dissertation was helpful. In it I had documented, then explored, three major areas a person needs to address in living his or her life: responsibility, or getting what you need from the world around you, such as money or recognition or power or a sense of contribution; relationships to others, which was managing interpersonal connections, priorities, and intimacies; and resourcefulness, or expressing that which is intrinsically motivated, from the heart and soul, whether through play or spiritual endeavors or creative expression. I knew that my inner life needed more space. As had so reliably happened other times in my life when I had been struggling, a teacher appeared. This time, it was in the form of a book.

In early March, a patient had told me about *The Artist's Way*, a book by Julia Cameron that offered a twelve-step program for enhancing creativity. Inspired by my young client's enthusiasm and progress, as well as by my respect for twelve-step programs that many of my patients had successfully followed, I decided to try it myself. As prescribed, I began to write three pages longhand every morning, letting whatever was on my mind glide onto the page without censorship. For perhaps the first time since childhood, when I had added brushing my teeth to a daily routine, writing these Morning Pages quickly became an essential part of my life, and has remained so all this time. Despite all my education and training, my own psychotherapy, David, and a network of supportive girlfriends, nothing has helped me more in being as clear and honest about what I feel and want, in observing my own stream of consciousness for a sustained period every day, in forcing me to pay attention to me. Giving myself that gift of attention means I no longer need to try to pretend I don't need it or to ask others to supply it. Not surprisingly, Morning Pages have become the ground from which my meditation and yoga practices successfully flourish. And they have definitely been a key to keeping my relationship with David as direct, "clean," free of illusion and clutter, liberated from neediness, and full of gratitude as I could make it.

Quickly, the pages showed me that I had been eating the intensity of my feelings away, rather than embracing them. I had ballooned to 132 pounds, too many for my five-foot-three-and-one-half-inch frame. I had been using food and the activity of eating to shut out exhaustion, frustration, and desires to play, to indulge, to be pretty, to create. A handful of trail mix or spoonful of ice cream supplied small squirts of energy just to keep going when I felt depleted or impotent. To silence my fears. To quiet the Brat, to deny all the neediness and yearning from all the years before David had begun to change my life. With him, I could feel understood. Rest. Sleep. Lie in his arms until I was ready to get up, just like I had practiced listening to my body when I was alone at the Maine cottage. With David, I could take the time to enjoy experiences fully, spending three hours on a delicious dinner, hiking until our bodies announced, *Enough!* or making love until we were satiated or exhausted. Slowing down to drink in the beauty of a sunrise or the harmony of Luke's white coat shining against the frost-covered grass that looked like green shredded wheat with icing. I could explore—the perfumes on the department store counters and their nuances, the utility of wrapping a scarf or shawl around shivering shoulders, the stillness in sacred moments of silently sharing a garden, a sandwich, a symphony. With David, I had found a partner who could understand the sparklies on the water, the facets in a diamond, the magic in eyes that dance with light. Finally, I was able to write:

I am so afraid. The deeper I go, the harder it is to let go—to love without attachment, to know he'll disappear someday—death, probably—and I'll have to deal with that, the pull to not let him in at all, to withdraw, do my work, run away from life. . . . I want to go live with David in France and write about what I need to write about and spend my days and nights with the joys of simple pleasures.

How do I retrieve discipline? The eating is foolish; how to feel the feelings, tolerate the exhaustion, excitement, pain? Somewhere down there is fear. I know the story ultimately ends unhappily—but why give up the wonderful moments from here to there—there could be years of them—for avoidance of what will probably come one way or another? And, of course, the larger danger is not letting myself love—we'll die someday too.

I came home from the hospital without a baby. Twice. I watched my husband die. Death changing what was supposed to be. Don't get too invested in outcomes. God has other plans. Do God's will. That's my prayer: Okay, God, help me see thy will and do it. . . . I am supposed to find what I most intrinsically am and be it—shine through, radiate across the being, illuminate.

Surrender remained my ultimate way to cope, what was left when all that was in my own power had been exhausted.

The Morning Pages helped me keep such private thoughts to myself and thus burden David less. I did not need to ask him to give what would never be in his power to give, which made his planning, perspectives, humor, analyses, and very different coping style all the more valuable. I had his material gifts as well. From the beginning, David had set out to surprise me, to bring beauty in all forms into my life and nourish me with it. As he had "warned" me at the very beginning, he intended to "court" me, for the rest of his (or my) life. The elegant earrings with the long carnelian drops and marcasite trim were only the beginning. *Reverie*, the Baccarat sculpture with whom I conversed; the sexy nightgown from the little shop on rue St.

Dominique; the necklace of faceted amethyst stones that closed with a unique gold clasp; the teapot shaped like a house, with its music-box mechanism playing "That's What Friends Are For"; the printed silk robe that will always remind me of springtime; the crystal heart earrings and necklace for Hanukkah; and, of course, the cat pin for my birthday. The perfect gold heart earrings and necklace from O. J. Perrin. There was the heavier-weight scarf in grays and tans for the fall, and then, when winter came, the warm shawl in the greens and blues and purples that looked like they had been drawn from the palette of Monet's *Nymphéas* or my office decor. The box of assorted "fun" earrings picked up on the Air France flight during the trip he had not expected to make when Sofia was born, and the *bôites* of teas and chocolates. The carefully crafted tapes of music he had long loved and the new CDs of music he hoped for us to discover together. Books and pamphlets supplemented articles and maps. Michelin guides introduced me to travel within France. Slowly, David's presence filled my closets and shelves and drawers, just as his words filled my fax machine and telephone and his existence filled my heart.

Yes, I felt indulged. Yes, I felt "courted." But above all I felt liberated, free to learn a new way of loving—that of giving and receiving, of an open exchange between two people, the only goal being to please the other, bring them joy and delight and resources they might need to be the best they could be. We wanted to begin and end our days by sharing, and to help each other understand the context of what had transpired in between.

Because all my contacts with clients were confidential, most days that meant David managed the majority of the conversation. We talked endlessly about when and where we could be together. David loved the adrenaline rush of it all. He wrote:

As I kept waking—or trying to fall back to sleep—I recited forthcoming trips and excitement of same. That excitement— all the things to look forward to, with anticipation of fun together—is my balance (defense) against the absence and the distance. I focus on all that's coming up: in two weeks we visit Normandy, less than three weeks later I come to Westport and we celebrate our first anniversary. Three weeks after that, Passover—seders and family, the Yale weekend, a stay of at least ten days. Ten days later, you come here and we combine romance in Paris with fun and gastronomy and wine and old/ new friends and romance in Burgundy. And all that—what a schedule!—only brings us to mid-May.

I was dizzy with feeling wanted, though I saved the more effusive and ruminating reflections for my Morning Pages.

In my fax conversations with David, I addressed aspects of my personality that could affect the process between us:

I'm an awful gear-switcher. All my energy goes into doing clinical work, and then it takes me forever to pay attention to analyzing data. Or even pay attention at a meeting. Sometimes even to what you wrote in a fax. I'm sorry if I miss responding to a detail here and there.

David was having none of it.

There is no "switching gears"—you're starting to use that as an excuse/justification. All of everyday life is a series of progressions from one thing to the next, waking up and having coffee and showering and dressing and then maybe reading, or writing, or shopping, or seeing friends or patients or colleagues—you don't "switch gears" each time, you just go on to the next thing/activity/thought/etc. The best remedy is to do/ act/think about other things, and perhaps "look forward" to that meal, but we keep on doing the other things anyway, if only to make the time pass, although there is also the satisfaction/ joy/reward of all those other things, too. And then—surprise— it's mealtime!

Each time we made plans for our moments together, regardless of which side of the ocean, we needed to coordinate with others who were to be involved. Integrating them into our world was tedious but essential. Meanwhile, I searched for alternative ways to use my professional skills, ones potentially offering more flexibility. David listened patiently as I considered the idea of moving into a consulting role in corporate America, advising developers of housing for older adults on how to best support and foster well-being in their residents. I could become *the* expert on the meaning of home and on marriage in late-life couples, including widowhood. The NIH grant I was applying for could fund research, and meanwhile I could locate and develop contacts at Marriott, a company just beginning to construct housing centers for older adults on the East Coast.

I had two difficult moments between those winter trips. The first surprised me. David became distressed about his relationship with one of his sons, a fear of increasing emotional distance. He opened up about this painful area that he had formerly kept hidden when I was neither expecting nor prepared for that kind of telephone call; indeed, I was deep into a project that required intense concentration. I did manage to "switch gears," but several faxes and phone calls were necessary before we could identify the source of the derailment of our normally excellent process and accept that we each had our points of vulnerability. Both of us could become upset about something that had nothing whatsoever to do with the other but that we wanted to be able to talk about, to explore, perhaps to complain or even cry about. And we needed a language to ask for what we wanted, to identify what we really needed. Distance, with its absence of physical reality and contextual cues, made intuitive empathy harder but even more important. We learned we both had to provide more information if we were not together.

The second challenge came when I did something well: making a presentation and then leading a breakout session at the winter Yale Alumni Fund board meetings. On one level, I wished David could see me at my intellectual best and feel proud of me. On another, I was missing the uncanny way our thoughts and minds danced together, either repeating the same patterns or complementing each other in a mirrorlike reflection. I was also aware of the distortions in those images that were more likely when we were apart. Finally, there was that mystical level, the one that had brought us into each other's lives in the way it had. I wrote:

> *Anyway, I kept wishing you were there—yes, to see me in action (you still haven't seen me at my best, although there was the Banff preview), but even more to share something intellectual. I'm feeling so hungry for that part of you. Last summer was so much fun—sharing ideas, concepts, analysis . . . I kept thinking how much fun it would be to learn things together.*

And then I mused:

> *It's hard to have meaningful conversations by phone or fax without the shared context—too much trying to describe, understand, communicate. Giving and receiving (though they too are, of course, wonderful), rather than sharing, then discussing.*

And then, perhaps to comfort myself, I became philosophical:

> *Yes, the angels in us belong to God—we see and love the light in each other, but trying to possess it would snuff it out, suffocate it. It needs air to sparkle and shimmer—the oxygen of breath, the nourishment of good works. But the more we each see, the more we shine. It's just important that I not be seduced by devils. Will you step in and protect me? Is that fearful or realistic? My history tells me I was naive not to believe they existed. As for concern about draining me, you got it right, David. You are totally different—and consciousness is what makes the biggest difference of all and is something I was incredibly impressed by from the moment I met you.*

In a concrete, as well as symbolic, response, David gave me permission to bring him a set of bona fide American jumper cables, guaranteed to work well at a fraction of the price in France. His car had broken down during a test-drive of a new route out of Paris toward Normandy for our upcoming weekend there. In letting me in to help where I could, he, too, was learning to accept being cared for and given to, even on the most personal level, regarding the maintenance and safety of the car he so proudly and confidently drove.

My plane landed at CDG around nine on the morning of March 7, and I fell into David's arms. We hurried to the always-gleaming Ford, and David navigated his way to the Autoroute that connected to the A-13, which then took us north and west toward Normandy. Soon we were following the Seine, passing exits with signs for Vernon, Giverny, les Andelys. After our first rest stop, jet lag clicked in and I fell into a deep sleep. We passed the exits toward Rouen, then Honfleur, Deauville-Trouville, Cabourg. I awoke somewhere around Caen, and the combination of transatlantic travel, time zones, fast driving in a fast car, and general exhaustion (plus extreme excitement?) had left me feeling sick. David left the Autoroute and drove to Creully. He parked the car and guided me into a café where he could get some Badoit and baguette to stabilize my stomach. We were already in the part of Normandy he loved most dearly, the Basse-Normandie area with the landing beaches and war memorials.

When we left the café, I realized we were standing in front of the Château de Creully, a fortress from the Middle Ages, complete with turrets and dungeons. From there we drove on narrow, winding roads to the coastal town of Arromanches-les-Bains, the man-made harbor that today is the home of the Musée du Débarquement. Following the coastline, we soon arrived at Port-en-Bessin, a fishing village nestled between Gold Beach and Omaha Beach, where we were going to spend our nights.

Before we drove to the château where David had reserved a room, he took me into town. We walked out onto the jetty that extended into the port and watched the boats as they entered and left the harbor, locks raising and lowering them to the level of the sea. We embraced, holding each other tightly, until we could breathe evenly again, feeling secure in our knowledge that we were in solid physical contact and could remain connected for hours to come. He steered me into a shop where a grinning Frenchman with a white beard, horizontally striped shirt, and navy sweater—right out of central casting—fitted me with a pair of dark blue Wellingtons. We picked up sandwiches and headed to the beach on the eastern side of the port, where we could feel the tickly crunch of mussel shells beneath our boot-clad feet and the slap of water against our protected calves. Cliffs rose overhead.

"See, it's really a lot like your Maine coast." David waved one arm toward the breakers and his other toward the rocks rising abruptly behind us.

"Not exactly," I said. "But it's very beautiful." I was wondering, *What is he thinking? The Normandy coast bears no resemblance to Penobscot Bay. Wrong colors. Shape. Sense of accessibility. Harmony. It is beautiful but sure is different. No, this does not replace the serenity of my protected cove in Tenants Harbor.*

After this orientation, David drove us to the gorgeous Château la Chenevière. Again I felt as if I were in a movie, this time maybe *Sabrina*, as we followed the woman who greeted us up the grand staircase to a room with a balcony that overlooked gardens. From the crisp white sheets to the heated towel bar, from the generous silk curtains with their tasseled tiebacks to the deep carpeting and Louis XV furniture, the room fit any dream I might have conjured up of a country castle that had been converted in service of hospitality. We unpacked and settled in.

David gave me a purple beret, earrings made of turquoise and amethyst stones, and a lighter-weight silk scarf in blues, greens, and purples that set them off. "Time for spring," he reassured me, grinning that grin. We drove into the town and down to the water for dinner. One of David's longtime favorite restaurants, overlooking the port, introduced me to Pommeau, the apple-flavored aperitif that remains my favorite to this day. We shared a startlingly fresh *plateau de fruits de mer*, that uniquely French banquet of fresh and mostly raw seafoods. Calvados, the apple-based brandy of the region, followed the tarte tatin we ordered for dessert. We returned to our romantic château. After a glorious night spent in each other's arms and a long, luxurious breakfast in bed, we dressed and were ready for the day ahead.

David gave me his best tour of his favorite part of Normandy. We began at a little-known spot called Le Chaos. We climbed down the cliffs and then walked along the shore, part of the span between Port-en-Bessin and Longues-sur-Mer. I looked out at the peaceful channel, pleasure boats and barges bobbing along on the picture-perfect day. Inside, I was thinking of my uncle and of a patient whom I particularly loved; both had been part of the Normandy landing. How in the world had they done it? And how had the experiences changed them?

When we returned, we found a *crêperie* where we could buy galettes filled with ham and gruyère for lunch. In the afternoon, we pulled on our boots and again walked along the beaches. We retrieved the car and drove to Pointe du Hoc, to climb among the bunkers built by the Germans for surveillance of the coastline during World War II. After much blood had been shed, allied forces finally overtook the strategic installation. We wandered through towns that had been destroyed—no home was older than 1945—and then turned back toward Port-en-Bessin.

At Colleville-sur-Mer, David pulled off the road into the parking lot of the American Military Cemetery. We walked quietly through the gates. There, overlooking the English Channel, stood thousands of symmetrically placed, brilliant white grave markers, each topped by a cross or a Star of David pointing toward the heavens. We squeezed hands as we walked among the graves, breaking silence only to occasionally read aloud the name, date, place of birth of a soldier who had crossed the Atlantic to defend the abstract notion of freedom. An alarming number of them had been in their late teens or early twenties. We reached the memorial itself, tears streaming down our cheeks.

"I understand now. At least, I understand better." Intuitively, I had known that my patient who had landed at Omaha Beach as a young soldier had lived a life of courage, focus, and perspective in large part because of his experiences during the war. I imagined memories he might carry. I remembered my response to him when he could not understand his adult son's worldview: "He did not have a war." By now I was sobbing. We remained in the cemetery until the setting sun sent streaks of orange and gold into the channel.

That evening, David and I stayed at the château. We shared one of those long multicourse French dinners, one that began with Pommeau and made its way through the *amuse-bouches*, the *entrée* (the appetizer), the *plat* (known in the United States as the entrée), apple sorbet drowning in Calvados to clear the palate, a salad course followed by a cheese cart. After Camembert and Livarot and Roquefort Papillon with veins so dark they were nearly ash came dessert; after dessert came coffee; with coffee came the *mignardises* (tiny cakes and cookies and chocolates); and, finally, there was Calvados. The day had stretched our range of emotions, tired us physically, and now ended with indulgence and beauty, gratitude for the good moments.

The breakfast tray, again brought to our room, was so filled with treats that David and I dragged ourselves away only by reminding each other that we really did want to go to Bayeux and that David had arranged to call on his artist friend before we visited the *Tapisserie de la Reine Mathilde*, the Bayeux Tapestry, which told the story of the Norman conquest and its aftermath in exquisite detail. We made our way to Clothilde's cottage in her tiny village, then climbed the staircase to her studio.

A radiant woman opened the door, clearly overjoyed to see David again. She invited us inside. They chattered away, fast and furious, as though they had not seen each other in far longer than the few months that it had been. Clothilde showed us the paintings she had been working on, and I was impressed by the range of art made by this woman who had never taken a lesson in her nearly five decades of living. She had one oil of red poppies, the kind that grow along the side of the road in that part of Normandy, that I adored. Later, in my

Morning Pages, I promised myself, *If David and I ever live together, I would love to have that painting hang over our mantel.*

After our gallery tour, Clothilde took us downstairs to share lunch with her parents and children. Her husband was working. Next, we toured the garden she had created with the same eye for color, balance, and harmony that she exercised in creating her easel art. David had been her angel, the support and encouragement that she had needed to pursue her passion for painting. He had urged her to exhibit publicly for the first time only a few years before, at the very Château de Creully where we had parked on our way to the sea. Finally, he had convinced her to offer her canvases for sale. He had an eye for what was beautiful, what was fine, what was talented, and here was one more example of his intuition's unwavering intelligence. And his knack for transforming lives in the direction of self-realization.

Clothilde lived close to Bayeux. We quickly found the medieval town, miraculously spared during the carnage of the War, and entered the museum, which held the famous needlework commemorating the Battle of Hastings: 230 feet of embroidered stories with Latin narrative allegedly created by Queen Mathilde, William the Conqueror's wife, along with her ladies-in-waiting, carefully preserved and attractively displayed. Art from the eleventh century was housed near a cathedral consecrated in 1077, in a town with pre-Christian era roots with a cobblestone pedestrian street running through it. David took a photo of us as we sat on a wall near the castle. Yes, this history mattered, and so did the present and so did the future. Careful links could show how they fit together.

At the end of the afternoon, David and I headed back to Paris. Somewhere around Vernon, we pulled off the road and found an auberge straight out of the fantasies of yet another filmmaker. I think it was Hostellerie au Bon Accueille in Bonnières-sur-Seine. Huge, open fireplace; long-haired, nuzzling dogs; plank tables with checkered tablecloths. The food was hearty and delicious, the man who served us enthusiastic and nurturing. We returned to the boat with our bellies filled with good food, our hearts filled with love, and our souls filled

with the beauty the days and nights had offered to us. David delivered
me to the airport the next day, and, once again, tears fell as I walked
through passport control.

Normally, I bypassed the duty-free shops. This trip, I unsuccess-
fully tried to buy a bottle of Pommeau. On the plane, I wrote to David:

> *They don't carry it. She suggested something "similar but
> without the apple taste"—that's like bringing olives back from
> Maine because they don't have blueberries.*
>
> *Oh, David, ain't we got fun? I refuse to let my body shut
> down this time: my heart feels as if it will explode inside my
> chest, brimming over with all good things. If it did burst, it
> would be like a piñata filled with precious things: jewels tum-
> bling out and Godiva chocolates (only the dark ones, heavy on
> the truffles, a few Normandy-apple caramels tucked among
> them); and satin ribbons; and a million twinkly stars released,
> like the sparklies on the water but millions of them—stardust,
> maybe angel dust. All these things would burst out, spill over,
> flood the body, burst it open, and light up the world. That's how
> strong it feels. And I'm not going to run away this time. I'm
> going to tolerate the wonder when we are apart like I now can
> when we are together. Thank you, thank you, thank you . . .*
>
> *The map [on the airplane screen] now. Arrow on Paris.
> You can see Rouen, the coast. Alive now. The landing a reality.
> Soldiers and sand and cliffs and liberation. Sacrifice—3,628
> miles from here to there; sixty-four degrees outside in early
> March. Who ever would have dreamed that the best years of
> my life would begin at fifty-two? You're right—this could be fun
> forever. Will be fun forever. Is being fun forever.*
>
> *The gentleness of Normandy. Coffee in a tiny village a pre-
> lude. The gates to the harbor at Port-en-Bessin. My marvelous
> boots! Perfect to touch and to walk in and on—permission
> granted to the little girl to kick and splash—and so adorable to
> look at on me, on my feet, now for you, stored in the trunk of*

your car along with yours. No, I did not miss the symbolism— nor your awareness of it.

Thank you again, dear David. Again you have shown me, rather than needed to tell me. How well you know that Mother taught me to reify words and that the words were lies and so I never feel as safe with words. Saying it doesn't make it so—but showing it insists that it is. So thank you for wanting my boots in the trunk of your car.

The images flow over, David: the clear blue sky in Bayeux, fog rolling in, hunkering down, mere kilometers away. The big things—the cemetery, the tapestry, the walks and views and vistas—including being lost in the fog—and the exquisite food, and, of course, the infinite details: a château (is that what you call your neighborhood hotel?) more perfect than I could have imagined, extraordinary baked treats with breakfast in bed, the wines and tastes, the man at the auberge, woman at the res- taurant, sweet concierge at l'hôtel. The sand and rocks and sea and shells beneath my feet, climbing cliffs and dunes and stairs to the tower, climbing up onto the quai, rather than across or down to it. The organization of the tapestry museum, the water wheel, picnic on the bench. Forsythias and willow trees and daffodils and even cherry trees bursting forth—greens and pinks and yellows against the austerity of winter. The warmth of Clothilde, echoing that of her home, that of her art, that of her moment in the universe. What a delight to be able to visit with her; what fun it will be to watch her evolve.

I thanked him for the earrings; the paintings on copper; the books and magazines; words, arms, kisses. By then, I had begun to write in French.

IV

Expansion of Self and Other

13

Celebration

*O*n March 28, David flew to New York for a long weekend in celebration of our first anniversary. I presented him with a découpaged wastebasket I had made for him. Words, map snippets, restaurant cards, ticket stubs, bits of brochures, stamps—and, of course, boarding passes—bore witness to our year together. One side was Europe and the other North America. In the tradition of an Easter basket, I filled it with other surprises: a tie with bunnies, chocolates, some pâté, a half bottle of champagne.

The next morning, drinking the coffee he had brought to me as I sat propped up on the pillows in the big bed, I wrote in my Morning Pages:

> *Hard to believe I met David a year ago today. What made me go to Paris? What made me know that, after thirty-three years of avoiding France, at a time when expenses were outrunning income, I needed to get on that plane? How could I have imagined David? Thank you, God—thank you for sending this good, decent, giving man into my life. Thank you for giving me the wisdom to see how good it feels being with him, to notice my heart, to act from my heart, to cut through my fears. Thank you for giving me the courage to manage the year, to notice my*

fears, to not get too crazed by them, to stand up for things that
were important to me. Thank you for helping me to be able
to know how it feels to love and be loved in this way. "Didn't
anyone ever take care of you?" he asked in Normandy. No,
David, not really. My first mother-in-law, a little. And Stuart . . .
Did he send David to me?

He liked the découpaged wastebasket I made for him. He
was touched—probably tired, late at night, and up for over
twenty-four hours—but he did like his gifts.

It really feels pretty "clean" with David and me. We both
give and we both get, and different kinds of things—our
resources are different. No, he can't "give" me a house and
home—but I can give those to him. And he can give me Paris
and Normandy—all of France, all of Europe—and respite from
the demands of others, from time being eaten up, stolen away
by expectations, hurt feelings. He's a good-feelings guy, nice to
be around, good energy—of course people want to be around
him.

We continued to celebrate on Sunday. A long walk at Sherwood
Island. After, a drive to Old Greenwich for Easter morning services
at the Albertson Memorial Church, a spiritualist institution that was
as conservative in its congregants and location as it was radical in its
perspective. The couple who together ministered to their flock chan-
neled dead spirits and led prayers for healing and wholeness. Sitting
there, David became more and more uncomfortable. He generally
liked new things, but this might have been a bit over the top, even for
him. Nonetheless, he had long ago accepted that I would open new
doors, and he was willing at least to peek inside them, and here we
were again, exploring another dimension.

That evening, the couple who had given me David's name came
for dinner. We served them a salad of endives, apples, walnuts, and
Roquefort cheese, accompanied by a sweet white wine that David
had brought off the plane, a gift from a flight attendant. Steamed

lobsters followed, and I must have made something chocolate for dessert; I was always making something chocolate in those days. David hosted in his characteristic fashion—chatty, gregarious, social, intelligent, and just a little outrageous. On Monday we awoke, spent the morning holding on to each other as though we could stop time if only we gripped hard enough, and then tried to cheer up Luke as he began to sulk while he watched David pack his bags yet again. Luke definitely understood luggage. This would be a nineteen-day separation; David was scheduled to return for Passover and to stay for eight nights.

As we headed for the airport, I began to feel resentful that I carried the entire domestic load—family, friends, home, and hearth. I was getting stuck with "meat and potatoes" while David got to do the "bells and whistles." Yet when I took my emotional temperature more carefully, I realized that I was just trying to block the pain. David was leaving and then would not be with me. Once again, I thought, *Tu me manques* ("you are missing from me") and how much more descriptive are the French words for a deep longing, a missing-ness— his warm arms around me, fingers digging deep into my shoulders, back, neck, spine, rubbing where it hurts, massaging the sore places away, recognizing them. I wanted to keep him with me—to keep our bodies connected, energies flowing back and forth across our spirits. Yet I knew I needed to take him to the airport, to say goodbye, to let him go back to France. What I wanted just did not matter, whether I wanted to keep him here when he was here or wanted to stay with him there when we were there. I didn't want to face the time it takes to reconnect and then disconnect—pull the plug, and the electricity stops flowing through. Some of it always seemed to get stuck in the wires, the spaces. I hated that this was so hard for me, but I didn't want not to do it, not to know it, not to savor the joys, simply because "switching gears" was, for me, so hard.

As we drove, the silence became heavier. I was aware that we were approaching the summer and neither of us had a clue what we wanted to do with it. Perhaps we both feared bringing up this taboo topic.

I had work to do: patients to see, manuscripts to write, new career options to explore, a life to manage, APA meetings in Chicago in August. I had a house in Maine to deal with, a bridal luncheon to host, kids to celebrate. I had many things that needed doing: ficus trees to trim, a garage to sweep, photos to organize into albums. Most of all, I carried this concern, this unspoken burden, that I did not want our relationship to become too difficult for David. I did not want him to go away because the hassles and expense of managing complicated logistics wasn't worth it. During the weekend, he had mentioned that his mother would have been very upset with the details of what we were doing, that she herself could not have dealt with all that moving, packing, coordinating . . . and spending.

More and more, I wanted to change my life; I yearned to share it with David. Was that crazy? Of course. But if my own history had taught me anything, the lessons were to take both my heart and my work life very seriously. We were going to have to struggle with this one. Driving to the airport, neither of us could leave the "room." The car became a finite container for conversation, so David confronted me:

"What's going on? What's bothering you?"

I was silent.

"I know you too well. This is not the silence when you are over-whelmed and become speechless."

"I'm going to miss you."

"We already know that."

"And all the work when you are here—it's really hard on me sometimes."

"So come to Paris."

"I haven't been invited."

"What are you talking about? Of course you are invited."

"I mean, specifically. I don't know when you want to see me again."

"Roni Beth, what are you talking about?"

"You need to drive the car. We both know that. And I haven't been invited."

"We settled that last summer. In Maine. On the deck of the cottage. We just haven't worked out the details."

"We settled what last summer?"

"That we are living together. Just in two places. You don't need an invitation."

"What do you mean?"

"You can't work there, and I don't know what I would do here, and if you moved over, we'd have to find an apartment in Paris, and we just don't have solutions yet."

I thought about what he was saying. Had we actually been living with such radically different perceptions of the nature of our relationship for nearly a year?

"If I had believed it were a real possibility, I'd have talked to colleagues who might possibly have contacts in France and be able to help."

"So start talking to them. See what you can find."

David was, of course, referring to that conversation in Maine when he mused about potentially living there and asked rhetorically, "Except what would I *do*?" Now, thanks to his reminding me of that and making it a reality, the proverbial elephant in the living room, which we had been carefully ignoring, had followed us into the car and, after this conversation, happily marched into his own quarters and away from ours. Speaking the unspeakable clarifies context and liberates energy.

I had clearance to begin doing research. I always did research, not as a stalling technique, just as a way of gathering information and confronting my questions and concerns. As every psychologist knows, structure and information bind anxiety.

When I got home, I listened to the message David had left while I was driving back to Connecticut. He described wandering around the first-class lounge of Air France, surrounded by personnel who knew him, yet feeling "lost," again.

In my NIH research grant application, I added exploring "the meaning of home." When were we "home," "safe," comfortable, and comforted—and when, indeed, were we "lost"? David and I were beginning to feel that home was with each other, regardless of the structural or geographical locations we occupied. I guess that is true attachment. I picked up my pen and wrote him the fax that would await him when he went to his office in Paris, directly from the airport, the following morning:

> *As I write, you are comfortably (I hope) seated in row 12, seat E (on the aisle) of AF007, flying high in the sky, somewhere approaching Ireland, I imagine, at this time. It's about 10:30 in Westport or about 4:30 in the sky, and wherever you are, my thoughts and hopes and dreams are with you.*
>
> *I loved being with you—watching you notice the patches of fat on Sofia's tiny feet, joke around with your sister, enjoy the food of the weekend with such gusto, walk with me on our beaches—convenient, if nowhere near as vast and full of grandeur as those in Normandy.*
>
> *I will leave a voice message of some sort on the boat, in case you decide to go home first. That way, either place there will be a greeting. And you will know that I love my beautiful gifts, my thoughts of you, and, most of all, the time that we share together. Ain't we got fun!*

The next morning, I wrote in my Morning Pages:

> *I can't just close up my practice and go do something else— or can I? Why not? Stop asking why and look at why not? Most of my life for others. Why not the beaches at Normandy? Why not the weekends in Burgundy, Sologne, the Loire Valley, anywhere—who cares? I do. Yes, I love my kids. But I'm not real important to them anymore, and I need a life, too.*

The days between the two spring trips that David made to the United States were filled with the usual busyness. I saw my patients, with and without emergencies, walked with Hope and Luke; volunteered for Yale and the Connecticut Psychological Association; worked on manuscripts and the grant application; cared for my dog, myself, and my children, too, whenever they were around. I attended a funeral, planned a baby shower, and ate breakfast with my girlfriends. Jennifer and Steve were going to take a short vacation in Maine before she began a new job; Danny and Stefani were together again and clearly in love.

The weekend after David left, I drove to Tenants Harbor to christen the cottage with a real street number, an honor bestowed by the village now that the rutted dirt road had been paved, and to make sure the hideaway was ready for spring visitors. I wondered why Maine felt so special to me, why the sounds of the night creatures, the foghorn, the bell from the lighthouse were so reassuring. Why did this place I never knew before 1986 feel like "home"? Then the thought was suddenly so clear: *Come here in the summer, Paris in the winter.*

I knew what *I* would do: write, paint, walk, and make love. And visit my as-yet-theoretical grandchildren. What would David do? Read, walk, make love—and maybe make music. This tight little cottage, with its high, beamed ceiling, always allowed me to ask all my questions and talk to God directly.

April 4, 1997, Morning Pages (written in Maine):

The land of the painted firs. They stand just outside my window. Eyes open, and the morning light dances on the water—too early for the sparklies but late enough for the pinks and peaches and grays to mix with the pale blue, reflecting the sky, grounding it, lines in my dream . . .

Telephone—David from Paris. I've got it backwards, he said. Change the organization of my life, then I can come to Paris—not move to Maine so I can change the organization of my life.

Still, I imagined expanding the Maine cottage, maybe even buying the property next door, and living there full-time, hopefully with David visiting for long periods.

> *We could teach our grandchildren to hear the quiet, to soak it up, to truly tune in to the moment, to screen out the noise—to be able to listen to God, to find a unique serenity, stillness, that they could use to nourish themselves forever.*

On the way home from Maine, I detoured to Cambridge to meet with Richard Hackman, my most cherished mentor. Since 1977, he had never failed to understand my strengths and challenges, both as a psychologist and as a person, and to provide wise counsel. This visit was no exception. I laid out my complicated work life and possibilities, explained the goals of simplifying and stabilizing my career, along with creating freedom and flexibility so that I could spend more time more easily with David. We reviewed options, and he finally listed seven career paths and instructed me to select five of the seven and explore pursuing them. Feeling more clearheaded, I returned to Connecticut, where I could get to work on the options.

But within a few days, I, too, felt lost again. In my Morning Pages, I wrote:

> *David gone. Clear there's no easy solution: David needs to earn his comfortable income to give us the ease of doing what we do. I need to stay here, since he can't guarantee me support there. And he can't guarantee an alternate means of support for himself here—and may not want to, and I may not want him to—and it probably is much less complicated and/or difficult than it seems. But that's how it is now, and the important point for me is that I get to have my life as I know it and as it becomes. But somehow this morning nothing seems real. I listen to the rain, know I need to get up, shower, walk the dog and deal with the car—and yet all is unreal, like walking through a dream, now a nightmare, not breathing. Is that fear*

or not wanting to feel the emptiness, the loss? Why do the pussy willows on the desk seem boring, the bunny with the cottontail mundane, the early-morning rain infinite? I feel like a repository for life stories, finally on the threshold of claiming my own. Decades of watching lives, seeing them up close . . . Now I want to live my own.

14

Ambivalence

*S*pring exploded. In my Morning Pages, I mused:

> *What is life, anyway? A series of memories—moments of enjoyment (or not) strung together into some sort of aggregate fabric. A quilt of colors—bright, intense ones or quiet, subtle ones. How would a box of ecru and sepia-toned collages look compared with the vivid and intense ones that I've always done?*

I was struggling to settle in, dig more deeply, stably, subtly, with less explosive change and more of a nuanced texture to my days and nights. Would that be possible with our intense connecting and separating?

Then the truth became clear. In one stunning, striking moment, when I could allow the fear to flow without distracting myself with one of my endless activities, I was able to own my role in my own unhappiness. In my Morning Pages, I wrote:

> *David, where are you? I need a hug. I need you to scoop me into your strong arms and hold me to you tight, panic subsiding. I feel the fear now, wafting over me, through me, dissociation on its heels. I feel the panic, its source: Fear that my life*

will be/is being swallowed up, that I have wasted most of my
life. Where is my life—getting out there in the wind and rain,
digging around in the dirt? I've been dressing for business, for
status, for "success." Yes, I want pretty clothes, but most of all I
want a life—a nonprofessional life.

Almost immediately, with these acknowledgments, I felt my
conscious attention liberated to work on all those projects I hoped
would help move me toward freedom, either through opening new
possibilities or through the honorable completion of commitments.
At the same time, my unconscious began to work overtime. Dreams
became nightmares, forcing me to confront the greed that surfaced
once I recognized the deprivation. First I tried to wrestle with it by
being logical, rational. In one of my Morning Pages, I wrote:

If resistance is fear, then what am I afraid of? Being suc-
cessful? No. I think I'm afraid of the devouring monster—that
I will unleash ravenous greed that will swallow me up, that I
will want to "do it all," "have it all," "be it all," and all at once.
Now what do I do with my greed? Think of trade-offs and pri-
orities—$2,000 would buy a new basic wardrobe; a long trip
(ten days plus plane fare?); a long weekend with the kids; a
big-screen TV; one-tenth of a car; four trips to Paris; a year of
Pilates, plus weekly yoga; thirty-three massages; forty days in
the city with modest lunches, or twenty days with splurges; a
week without patients; twenty inexpensive wedding gifts or ten
expensive ones; a week at a ranch (not counting lost income);
fifty books, more if novels, less if technical; six-plus cashmere
sweaters; refinished wood floors (maybe); summer plants with
$1,800 left over. Lots of choices to be made. What do I need to
nourish me?

Help me, God—what am I struggling with here? Five hours
can be five hours of worry; half a day at a museum; two movies;
cleaning many closets; half of a book; half a day at a day spa;

travel time between Westport and the ashram; preparation for
the shower-luncheon; returning phone calls; playing solitaire;
taking a long nap; going shopping; reading the New York Times;
horseback riding, complete with travel; writing the grant. Again,
choices—but the moments for them will never come again.

While I was working and agonizing, David went to Normandy to enjoy his four-day spring weekend, a staple in the French calendar, with its three extended holidays during the month of May. While he climbed the cliffs and wiggled his toes in the sand, I wrote science and tried to generate clarity. I struggled with the historical roots of my need to feel "competent." Most vivid were the memories of San Francisco, flights out there from Connecticut to deal with—care for? about?—my mother as she became ill, began to die. How competent I felt. Checking in and out of hotels, renting cars, in and out of airports, planes, acting like an adult in something that mattered. Gathering and evaluating information on medical and residential options. Consulting with doctors. Arranging for housing with increasing levels of care as her health deteriorated and getting her moved from one place, from one life, into another. Again and again. I could take responsibility (and behave responsibly) even when she could not. Never had. Nothing new in that theme: by taking charge, taking care of whatever, I reassured myself I would not repeat my mother's dependency and the manipulation that had grown from it. Thus repeated a theme of my entire adult life: regardless of psychic, physical, or financial cost, I would take care of that for which I was responsible. Starting with myself. Depending on someone else was foolish at best and an invitation to blame him or her at worst.

Now I was again moving toward balance. While I was proud, grateful, and relieved to be putting money back into the bank, instead of taking it out, exercising with some regularity, and enjoying the luscious moments of sharing with David, I pondered my capacity to continue working so intensely over long hours and began to long for the vulnerability of dependency. And I wanted David to be more accepting of that vulnerability, both in me and in himself. I wanted him to see the relationship as a partnership, more than just a conduit for fun and games. I knew that my turbulent fights with internal monsters, clearly of my own making, *were* illusory. I was afraid that I (they) would drive him away. Another echo of the Snow White theme—I needed to somehow neutralize my internalized mother, the greedy and devouring monster who was trying to kill me. Ultimately, I understood that I needed (again) to be impractical, no matter how much fear I would then need to address. Staying "safe" was not the answer. Meanwhile, I faxed David the abstract for the grant proposal. It represented one route to a new work configuration. He sent back lucid remarks, helpful ones, especially, sweetly, those that suggested I follow the NIH instructions more precisely.

I returned to France on the Ascension weekend for the HLSAE annual junket, this year in Burgundy. The weekend in Dijon began a pivotal period in our relationship. The closeness, the sharing, the chemistry and sheer magic of being with each other had finally reached a point where we both had to confront our worldviews and, if we were going to continue together, the imperative of changing patterns and perspectives that had, until then, permitted each of us to feel safe, independent, able to take care of ourselves. For me, the questions revolved around where I felt most vulnerable—would it be okay to be feminine as well as "professional," impractical as well as responsible, dependent as well as the rock others relied on, expressive as well as reticent, free to acknowledge my longings and desires as well as disciplined and grateful for my blessings? For David, the issues were more subtle: he had created a self he liked, a lifestyle that made him happy, beliefs that stood him in good stead. What would it mean to allow a broader space in his life for this woman with her commitments to social involvement and connections, her messy routines with too much on the calendar and even a dog, albeit an adorable one, who could be guaranteed to occasionally pee or even poop or vomit on spaces recently cleaned? And how in the world to balance the two cultures, one he ran away from, another to which he was fiercely, though

ambivalently, attached? And how in the world could he let himself
depend on someone else for just about anything?

The first big fight during that trip came on the heels of one of
David's typically sweet and generous gestures. I had proudly come to
Dijon wearing a pair of new navy Ferragamo ballerina pumps, my
first and only pair ever, bought after agonizing over the expense. I
rationalized the purchase on the basis of comfort and the notion that
they would last forever and not go out of style. The pumps did not like
the downpour that greeted us in Dijon. By the time we were halfway
back to the hotel from the museum, their leather soles were soaked
through. David steered me into a shoe store and insisted I try on a
pair of sturdy canvas, sneaker-type walking shoes with rubber platform bottoms. Sheepishly, I thanked him. As he punched the code
for his debit card into the clerk's machine, I leaned over to kiss him. It
was, admittedly, a fairly enthusiastic kiss, but this was France, where
people engaged in outright sexual behavior in public. David pushed
me away. And I was mystified.

After our expansive displays of affection in France—embraces
on the bridges, on the quais, on the walkway at Port en Bessin, in
Bagatelle, on the Champs-Élysées, above all in airports—and after his
consistent irritation when I refused even to hold his hand in public in
Connecticut, lest a patient see me and become curious or confused—
David was insisting that a thank-you kiss in front of the salesgirl in the
shoe shop in Dijon was "inappropriate." I was crushed, bewildered,
and overcome by shame. Why would the French culture accept all
manner of settings for open seduction and yet create a taboo in this
instance? The psychologist in me decided something else must be
bothering him. Was he suddenly afraid that one of his HLSAE peers
might wander along, see us, and judge either of us poorly? Why was
he suddenly judging the behavior? Or was he worried that the salesgirl might feel less freely attracted to him (he *is* magnetic)? Or that
the affection between us represented more closeness than he wanted?
Was he afraid of where we might be headed? Did he want more literal
distance?

"David, help me understand. You usually can't get close enough to me in public, especially in France."

"Not in the shoe store."

"What do you mean, 'not in the shoe store'?"

"It's not appropriate in a shoe store."

"You've got some kind of a 'rule' going on here that I don't understand. What is it? Why is the shoe store different?"

"It's not a 'rule.' It's just not appropriate. How things are done."

"Sounds like another one of your rules. I can follow—or challenge—it if I understand what it is."

"It's *not* about rules. You always want an explanation for everything." He was getting angry.

Silence. No hand holding.

We limped through the evening festivities, four varieties of foie gras, snails prepared in a shallot cream sauce, perfect scallops and succulent lamb, dessert tables that were an embarrassment, wines from the region flowing. Over the weekend we slowly relaxed, helped by wine tastings, conversations with David's old friends, the black-tie gala, a visit to the basilica at Vézelay on the way back to Paris.

But by Sunday night, back in Paris, as we walked across the Invalides to Pizza Veronica, the air between us again became tense and the slight distance that had accompanied us throughout much of the weekend began to grow. Conflict ripening. David was walking a little too quickly and speaking a bit too brusquely. The next day, when I tried to work at my desk in the office next to his, I began to worry that he had had enough, too much. Throughout the weekend, he had been ignoring opportunities to touch, be physically close. Was he just afraid of letting go, of having to say goodbye so soon? Was I? I decided to delay thinking about that until the next day, when I needed to leave, but then trying to pretend it didn't matter when it mattered a great deal did not work. I pictured going home with no more David in my life and could feel the emptiness I had known after Judith or Matthew died or, even worse, Stuart. The color and dimension drained from my life; everything felt bland and flat, inside and out. I moved through days feeling as though my feet were trudging through wet sand. All that was in my heart and could no longer be shared was stuck there, making me feel swollen, heavy.

All I wanted was to love: love the baby, the children, the man. Now David. Intolerable deprivation. I felt starved for the freedom to give love, attention, affection; it was hard to conceive of overdosing. I knew I needed to keep taking care of myself, or I risked being too emotionally exposed. David would have to be responsible for his own feelings. Over the weekend, he had been complaining about what he perceived as my insistence that we had to "talk about everything"—yet I had been notably quiet, my natural, introverted style, speaking only when I needed to and silently appreciating moments of awe and those spent in communion.

Was there something that I was not talking about? Maybe. That I was starting to feel homeless. I had a house, a cottage, and access to a houseboat yet really felt at home only when I was with David, wherever we were. Home is where the heart is, where the loving takes place. Truth was, we did it better here.

I wanted to move to Paris to be with him. We didn't talk about that. It was not a simple thing: there would be many problems to be addressed, details to be worked out—but they were only logistics. I began to spin scenarios. At some point, perhaps Jen and Steve could even live in the Westport house for a year. She had this new job in Connecticut, and it could be convenient for them. Signal Lane could remain a place for me to stay in the States, yet the day-to-day responsibilities could go to them in exchange for a home. What would it cost me to live in France? How much of my life could go on hold? It was a moot question at this juncture, but how would I feel if I didn't do it? I did grasp that I could not "always go back," because I *couldn't* always go back. The patients wouldn't be there—and what would I do? How would I figure it out? I felt sure that I *would* figure it out, but then, David was a central part of the equation. I needed him in more ways and more deeply each day—and it terrified me. The real issue, in my own mind, anyway, was that I hadn't been invited. On some level, I knew I needed to put my faith in God and just let go, but I continued to flail around, grasping for some possibility of control.

It all exploded our last night together on that trip. Following a somewhat sullen dinner, as we made our way across the bridge, David began, "The trouble is, you always want an explanation for everything. Why can't you just accept that some things are appropriate and others are not?"

"Who gets to decide what is appropriate when? I just want to understand how these decisions get made—or perceptions get formed."

"There you go again. You always have to make everything so heavy, complicated."

"I'm not complicating. I want to understand what triggers what feelings in you."

"You always have to know what I'm feeling. And why. Stop being a psychologist." By now he was screaming at me. We had reached the boat. As we undressed, any lingering efforts at politeness came off with our clothes.

"I can't stop being a psychologist. It's part of how I am, who I am. And I can't let you change that in me. I've been trained too well and fought too hard for it. Besides, it's my path to independence. I can't do this. This relationship is not going to work."

His face deep with lines, red with rage and distorted with denying his own fears, he let loose one last, booming tirade.

"So this relationship isn't going to work? What do you think we are doing here? You are so negative, such a complainer, so ungrateful. I could get real aggressive right now. Where were you a year ago? How many trips to Paris had you made?"

I was stunned and silent and wound up cowering into my side of the mattress, sobbing. *No, David, I had not been flying to Paris for weekends. I had not been dining on foie gras and magret. But I had begun to put my life back together after a tough period. Some years before I met you, I made a big mistake: I loved unwisely. Am I now unwise in loving you? Will I never have the feeling of sharing a life? You do. I don't. Your life is much simpler. Yes, you have changed my*

life, and no, it is not worse. But it certainly is more complex. I craved
reassurance, summer plans. I was yearning for plane tickets, their
reassurance.

David saw that my body was curled into a ball, shivering, shaking,
that the sobs came from the depths, that I was hurting, and he realized that we needed to address the little-girl state that his tantrum
had provoked in me. Lawyerly arguments had not worked, nor had
intimidation. He put his arms around me and, again, rocked me back
into my adult. We managed to work through it. The psychologist in
me wondered if the underlying source of all the conflict that weekend
was the reality of yet another too-brief physical connection followed
by a wrenching separation.

The next afternoon, on Air France flight 006 bound for JFK, I
wrote to David:

> *The tears were good—at least for the first time I feel fully in*
> *my feelings, not the horrid numbness of last May or the illu-*
> *sory "everything's fine" of other trips. . . . As AF006 heads out*
> *over the Atlantique at 505 mph somewhere a bit north of Cork,*
> *Ireland, an hour and twelve minutes into the flight, I thank*
> *you, David. For the days, for the nights, for the moments. For*
> *the sun and the rain and the shoes and the teapot . . . and crois-*
> *sants with good butter and tiled roofs and roadside stops with*
> *clean bathrooms and comprehensible pay phones and rolling*
> *hillsides complete with microclimates. For an office to work in*
> *and park to walk in and bed to share.*
>
> *Dreams of stepping on and off the boat, on and off the quai,*
> *on and off the airplane, on and off the switch that turns on*
> *the lights in my life. Thoughts of home, of hearth, of heart.*
> *Work you need to do, I need to do. Lives filled with distractions,*
> *attractions, main events. Babbling now—not wanting to let go.*

Not really complaining, David—just not black and white. Most of it is wonderful; letting go is hard. . . .

I think the "lost" feeling is simply a form of homelessness. I thought I knew where I was—especially the notion of having made the "home" (safe and loving place) I'd never had—and now it's all turned topsy-turvy. Patience, please, while I reorient, adapt, look around and see where I am. I guess that means discover my contexts or rediscover them. Is this too "heavy"? Too "analytical"? Too complaining? Just trying to find some words—really the best (i.e., most constructive, healthy) thing you can do with feelings—when you can't make love or reach over and touch a cheek, hold a hand, pat a shoulder, straighten a stray hair.

A welcome-home fax greeted me. David wrote:

Hope the "landing" is/was so far "soft"—that the flight was easy and uneventful, the drive home likewise (no traffic, no car problems), that you have recovered Luke, and that there are/ were no disasters waiting. So much for the material inconveniences. As to the emotions and feelings, I know them and share them. I miss you too. I would love to find you "at home" later, or to leave the office with you, as we did yesterday. We'll both "cope"—but neither of us has to feel good about it.

An e-mail jolt also awaited me. The EPI business office announced that my grant application could not be completed and submitted unless I had a Human Investigation Committee (HIC) protocol pending. And the HIC process would require a whole additional layer of papers and procedures. With signatures. I certainly was "home" again. The house welcomed me back to its bosom—gray carpeting that needed cleaning in the bedroom; fluffy new pillows on the bed; fibers holding energy, memories, history. The grown children and those patients whom I loved. David remained in the Paris that he adored. A place,

not a person. One that brought out what he liked best in himself. But I
myself loved Maine. For the first time, I could understand. I knew that
my feelings for David had a great deal to do with who he was, but I
also appreciated that they were about who I was when I was with him.
Just like being in Maine helped me dig more deeply inside myself,
being with David helped me reach beyond myself in a uniquely nourishing way. The couple we were creating had a lot to bring to us both.

Our routines returned. Madeline began creating a scrapbook
about Bill's life for his seventieth birthday; we agreed she could use
Danny's room as a studio, come and go with her own house key as
she pleased, so that she could keep the project a surprise. My patients,
unaware that I had been away during my short trip (I had called in for
and returned messages with strict regularity), did not feel a need to
punish me for perceived abandonment. David and I began to discuss
summer plans in earnest.

Time itself had shifted to a different experience with David in my
life—days floating into each other, months melting, time punctuated
by sharing or not sharing, missing him, catching up and preparing
as he left and came back. Seasons brought new joys, along with their
colors. As the calendar pages turned, would the novelty continue?
Would the opportunity to share permit it all to ripen, deepen? Or
would being together take on a feeling of "been there, done that,"
ennui born of repetition? Would we continue to be able to see the new
in the lights, the shadows, the soul? David was caught in the timeless-
ness of Paris—age-old monuments remaining the same day to day,
meticulously tended—and the stable background against which daily
life marches along: an old shop closes, a new one opens, a restaurant
changes hands. Imperceptibly, his children had aged; so had he. He
had done it all—lived there, done that—all the glamour and charm
that a life in Paris in the '70s and '80s and early '90s could offer. He
had places to take me, share with me, be with me. And I wanted to be
there, by his side, walking to work, home, across the city, on the quais.
I wanted to think of Paris as a home, a place with my own connections.

Was that what home was? A place with one's own connections? So then the place where the connections were most meaningful must be the place most home. Questions then become: what makes connections possible and what makes them meaningful? I did not care where I was, as long as I was with him. But was that really true? I did have other connections, important ones—friends, colleagues, most of all my children and Luke. How meaningful were they? The instrumental part of the "home" I had created was important: meeting family needs, getting help in maintenance when I needed it, working in a setting that embraced my clients and me. I felt worthwhile and competent because I could help others to find freedom to be who they were. Roles could be replaced in time, but Jennifer, Danny, Steve, and now Stefani were irreplaceable. And then there was duality in my work. I agonized: How could I continue to do both science and clinical work much longer? I was torn in two directions—was it time to give up one or the other?

The immediate question was summer. Choices. We could be together in Maine. Or in Paris. Or anywhere. I wanted to let myself go to France. Out on the boat. In July or August. Could I do it? Take the time? Could I *not* do it? Fail to take the time? Go early July? Then David could come in August—but could he take time to go out on the boat while he was working in July? It was an appealing solution: half July there; half August here. Only June would be barren, and perhaps he could come to the United States for a weekend. We could breathe in the honeysuckle-saturated air together.

Late at night, only days after my return, I asked him if he really did want to have me in Paris in July. I could feel his grin across the ocean. In his next fax, he wrote:

> *Just to confirm that yes, absolutely yes, I would be very happy if you could come for a long trip in July, those dates or others, whatever is convenient. Already all excited—and in particular about going out on boat. Can't wait!*

And so, even later that same night, I got three quotes from three airlines for round-trip, high-season New York–Paris fares and reported back to David. At $1,016, Air France was the least expensive—though definitely not the $279 special fare of that first round trip. I put a hold on seats, to be confirmed within forty-eight hours. David went into high gear when I told him. In his inimitable fashion, he spent whatever time it must have taken on the line with his Air France reservation agent, and at the end of the call had arranged that he would come to Connecticut for a long weekend, June 12–16, and attend the wedding of a friend's daughter with me. After that, I would fly to Paris on July 2 and we would go out on the boat for a few days before I left on July 15. David would fly to New York on August 12, go to Chicago with me for APA meetings, and return to Paris on August 19. He would come back for a long weekend to attend another wedding, in Maine this time, over Labor Day weekend, August 29–September 1.

He had booked all the transatlantic flights on Air France, using his accumulated miles for my otherwise expensive trip during July and finding reasonable "kiosk" fares for his own trips. In addition, as he pointed out (with the twinkle that emerged when he was teasing), he would receive mileage credit for all of his trips because he himself would be taking them. More miles for us to then use together. I was ecstatic.

My work showed it. The next day I managed to secure an HIC number, complete a good bit of the additional requirements for the grant proposal, and plan a bridal shower for the young woman who would be married in June. At the party I would ask each guest to complete three file cards with recipes—one for "a happy marriage," another for "a happy home," and a third for "a fulfilling life." The resulting album would become my own shower gift to the bride-to-be.

Meanwhile, I sensed a backlash after David's excitement in buying all those plane tickets. The next day, I wrote in my Morning Pages:

Funny note to end a conversation: booking four trips in the next three months and then cautioning me to wait, that it was impulsive—and then the remark "The woman at Air France told me it would be a whole lot cheaper and less complicated if we lived in the same place." I said, "I'm willing." He said, "I know." Silence. End of conversation. Me feeling like I had broken all the rules. I guess David doesn't know about my ambivalence. Does he really think I don't have any? Does he really think I wouldn't have issues around loss, identity, novelty, learning new things? And about him? I like controlling my life 100 percent. I like not answering to anyone, being free to follow my nose.

At the same time, I was once more aware that David was out doing whatever he felt like doing while I was in withdrawal, missing him. He knew that my life was rich with texture, meaning. And I remained anxious that he would never want to live in the same place with me, that he would get sick of me, that something would make the relationship doomed, impossible. He needed space—lots of space—to work it all out, and I needed not to get clingy. I had to believe it was scary for him, too. But I could not think of any better way to find out what it was like to be with him over time than to spend a real holiday period with him in Paris. July was perfect. And somewhere deep down I understood that a real vacation was exactly what I needed.

I accepted that there was much of David's life I would never know or be able to fully appreciate. I did group what I admired in him. Lots of energy. Integrity. Passion. Intensity. Courage. Willingness to do the nontraditional. Making conscious choices and taking the time to enjoy himself. Doing what made him happy. Acts of kindness. What did I *not* associate with him? "Making a difference"—neither a big ego needing to feel showy nor a driving sense of altruism. He did it in small, silent, near-invisible ways. Were those qualities I aspired to? You bet. And his very sharp mind. An incisive ability to analyze, organize. I was in love with a man who encapsulated qualities I hoped to realize in myself. No surprise there.

I was reexamining my life. What would I be doing if I weren't writing this grant proposal? I could envision long, luxurious hours threading through spontaneous days—sparse patient hours punctuating the velvet flow of a flexible life. Would I learn to focus on me and *all* my needs? Get exercise and eat properly and work at loving and allowing loving? Would I take the time to appreciate Luke, still wet from the rain, jumping onto my bed, crawling under the covers, scratching his chest at my feet? How sweet he could be; how dearly I loved him—symbol of natural loving, goodness, dignity. Sweet instincts—wonderful enthusiasm, hippity-hop, over the pillows, now into them. His lovability lay in simply being himself. Could I somehow make peace with the pleasure I got from producing—a paper, a meal, a product, an idea, a party, a plan? Producing had been my main source of pleasure prior to meeting David; it was so much more fun than merely responding to demands of the days. But David had brought me a whole new world—the world of just being and paying attention to the information available through all my senses. It was important for me to acknowledge that producing is fun; responding usually somewhat less so; and a third dimension, receiving, a source of joy I had yet to learn to tolerate. A step further: I needed to practice giving to myself.

I kept examining the possibilities of two very different lives—the romance of Paris or family life in the United States. I wondered, *What does David want? What do I want?* I had to admit that I liked being married better than being single—the stability of a shared life, of being able to dream a joint future, of having a set of collective concerns, the fun of sharing some memories. Someone to look after my welfare, let me look after his. Like the coat of the Velveteen Rabbit, all those years of caring and sharing brought transformation and let the patina grow, a deeper beauty shine through. Yet the pain of my bad past decision made me suspicious of my own judgment. The previous summer, David had proclaimed, "Someday you'll trust me, Roni Beth." By June 1997, I struggled with whether I did not trust him or myself.

In Paris, David went to art exhibits and movies, began to have aperitifs and eventually dinners in the home of Jacques and Corinne, and worked on his legal matters. He stayed in touch with his sons and his sister, continued to entertain visitors who passed through Paris, and tended his boat. He watched the French election results on television, read the new Ed McBain novel, and complained about French income taxes—54 percent plus substantial social charges on top. I said, "You can always come here."

Silence. Finally he answered, "That's a thought." He was aware he was spending most of his time thinking about or planning to be with me. He began to play with possibilities. What might he do in the United States? He could get a few clients; he could retire. He could do something radically different, too, couldn't he? I remembered what he had said on the deck of the Maine cottage the summer before: "Except what would I *do*?" At least now he was thinking about it.

15

Playtime for My Inner Child

Memorial Day weekend, Dan and Stefani came to Connecticut. I wrote to David:

> Luke sat at the table totally properly, and then we taught him the word "jump." Actually got kind of fancy with it, making him switch among "dancey-dancey" and "sit" and "jump." I told Dan and Stef that I was thinking of taking him to France for a visit, and we all agreed that he would have a very nice time.

All was right with my world—a man who loved me, although from a literal distance; children who were launched into adult lives yet returned to share precious moments; a dog who felt like my ever-present angel, bringing joy and laughter and an intense reminder that the present was the ultimate reality. With Luke around, I never got too stuck in memories or in dreams about the future.

I became more and more excited about the long summer trip that David and I had begun to plan, a major experiment in "giving to myself." I was going to Paris and I was going to play. When I asked David about his own recreational history, he thought about it. There were the trips on the rivers of France in his barge with his boys every summer. The ski trips in the Alps, also with his boys, in winter. The

Harvard weekends. His wanderings around France. An occasional day or two away with a woman he had been seeing. But a deliberate, planned, scheduled vacation just for himself? He remembered only one dismal week at a Club Med many years earlier. He was as excited as I was about the July trip.

Visions and discussions of it kept us focused through our respective June days. David was busy monitoring the level of the Seine, dealing with leaks in the roof of the barge, being the "eligible bachelor" assigned as a table partner to attractive women at Princeton or Harvard events, and working. On my side of the Atlantic, I agonized over and managed to submit by deadline the fifty-three-page, single-spaced, signed-off-on grant proposal, hosted yet another bridal shower, made sure the Maine cottage was ready for summer rentals, kept my practice and house and volunteer responsibilities running smoothly, and finally even treated myself to a sexy Italian sundress on sale for $20 at the store next to the copy shop while my grant proposal was being run off.

David had brought French canine antinausea pills so that my puppy could enjoy the long drive to Maine with me and, if they worked, potentially travel to Paris. They did work, but when I became aware of my own exhaustion and my hope simply to take care of myself for a few days, we dropped that possibility. I needed a real vacation. The night before my departure, suitcase and carry-on prepared, David told me to unpack the electric curlers; he had bought me a 220-volt set that we could keep on the boat. That announcement caused my determination to keep it light, just have fun, acknowledge that most of my worries were ridiculous, to skyrocket.

David and his Ford were waiting at CDG. Air France flight 009 came in as scheduled, 11:50 a.m., a little later than my usual flight, but this trip had the benefit of leisure. David whisked me through the center of the city, relatively free of the early rush-hour traffic we routinely encountered, and hoisted my suitcase onto the boat. I followed him, noticing how shiny the Berreti's decks and windows seemed, how clean the new tarp on the roof.

I began to descend the short staircase from the driving cabin to the kitchen, and then I saw it. Right in the middle of the room, opposite the tiny refrigerator and two burners. A huge purple ribbon with streamers tied in a bow around the handlebars. A new bike. A new *mountain* bike. *My* new mountain bike. The information sank in slowly, filtering through layers of awareness, too much to take in all at once. And then it reached the little girl. She burst into tears, giddy with delight, and began jumping up and down, unable to contain the unbridled glee that ripped through her whole body. No words, of course. *How did he know? What made him do something as perfect as this?* In a flash, I grasped that I had to somehow retrieve my adult: David was already explaining the equipment, and he expected me to be able to pay attention. Not only had he bought me a bike, but he had bought *accessories*. I had *never* owned accessories. And here were saddlebags, a water bottle and pump, gloves, a tool kit, a gauge for the tires, a bell, lights front and back, and even, astonishingly, a small gadget that attached to the handlebars and could tell me speed, distance, all manner of current or cumulative data, in both kilometers and miles. I was overwhelmed. Not breathing. Ready to hop on and ride it across the living room. He promised me we were going to buy and install a bike rack that afternoon, and then we could pedal through Paris together on the weekend. We would store my new *vélo* in its new home at his office, parked in the back room, keeping his own bicycle company.

I was far too excited to indulge in my usual extended nap. We drove to the bike store, avenue de la Grand Armée, a bit beyond l'Arc de Triomphe at the Étoile, and selected a rack. Discussed L.L.Bean with the salesman, a dedicated fisherman who knew the company's catalogs. Always important to converse about something meaningful with those who help in French stores. It's seen as a marker of respect. Almost as important as the mandatory "*bonjour, madame*" or "*bonjour, monsieur*" upon entering. We stopped at David's office. He had suddenly become busy with legal work again and had some papers to review. I went for a walk in the park. Dinner at Du Côté 7ème.

Together again. This time for twelve nights and thirteen days. And I had just arrived.

The trip approached perfection. For the first time since we had met, I was in Paris for enough time that the jet lag could dissipate early and leave no agenda beyond our being together in its wake. Add the warmer weather and plans David had made, and this was a vacation crafted from dreams. We spent Friday in the office, but then, showing off his impressive capacity to switch gears, David left professional concerns behind and prepared to take his girlfriend to the ballet at Opéra Garnier.

I had been in the building once before, in 1960, with my father. We had gone to see the visiting Bolshoi Ballet Company dance *Daphnis et Chloé*. But I was sixteen, not fifty-three, and it was my introduction to quality ballet, not an extension of exposure to what had become my favorite performing art. We climbed the grand staircase and were directed to orchestra seats about halfway down and slightly left of center. The red velvet fauteuils welcomed our bodies with a hug, dignity, and warmth. Above us, the domed ceiling painted by Marc Chagall almost shimmered as the lights that encircled it accentuated the animated life depicted in vividly colored scenes of performers creating music, dance, drama, art. A deep stage stretched in front, balconies behind. Outside the theater itself, more staircases led to the central floor, the one with room after room filled with mirrors and chandeliers and parquet or marble floors and carvings and paintings and all manner of decoration. Of course, the building *was* a palace, a palace dedicated to the arts. I watched women who never wobbled in their high heels wander around with that unique French walk, part glide, part saunter, the one that screamed, *Confidence! Sexuality! Female here!* Makeup understated, outfits stylish but discreet, accessories ideally selected, voices lyrical. This time, both the little girl and the adult were enchanted. I worked to keep my breathing even.

Sylvia, a stunning two-act piece choreographed by John Neumeier and set to a score written by Léo Delibes, offered gorgeous music, dancing that made more statements about gender than my entire library on the topic, and staging that evoked a gasp from the audience when the curtain was raised on Act Two and the transformed forest huntress Sylvia stood in a ballroom, draped in a strapless ruby-red gown, and was soon surrounded by men wearing sharply tailored black tuxedos with crisp, formal white shirts. The story, a love story, told of the tribulations of liberation. Sacred groves, god-inhabited places, cavorting fauns and dryads, Eros and Bacchus, the joys and pleasures of loving, the intoxication of music and dance. A woman saved from dedication to her work, her dharma, who rejected diversions both evil and sublime and then was ultimately released, permitted to slip into the arms of her lover. Had this story been written just for me?

After the ballet, David took me to dinner at Café de la Paix, the institution across the street from the Opéra that had welcomed theatergoers since 1862.

"Is this what you had in mind when you said you wanted a vacation?"

"I don't know what I was thinking. This sure counts, though."

"I wanted you to see Paris at its best. Its most creative. Sparkling. Innovative."

"The beginning of Act Two, when the curtain rose and she was standing there in that red dress . . ."

"I know. It's like us. All mystical and otherworldly and then suddenly—boom!—into a modern-day reality. Fun, isn't it?" David understood the way our relationship kept skating across frozen lakes of time and place, occasionally dipping into melted territories, then gliding back onto traversable terrain.

On Saturday, we put our bikes on the new bike rack and drove to the cycling paths in the Bois de Boulogne. I was nervous; years had passed since I had last ridden a bicycle, and much about this 1997 mountain bike was new to me. Happily, as I pedaled through the

Bois, I learned to operate the twenty-one gears and hand brakes. Each increase in competence brought exhilaration, confidence, freedom.

Sunday, David and I drove to Sens, one of those storybook Burgundy villages on the river Yonne that just happened to have a festival of costumed local groups presenting their folk dances on a portable stage in the center of town, around the corner from the cathedral. As evening approached, we made our way to Hôtel de Paris et de la Poste, home to one of David's favorite dining rooms in the whole country. He had made reservations and knew what we were about to encounter. From *amuse-bouches* (served with aperitifs, before any appetizer), to Époisses (a typical and particularly smelly local cheese), I discovered new tastes, presentations, deliciousness. I was beginning to feel decadent, without the guilt.

"This is what a vacation is for. New perspectives, experiences. Letting in space once the clutter of burnt-out neurons and cells can be brushed away."

"Yes. That's what I want."

I paused.

"But you live this all the time, don't you?"

"I live in the beauty all the time. With the balance and harmony of it. And it helps. I don't get overwhelmed with the material level of things, like so many in America do. That's why I wanted to live here. And I wanted to ride my ten-speed bike."

"Not a metaphor."

"No, not a metaphor at all. Even if yours has twenty-one gears."

While David worked during our first week together, I explored the quartier surrounding his office—Musée Nissim de Camando, Parc Monceau, the covered market on rue Lisbonne and the street market on rue de Lévis. One night we were invited to Jacques and Corinne's home for *millésimé* champagne before walking to Carré Kléber, a few blocks away. Another night, we complicitly introduced David C. to

Jean-Michel, imagining that their professional lives, skills, and interests might intrigue each other. They did.

Midweek, we prepared to use the extended Bastille Day weekend
to discover France from its rivers, driving the Berreti to Samois, some
eighty kilometers and six locks away from Paris. After casting off all
lines, water, phone, and electricity, David solidly situated us in the
Seine's right channel, going east toward Notre Dame. He smiled that
impish grin and invited me to drive. Determined to ignore my protesting comfort zone, I guided the twenty-five-meter barge alongside
Notre Dame, past Île St. Louis, under one bridge and then another.
David noticed that a gauge on the control panel had begun sneaking
up toward the red zone.

"It's moving a bit too rapidly," he said.

"Either the gauge is broken or the engine is overheating."

"Maybe the winter freeze did some damage to the motor. I think I
need to take the wheel."

David guided us to a spot where he could tie up along the Jardin
des Plantes, a great place for a picnic. We could give the engine time
to cool down. Except it didn't.

"It's a holiday weekend. Getting help is going to be hard. In a village it could be impossible. I don't think we have any other reasonable
choice."

David was deeply disappointed. He wanted me to share the experience of river travel, to know what had made his summers with his boys
so meaningful, the idiosyncrasies and near-constant maintenance of
owning the boat so worthwhile. After a picnic on the quay, we limped
back to Paris, towed the final stretch of the Seine by an accommodating river-police boat.

Once we were securely reconnected to water, phone, and electrical sources on the quai, we faced four days full of possibility prior
to Bastille Day. David generated a plan B that allowed us to use the
carefully selected provisions we had stocked for the trip, take advantage of the bicycles, see a bit of the countryside, and remain disconnected from the world of work. One day we hiked through the forests

of Fontainebleau and explored the galleries in Barbizon. Another we traveled to the walled village of Moret-sur-Loing to see its medieval heritage, picturesque mill with two water wheels, ancient church, and excellent rum-raisin ice cream. On a third, we biked beneath the parasol pines of the Bois de Boulogne and I felt (almost) like a native.

I watched David shaving—rough beard made smooth, testosterone bubbling beneath the surface. And wondered, *How do I leave this? How do I go from hugs and kisses and so much more, soaking in one another's energy, to the pace and content of my American life? The challenge is to live it with even more reverence. Savor what I do here. Is my stomach upset because I'm facing the final weekend? The end of a dream-come-true vacation?*

During my weekend in Paris in March 1996, I had imagined perhaps returning for a week—maybe even two—at some later date. This was my seventh trip to Paris during barely more than a year; David had traveled to the States nine times during that same period. Somehow we *were* managing to do it. I was no longer paranoid about other women, at least not *all* the time. No longer needing the intensity of reassurance, at least not *all* the time. I had more energy free to enjoy it all, at least *most* of the time.

We floated through our final weekend in a blur of romance. Wherever we went, whatever we did, it all turned to magic. We were in love. The fireworks for Bastille Day were no match for those between us; the blaze of glory when France's finest flew over or paraded down the Champs-Élysées only reflected the triumph we felt in being with each other.

Our last evening together, David took me around the corner to a restaurant on rue Cambon, just off the rue de Rivoli, where we had never before gone together. He had often told me of stopping at Brasserie Flottes for dinner, and I had begun to wonder if he did not take me there because that was a special destination where he took some other woman. He laughed when I shared my fantasy and explained that he considered it his neighborhood hangout, not quite worthy as a "date" destination. The restaurant quickly became a favorite for the two of us, a comfort spot where we returned whenever we wanted reliably excellent traditional food with personal service. Carpaccio; endive, walnut, and Roquefort salad; roast chicken I can still taste; steak tartare. They knew David well there: he and his book of the moment visited often; he and the maître d' routinely exchanged movie reviews with appreciation for each other's judgment.

The whole trip had been light, airy, fun beyond anything I had ever known. The little girl and the woman inside me had made friends and were ready to take on the tyrannical superego, that part of me that refused to listen to basic needs or natural inclinations or even reason. The part that was driven by "shoulds."

Then a funny thing happened that last evening. We had walked home across the rue de Rivoli, in front of the Jeu de Paume, marveling at the lit obelisk and fountains, still surrounded by the reviewing stands that had been set up for the Bastille Day parade. We watched the Eiffel Tower glow as we strolled along the river, hand in hand, I in my skimpy new sundress and David in his jeans and jaunty cap. A slight detour for a hug on Pont Alexandre III.

And then there it was:

"Roni Beth, I want to spend the rest of my life with you. I don't know how we are going to work it out; it's complicated. But we are going to find a way. I promise you. Just like I found a way to bring you back after I first met you. We both know we are meant to be together."

I looked at him, flooded with feelings of being understood and cared for. A tear trickled down my cheek. And then another one. My knees wobbled a bit, and I leaned more dependently into his arms. He caught me as I began to collapse and hugged me even more tightly. I probably mumbled something like, "Yes, I know," but words weren't necessary; David could feel my joy and surrender.

V

Decisions

16

Invitation

I returned from what had been labeled a "vacation" with a new perspective on my entire future. I was going to share it with David. Indeed, soon after that trip, during a phone call when I was complaining about confusion with a patient's insurer, David asked me to please not sign anything that was even remotely contractual unless he took a look at it first. After years of dealing with vendors, bankers, repairmen, and insurance agents who treated me somewhat to seriously disrespectfully, presumably because I was a woman, his words sounded like music to me. A little scary, too. I knew I needed to continue to be responsible for whatever I did, never to cede what I had so painstakingly learned, but now I could really share burdens, confusions, joys and consequences of decisions with another person who cared.

In Paris, David once again said he felt "lost" when I left, even though this time I had done the leaving and he remained very much at home on his boat, in his office, in his city. He wrote:

And yes, we celebrated life—life as a joy and a wonder and a sensual pleasure (i.e., in the broad sense), but also as in your life, my life, our life together. And I love you.

We both knew we had uncharted territory to navigate ahead. For both of us now, "lost" meant yanked away from the feeling of wholeness we could share in person.

While I caught up on two weeks of phone calls and chores, David dug into the work on his desk and prepared for his sister's arrival in Paris for a vacation with her boyfriend the following week. I reflected on the separation:

Loved my good-morning fax, too—somehow a warmth, reassurance that through the "sound" of your "voice," you and I continue the intimacy even when we are separated.

The faxes had begun to feel like threads of silver silk that kept us connected across the ether, at times transforming into strands of spun gold, even stronger, brighter, more iridescent, like the lights on the Seine—dazzling in sunlight and still there even when the weather didn't permit us to see them as clearly.

Our conversations turned more intimate as we began to talk openly as committed partners. Because our children had been the centers of our emotional lives, we now were struggling to define new roles with them as adults, both individually and as a couple. We agreed that we liked their relying on us to take care of details, especially those of a practical or logistical nature. We had both looked after our parents more than they had cared for us, and there seemed something fitting in this more "normal" arrangement, parents caring for children. Besides, we had become skilled at it and could now also share adult-adult companionship—a better basis than neediness or shared history for bonds with our grown children. I remained grateful that my kids felt so free to come "home," although they understood they now needed to *call first* whenever David was visiting. Just like he knew to censor his own phone messages when they might be around.

With Paris a possible permanent solution on the horizon (although I still thought that I did not have an actual invitation to move there), I became even more introspective about my current work life. I was tired of trying to avoid bumping into my patients in public places, especially when I was with David. I wanted a consistent identity, one in which patients would not be disturbed to find me disrupting their transference fantasies once we were outside the consulting room. As long as I remained a fairly "blank screen," they could project whatever they needed to onto me and we could both learn about their unconscious expectations from their distortions. Nowhere were those more powerful than in the way they imagined my personal life, especially my love life, to be. Once, when David and I were walking Luke hand in hand on the beach at Sherwood Island State Park, we encountered a patient who knew that I was single. She was deeply disturbed at her immediate conclusion that I had been deceiving her, hiding all manner of secrets. The reality was that she had never asked.

In addition, I was exhausted by occasional clients who were "energy vampires," people who were invested in avoiding the issues they most needed to confront. They could suck the air out of my office with the suffocating vacuum of lies, repression, or denial. I wasn't all that crazy about the science, either. I did love the actual work of it—solving puzzles, asking interesting questions, testing possible answers to them. But the industry of social gerontology epidemiology was problematic. There was an aggressiveness, a competition, an "in group" aspect to it, and I did not want to make the required moves, play the political games.

I tried to stay focused on the broader themes of my life, seeing events in it as markers leading me toward some higher purpose or destiny. Across the years, my greatest challenges had been learning to love, learning to be loved, learning that loving is not always safe, learning to love myself, and now learning to permit the free exchange of loving feelings, to understand, as a new way of loving, *je veux te faire plaisir*. Translation: "I want to give you pleasure," rather than "I want to please you." Another example of culture embedded in language. Far more than caregiving, or even passion, this new kind of love was about simply bringing joy and pleasure to each other and sharing whatever was.

I wrote my thank-you note to Jacques and Corinne (in French, *bien sûr*), and picked up tick- and flea-prevention meds for Luke at the vet. After attending to some other details, I indulged in a detour into Barnes & Noble, where I stumbled upon Adele Puhn's *The 5-Day Miracle Diet*. Again, a deeply needed teacher had appeared. Here was an explanation for my difficulties in dieting. I resolved to begin following her recommendations immediately, and did, and her approach changed my relationship to food—to my energy, to myself in my life— forever. Perhaps most important, I came to appreciate how much I used food to provide energy when what I really needed was a nap or at least a few minutes of serious meditation, especially when my emotions were drained or my neurons fried from too much sustained concentration. With a new understanding of my own blood sugar level and its consequences, I started down a path that put me comfortably back into my closet, with its size 6 wardrobe, and let me feel good again about buying underwear. Maybe now I could stop worrying about David's leaving me if I ever became fat and unattractive, seduced away by an irresistibly gorgeous tea lady or dinner partner at a Harvard event. I had found a method to prevent that from happening and could muster enough self-discipline to run from the sugar addiction that had a life of its own. I could harness my professional training in consciousness for my own benefit, freeing precious energy, and turn my attention to the next challenge, achieving financial independence so that I could move to France or anywhere else we might decide to settle. Half-seriously addressing my primitive but unreasonable fear of not being able to take care of myself, I began to buy lottery tickets and imagine what I might do if I won. It was clear that my lifestyle provided all I wanted or needed and that, if I could secure it indefinitely, I would give away any extra money while David and I rode merrily into the sunset.

Weeks before his already-scheduled eight-day mid-August trip, David bought Air France tickets to come to the United States for the Jewish holidays in the fall. He investigated another, more expensive set of tickets for me to slip in a long weekend in Paris in September, after his own trip to the United States in August and between his trips on Labor Day weekend and October 1.

We began discussing the possibility of bringing Jen, Steve, Dan, and Stefani to Paris with me, perhaps around Christmas, so that they might better understand the world into which I kept disappearing. They could stay at a hotel across the bridge in the 7th arrondissement. Even though all except Steve had actually been to Paris, they had been young and seen the city through adolescent eyes, bridges and bars predominating. We wanted them to experience it as we did, walking the streets we walked every day, eating the food we ate, living the rhythms and sparkle that comprised our life when we were together in Paris.

In Connecticut, an invitation arrived for a Yale dinner dance with David's name written on the envelope, along with mine. My staff liaison at the Alumni Fund office, a woman who had thoroughly enjoyed meeting him the previous spring, had added David's name on her own initiative. I faxed both the invitation and a copy of the envelope to him. Suddenly, the practical implications of trying to share a life on both sides of the Atlantic popped into place: How could he possibly schedule yet another trip, this time to accommodate an event at which, as cochair of the Graduate School Alumni Fund, I was to be a featured player? We held off discussion until the implications of becoming a "couple" in the eyes of the extended world could sink in.

Renee and Matt were coming for a weekend. I wrote to David:

Renee thinks that a wedding between Ann and Gus is in the stars for next summer. That will be a big deal. Ever been to a real Greek wedding? Talk about ritual, tradition, and a lot of food . . . The food will be as good as Greek food can get—and I happen to adore Greek food.

I was announcing one more event on US soil—an event important to me. My best friend's daughter was getting married—a girl I had known since birth and mentored during her high school days, whose graduations at Princeton and then Harvard I had attended, for whom I had written recommendations for her PhD program at University of Pennsylvania. My roots in our relationship ran deep. David would be facing attending our fourth wedding as a couple within our brief time together: the Episcopalian one in Westport the November after we had met; the Jewish one at a catering hall in West Hartford the following June; the upcoming wedding events in York, Maine, on Labor Day; and now a Greek wedding in southern New Jersey on some undetermined future date. There was also the wedding I had missed entirely because of a conflict with professional meetings and the other one I had gone to alone when David was in Paris.

He was being a good sport about all these invitations and about the intense social nature of my life, but it did seem to leave him resentful of having less time alone with me than he would have liked and of having far too much of his life organized around other people's constraints, demands, plans. I knew he went along with it because it *was* my life and these people were an important part of it, but I also knew that he felt at a loss to understand why they mattered as they did. He was also probably thinking about ways to minimize the disruption in our romance.

In Paris, David confronted the quiet in his office, the silence in summer streets, the near emptiness in restaurants, the hush in parks as Parisians began their August holidays, closing up businesses, small shops, apartments, traveling north or, more often, south, leaving paid employment behind. When seven million French people (out of fifty-five million) were on the roads, television showed hundreds of kilometers of *bouchons*. David kept me apprised.

And then, on Sunday, August 3, 1997, in the middle of a phone call:

"Roni Beth, I think you need to move to Paris."

Startled, silenced, my heart pounding, I reminded myself to keep breathing. Eventually I managed a nod, although of course David could not see it. I could sense his growing irritability as he awaited a response. Yes, I had repeatedly explained this instinctual silence of

mine, but he needed feedback—especially across a silent phone line—
as much as I needed time to let what was happening settle in.

"Well?"

I sputtered, "Delighted. Thrilled. Absolutely. But this is *big*. I need
some time to digest it."

"What's to digest?"

Still being the psychologist reluctant to make assumptions, I wasn't
positive that he intended for us to actually live together. Perhaps he
wanted only for us to be on the same side of the Atlantic.

"What are you proposing?"

"Come. Live with me. Not sure where. Or exactly when. But
we've had enough separations. Lots of choices. But we'll make them
together."

"Yes. Together. Make them together. In France. Yes. Thank you.
Great idea. I'll call you later. Or, if it's too late, I'll write to you. Thank
you. Together. In Paris. I love you."

Once off the phone, I began playing with possibilities. Again,
research was my go-to coping skill when I faced a challenge. After
analysis for decision making came research to manage anxiety and
help solve a "problem." This was a double one, involving both complex
emotions that needed acknowledgment and elaborate logistics that
required coordination, I began an earnest study of *FUSAC*, a French/
USA weekly newspaper that listed job openings, apartments, and
other information of interest to expats. I thought about work options,
mastering the language, housing. In a scattershot response from the
essential to the trivial, I asked David if he could investigate rules on
residence and work permits and if he could contact Espace Vit'halles,
a health club advertising to English speakers, and obtain a brochure
listing services and programs. I hoped it offered both yoga and spinning. I would contact APA to learn about licenses for those who lived
abroad.

Yes, I would move to Paris. Rather than looking to expand, I would
contract. Rather than meeting new people, I would say goodbye to
those I knew. Especially many whom I knew well. Closing my practice

and leaving my patients, friends, and close colleagues was going to be hard. But nothing, no challenge, no obstacle, compared to moving far from Jennifer, Danny, and Steve. *Children* were supposed to leave home; their parents were *not* supposed to leave them. At some point, soon, I would need to tell them. The relationship with David was no longer only a source of delightful surprises and fun.

Tons of logistics required attention: housing, residence permits, closing a practice and collecting my scientific files before I left. And there were the bigger issues: letting go of what I had been rebuilding, going into the unknown to construct A New Life. David, with his sweetness, curiosity, energy—I would need to learn to lean on him, rely on his mind, his caring, his gentle lovemaking. And there was the whole notion of reliance itself—what would it mean to me dynamically to depend on someone else? The French language was the key to adaptation. What would it take to become fluent? Of course I *could*. I had learned all kinds of things, most of them as an adult. Homemaking. Parenting. Psychology. Epidemiology. Even a modicum of mechanical and technological mastery. The latter took many repetitions, but here I was, fluent in Word 6.0. What was essential to do before I could go? Sell the cottage? Perhaps also the house? Collect additional research data that I could analyze there? Plan to go to Paris in December for my birthday on a reconnaissance trip? I contemplated the fun of looking at housing, a favorite activity throughout my life. David was already researching prices, sizes, styles, and locations of apartments and sending information in his faxes. Transition: How to do it? New people. New life. I loved the idea of renting in Paris for a while—*then* buying. I would require experience there to appreciate *living* in the city. David and I had different decision-making styles. Making decisions together would inevitably involve several iterations and most likely some mistakes. Paris was probably an ideal place to make them.

I needed him to get to Connecticut; we had so much to discuss. Besides, sometimes this was scary stuff and I wanted to be in his arms. Letting go—of friends, patients, my pretty house, treasured belongings, the status I *did* have. Not the children. I would never let go of them. I told myself that distance would not require letting go, only creating new ways to interact, to stay connected. We would find them. The goal would be flexibility. I imagined reinventing my work life, creating a writing-lecture-workshop career, "making a difference" in a personal way both on a group level and potentially at a geographical distance, no longer one-on-one. I also wanted to make art. Not just my home and life as works of art—I wanted to create something beautiful that emerged from a very deep place, preferably through painting pictures with words.

I told Jen and Steve that I was moving to Paris, and they were pleased for me. New life coming. Looking forward to visits. I would keep them posted. I delayed telling Danny. As independent as he was, he and I were close, and part of the security in that closeness was that we knew where and how he could always reach me should he want to check in. He could be as free as he needed to be, at no risk to our bonds. That was going to change with six time zones and the Atlantic Ocean separating us and demanding attention.

I began to ruminate, deliberating about decisions and their consequences. This was a great opportunity to ask myself again, *Do I really like the color blue?* a phrase coined by a patient when his own life changes gave him an opportunity to revisit how he really felt about all manner of choices he had made previously and could make in the future. There were so many options now, but they basically boiled down to what I wanted to carry with me and what I could leave behind.

No more stalling. I finally spoke to Danny, and it went something like this:

"Dan, David and I have been discussing it, and I've decided to move to Paris."

"You what?"

"I'm going to move to Paris. To live. With him."

"To live. In France."

"Yes, Paris is in France."

"I guess you want to be together."

"We do, Dan. I love him. And we can't keep doing this, all this travel."

"So you've thought about this. What about your practice?"

"I'm going to need to close it. And that's going to be hard."

"When?"

"When am I going? I don't know yet. Not immediately. I have a lot to do before I can go. But probably this winter."

"Forever?"

"I don't know, Dan. That's the plan. But we both know plans don't always work out."

"Where are you going to live?"

"I don't know that, either. Probably on the boat at first."

"What about the house?"

"No decision right now. One step at a time."

"Luke going?"

"Of course Luke is going."

"Lots of changes."

"Yes, lots of changes."

"What else is changing?"

I thought about his question.

"I guess that instead of you and Stef and Jen and Steve coming over with me this winter, you'll probably be coming over to visit me. Maybe March. Early spring."

"Oh. Okay. Cool. I want you to be happy, Mom. If this is gonna do it, go for it."

"So you really do need to let me know how your names are spelled on your passports."

"I can do that. I'll talk to Stef."

Air France had a promotional winter fare of $379 round trip through the end of March, and Steve had spring vacation time; March 13–21 would be perfect for the kids' visit. The fare was going to expire the following Thursday. Buying tickets for them to visit—without one also for me, assuming I would already be there—was going to be our first concrete act in moving me to France.

Across the ocean, David had *"been having fantasies—probably not very realistic or practical—about already having an apartment or house that we rented, so that the kids could stay there, us on boat. Even if only fantasy, it's a* fun *one . . . Lots to think about/talk about. And fun of it all."*

I was beside myself. It *was* going to be so much fun looking together, doing research together, developing a dream together, planning together, then living the reality, no longer needing to say goodbye or to send faxes into the night simply because blackout zones that lasted for many hours each day made it hard for us to tell whatever we wanted to share in the moment in which it occurred. For the second time in my life, I had a true friend who wanted to share all of life with me—a playmate, a lover, a partner, a sounding board, a source of moral and emotional and practical support. Uncannily, right out of my research, a relationship style associated with good spirits and longevity. Sharing laughter and beauty and fun gifts and food and the very best parts of me. Accepting the vulnerable, demanding, or dark parts. Who understood biological needs and the importance of honoring them, preferably in a way that brought grace, balance, harmony. And pleasure. I wrote to him:

> *We both need to remember that your sense of timing is better than mine. I need to practice being willing to rely on it (is that too much "responsibility" for you?). Luckily, some of our similarities (liking to look at things from multiple angles, not needing to do perfect, being excellent problem solvers) will feed off each other in a really positive way. It's so much fun—even the work becomes fun.*

We generated ideas, possibilities. Maybe Jennifer, with her new office located in the next town, would want to stay in the Westport house sometimes during the winter and avoid her long commute to New Jersey. She and Steve planned eventually to move across the Hudson, somewhere between his job in Manhattan and hers in

Connecticut, but they had just moved into their pretty house in Glen Ridge, New Jersey, and were not in a hurry to leave it. Or perhaps Scott would want to move his family into the house, rent it at a reduced rate for a while. He and Stefanie could try out suburban living, including the commute, and have plenty of space to do whatever they might want to do. Stefanie could even play my precious piano. The expenses would be lower than those of the apartment they were in, even with a larger heating bill.

When should we put the cottage in Maine on the market? Trying to maintain a *second* home from across the ocean, one that we were unlikely to visit, given that our children and his sister lived in the greater New York area, was foolish, wasteful. Besides, I wanted the money that I could get from selling. I was going to need to liquidate assets, maybe from both houses, to support myself. Who knew how long it would be before I could earn income in a country that had so many irregular verbs and tenses needing conjugation (to say nothing of 246 different cheeses)?

David responded with sensitivity:

> *I am extremely excited about plans to be together, live together, make a home in Paris. Yes, putting it all together and the details are a bit intimidating, sometimes (seem) overwhelming, but that does not change the excitement and the wanting. Is that clear? (And, yes, of course, I know the life-choice issues are greater on your end. I understand that, and that is what makes it scarier.)*

David dealt with the summer-vacation trickle of work that crossed his desk, kept finding new routes where we could ride our bikes, and consulted me on wardrobe selections for his upcoming trip to America. He remembered the drill at APA meetings, this year convening in Chicago, but we also planned to go spinning together. Should he bring his toe clips? His helmet? A suit? He was teasing me.

Danny came home for a weekend. Late at night, he flopped down on my bed for an increasingly rare extended conversation, all about life and love and friends and change. He was about to be best man at two different weddings—Newport the following weekend and Maine over Labor Day—and his father's family was celebrating some milestones. My son counseled me on identifying when a person was never going to change. He said it was when they had just given up, packed it in, closed off to what was new. In addition to wisdom, in his own unique style, Danny was giving me permission to follow my heart into the unknown. He was telling me that he understood, even though we both knew that the geographical distance might challenge us and promised to be painful at times.

Jennifer and Steve landed at the house for an overnight that same Sunday, following a party with Jennifer's new work team. We had breakfast together Monday morning, I saw patients all day and then got to bed so that I could be alert the next day when I met David at JFK at one o'clock. He and I looked forward to a precious evening of being together, just us two, in material reality the first day of his visit.

The day after he arrived, we went to New York to see Scott, Stefanie, and Sofia. After hamburgers with boutique beer at the Cowgirl, just a few blocks from the Archives Building, we came home to pack for our early flight to Chicago the next morning. The Saturday night that was his fifty-seventh birthday, thunderstorms with torrential rains paralyzed the Windy City—one of those Midwestern storms that make sidewalks look unused because they are so well washed and make the August corn pop up all at once. Taxis could not navigate downtown streets, and the city halted. We, along with thousands of other convention attendees, were held captive in our hotels. Finally we accepted the reality, called the restaurant to cancel the reservation made two months in advance, and slid onto the last available barstools in the hotel lobby's lounge. Feeling pretty in the size 6 white cotton dress with décolleté that I had proudly managed to fit back into, I enjoyed being overdressed. By then, the only food left was nachos. So there we sat, switching gears and swallowing disappointment, grateful above all that we could be together to celebrate his birthday.

Suddenly we saw our good fortune and began to laugh. We continued to giggle all the way home to Connecticut the next day. David stayed with me in Westport for two more nights, long enough to thoroughly confuse Luke, and then boarded Air France flight 011 Tuesday afternoon.

After David returned to Paris, I revisited the fantasy we had explored—renting Signal Lane to Scott and Stefanie—and laid out the idea for David. He found it intriguing but cautioned that we should wait to make decisions until we were together and could anticipate possible consequences of various choices. I signed up for some one-day computer courses, hoping to beef up my software skills before I left my native language on the other side of the Atlantic. I wrote long lists of possibilities: what to keep, what to sell; what to bring, what to store; when to leave, when to return; how long to plan to be away, how to recover should it not work out. I was reassured by my yoga teacher's quote, long ago taped onto the refrigerator door: *In order to discover new lands, you need to lose sight of the shore.* Every day I read it many times, touched it, etched it in my brain. A mantra.

Now I really did have to address telling my patients. First, I made lists of people to whom I might refer them and cleared possible referrals with other therapists: Were they taking new patients? Any particular restrictions? Preferences? And then, one patient at a time, I decided how long we needed for a proper "termination," knowing that a large part of the work of long-term therapy is accomplished during the final phase. I also knew that some of them would be furious. A therapist is *not* supposed to leave a patient. Closing a practice is *not* an act to be taken lightly. I expected that some might need to leave me before I could leave them. This task would be one of the hardest in my life. Redirecting my attention to the simpler logistics of travel or moving could easily become a way to avoid going through the difficult process that both my patients and I needed to experience as we said goodbye to one another.

I kept trying to explain the psychological enormity of the task to David. That simple solutions like setting a date and then closing the door were not feasible, were irresponsible—indeed, unethical. And could even cause harm. I was going to have to do this with 100 percent presence and attention. And he needed to remember that I had difficulty "switching gears."

Alongside this upcoming change in my life, daily demands continued. I did not want to lose "the present" as I planned for a new future. So the period became one of practicing balance, moving back and forth between the quotidian tasks of laundry, phone calls and faxes, trips to the market and cleaners and fulfilling commitments to clients, to the Connecticut Psychological Association, to Yale, to friends and family, and to my relationship with David and all it represented.

Together, David and I began to discuss Thanksgiving. Did he want to come to the United States this year? Would Scott, Stefanie, and Sofia want to join us? What would I do about coordinating with Renee and Matt? My one traditional holiday was not to be casually ignored; after all, it was all I had had for years, and it was important to me and to my children. (Christmas did not count; we were Jewish. I got it by default.) But Jennifer was married now and had two divorced in-laws; Annie was heading toward marriage with Gus, a man with a large local family; Dan had Stefani and her family in his life; and Nick and his wife were living in the Midwest. Renee and I needed to allow our relationship to evolve along with the lives of our children. Conversations debating options continued for weeks while we articulated and debated choices.

The summer drew to a close, and, as planned, David boarded Air France flight 006 to arrive at JFK in time to get to Westport before a movies-and-dinner date with Bill and Madeline on the Friday of Labor Day weekend. Later that night, Jennifer and Steve, Dan and Stefani arrived at the Signal Lane house so that we could all depart early the next morning. We caravanned to southern Maine for the wedding of Danny's closest friend, in which he would serve as best man. Saturday night, Dan and Stefani went to the wedding rehearsal and the dinner that followed, while Jen and Steve and David and I circled the lighthouse to locate a lobster restaurant overlooking York

Harbor. Aware that he was about to take their mother (and mother-in-law) far away, David offered conversation, wine, humor, anything he could think of to lessen the tension. In the end, the four of us confined in one car, Jennifer observed, "David, you're trying too hard."

Startled by being addressed so clearly and directly, especially by someone a generation younger, David got the message. He did not need to entertain or impress or even lavishly feed these loving adults. He needed only to be himself, and they would accept him.

After dinner, we all joined an informal reception where out-of-town visitors were gathering, and then retired to the bed-and-breakfast where we had reserved our rooms.

In the morning, we woke to smells of bacon and eggs, sticky buns and pumpkin muffins, coffee and cinnamon-apple tea. But as we descended the stairs toward the dining room, we sensed the quiet that signals some sort of disaster. The dining room remained empty. Instead, guests gathered silently around a television set in the parlor. We joined them. David took my hand and squeezed it, hard. Even before the broadcaster began the commentary, he could see what had happened. A horrible car crash had taken place near Place de l'Alma, just where the Cours Albert-1er goes into the tunnel under the large plaza. Photographs identified Princess Diana. Princess Diana leaving the Ritz Paris. Getting into the Mercedes. Being followed by motorcycles. A crash. Pictures of Hôpital Pitié-Salpêtrière in the southeast of Paris. An announcement that she was dead.

A tragedy unfolding less than a mile from David's home. Whole nations in mourning. Confusion, allegations, interpretations. And here we were on Sunday of Labor Day weekend at a bed-and-breakfast in York, Maine, about to attend the wedding of two young people who had fallen in love during freshman year of college. The disconnect was palpable.

David's heart bounced back to Paris; mine remained in rural Maine with local American reactions. The difference was striking. Our respective cultural training and attachments managed to briefly derail our usually fierce bond. To his credit, David's gift for being in the moment kicked in and we celebrated with the bride and groom at their ceremony. Later that evening at the wedding festivities, we danced enthusiastically. David's jacket, dripping with sweat, bore testimony to our intensity—part tension release, part tribute to the young couple. Surreal. As was the eleven-hour road trip the next morning direct from York to JFK, one typically made in half that time. We snaked through holiday traffic, practicing patience as we inched toward getting David to Air France flight 007 before its 7:45 p.m. departure. Someone at check-in must have seen the distress in his face; he was given a free upgrade to first class.

17

Responsibility

$\mathcal{D}$avid moved effortlessly back into his world. His client Jean-Michel launched *Goosebumps* in France that week, with a fully catered public reception held in an appropriately spooky abandoned metro station one night and a gala dinner for a privileged group, David of course included, at Pré Catalan the next, while Paris continued to buzz with both information and speculation concerning Princess Diana's tragic death.

Meanwhile, in my journal I tried to wrap my arms around the changes that were upon me:

> *New month. New season. New plans, perspectives. I need to go. I know that I need to go. I know that I can't not take the chance. Driving home. Hours in the car between Maine and JFK airport. David cursing, complaining, criticizing—and my awareness that he was just doing his characteristic adaptation to anxiety or pain, that I could recognize it for what it was and not be upset by it. What was annoying became endearing; what was difficult became manageable. Am I losing my resilience? (Here I give an example of it and, in the next sentence, question it!) No, I worry will I be tough enough to roll with the tight spots, do what must be done? Start keeping names and numbers for*

a database, make it easy to change addresses, start a database
for France, start a series of folders of things to be done—or an
outline. But the current commitments are key. If I have a target
"announcement" date, the end of October, Yale convocation
weekend, I could have eight weeks of getting ready—learning
French and the computer, doing things that need to be done,
getting my body in shape—this separation from David won't be
so awful. After all, I'm going back to Paris next Wednesday. But
it's all so much work—the planes, disruptions, planning, pack-
ing. The toll of travel extends beyond moments spent in transit.

I began preparing for the change financially. Gary A., my financial advisor since Stuart's death, listened carefully as I described my situation, challenges, and dreams. In the short term, solutions were easy: an investment was about to mature, and I could access the cash to cover the transition. In the longer term, I needed an income. Gary appreciated the passion behind my dreams to become a writer. He had a lawyer friend who had developed a specialty of consulting with writers, and Gary suggested I contact him. The man's secretary set up an appointment and told me to bring a résumé and writing samples when I met with her boss.

I also made an appointment with my own psychologist. Yes, I wanted to—intended to—live life. But all those decisions and all that loss promised to be hard. Especially the loss. I knew that I had "worked through" earlier grief—allowed full experience and expression of all the complex emotions embedded in the experiences. So I was well aware that the roller coaster was about to take up residence in the home where I had so carefully constructed restricted zones dedicated to balance and serenity. I would have my own rage to deal with: at those who refused to let me be helpful when they needed to believe no one could help them; at myself for wanting to believe I had power that, in my rational mind, I knew I did not; at the patients who didn't value uniqueness I had brought to them; and at myself for wanting to feel "special." Then there was my guilt (over putting my needs and wants above those of my patients) and their fury (at me for leaving them) and potential jealousy (for about a million reasons, both real and imagined).

It was all very intense and scary but all a necessary part of getting from here to there, so I knew I just had to go do it. My therapist agreed that the more time my patients had to adapt to the idea, the better their adaptations would be, the more likely it was that the terminations could be a growing experience for them. For me, too. I moved the announcement date closer, even though my departure date was not yet set.

I bought a handbook on the nonlegal aspects of closing a practice and sent David sections from it so that he might understand the reasons why I needed moral support from time to time. Some of the advice was relevant to change in general. I wanted to keep us on similar pages, to open up dialogue, to guarantee that things that needed to be talked about did not become taboo. Of course, me being me, at each step I wanted reassurance that he really did want me, that he had thought it through and realized that I would be fairly dependent, at least for a little while, and that he might feel crowded, especially on his boat.

My Maine realtor called to say that a client who had wanted to buy the cottage but had not had the money for it the previous spring was now more solvent and wanted to buy it. On the realtor's advice, I listed the property for sale again. It was a hot market, so she suggested $239,000, instead of the $225,000 of the spring before. I spoke to my accountant and learned that federal taxes on the sale of the Westport house would be about 20 percent of the net gain if I had worked in the house during the calendar year in which I sold it, but only about 10 percent if I had not. These two events led me to write to David:

So I am strongly inclined to shut down the practice sometime in late December. I do hope that you do not feel that I am pushing here, but there are practical issues at stake. And I guess if we really both want it to happen, going public—announcing

the decision to patients and organizations and friends and the
world—is an inevitable part of the process. I know that it's no
turning back, so it's scary. But my Artist's Way book says, "Leap
and the net will be there," and I'm ready to leap.

I also knew that getting ready makes you ready. With college, a new job, marriage, childbirth, parenthood, relocation, even divorce or bereavement—virtually any major life change—the evolution of identity comes in passing through difficult moments along the way from there to here. Indeed, I often asked a patient, "What are the most difficult moments you anticipate along the way?" and, "How can you best cope with that?"

Jennifer came for dinner and slept over. Her frequent companionship was invaluable to me as I navigated my way through the transitions. As always, I loved being with my daughter. I would watch her be her capable adult self, juggling her work and relationships and home and trying to maintain time for fun and acts of kindness, and I was in awe of her. I knew that I was the mother and she was the daughter—but on some level she had always felt like an old soul come to raise me as much as I raised her. And oh, how we could laugh together!

Predictably, the next morning, David sent me the reassurance I needed:

I am, often, intimidated (also impressed) by the amount,
number, complexity of things you have to (and do) deal with,
plus the number of activities and commitments and obligations
you are constantly juggling. I guess that is why you need lists,
and "processing" and consulting. But, yes, of course, I do under-
stand and continue to try to provide reassurance and moral
support and encouragement—and not to show my own anxiety
in face of all that complexity. (Way back, you said and we noted
that your life was and had been difficult and complex, mine easy
and simple—which may explain why I "think things through"
much less, even though you have a different impression, so a lot

of this is intimidating, which may be why you insist on every-
thing being open and talked about—since you do, quite accu-
rately, sense my sometimes avoidance of issues, what you call
the "taboos.") All that to simply confirm that I am as scared—in
my different ways—as you, but together we can discuss and
provide mutual support; will be easier in person (next week)
than on paper or by phone. . . .

As to your coming here, us living together, making a life and
making a home together, that is all wonderful and I want to do
it with you. . . . I am aware of everything that this represents
for you—the risks and difficulties and complexities—but I also
know all these problems are greater for you, and that is why
my concern is for you, not for me (and, on that level, I have
not thought enough about details, focusing more—to use your
image—on what makes me happy and doing it). Perhaps you
really don't see or feel or appreciate to what extent I am or can
be irresponsible, and can (sometimes) act on impulse, confident
in some instinctive way that "it will all work out"—or that if
it doesn't, then there will be another solution. Bad example,
but I bought the boat in 1982 with the very clear notion of not
thinking too much of risks/consequences—too much logic or
rational thought might have concluded it was a dumb idea (but
it wasn't, and I've enjoyed it, fifteen years, and maybe it is time
to move). . . .

He agreed that my reasoning for selling the Maine cottage was
sound and then went on to analyze his own cash flow a bit. France
was *not* the United States. David's tax bracket at the time was some
54 percent—and it kicked in at an equivalent of about US$35,000–
$40,000. Dealing with money, the role of money, the buying power of
money—all were different in France. Again, David's similarity to the
Little Prince came through: Why in the world would a person spend
his precious days counting and recounting coins (or even bills or stock
certificates) when he could be watching a sunset or eating foie gras?

I struggled with the enormity of what I was doing, closing the door on a life I had painstakingly constructed over more than two decades. My continuing, biggest fear was still that David would no longer want me once I had dismantled my nurturing and relatively secure life structure. (I kept hearing *The Rules* or my mother's voice warning that a man's strongest motivation was the chase, the conquering.) What might I do then? Did I need a plan B? Actually, the alternatives were not too awful—first thing I'd do would be to take some time. I could rent a place for a while, put stuff in storage—it would be expensive, but I could do it—and take a *long* vacation, no demands at all, let my head clear. And when I was clear, I trusted, I would know what to do. Faith. I wondered if the door to university teaching in America had slammed shut when my age had passed fifty. But maybe I could teach in France? Could I sufficiently master the language? Probably. Did I want my computer? Yes! One of my few certainties was that I wanted to write. David assured me that possibilities would open up once I lived in Europe, once we were sharing the same time zone and activities and points of reference.

Tending to more essential matters, I decided to go in person to the French consulate in Manhattan in order to investigate rules concerning visas, residence permits, formalities that might be required because I was moving to France.

While I gathered my wits, official papers, and luggage for the four-night trip to Paris in the middle of a busy September, I let some of my deeper yearnings surface. Not only did I want to be with David, but that nagging internal voice kept reminding me of my dream of writing, along with its accompanying fears:

> *Probably won't forgive myself if I don't try. No one reading it? That is probably the biggest fear—maybe because I don't read a lot of* [self-help] *books. Think of the whole country, not just New York, sophisticated cities. Think of people who don't get a lot of good stimulation, information. Indeed, think of whom I would be writing for. One population is my patients—write for*

G., hoping to bring light back into her eyes. Write for A.—here's
why people would want you, would want to be your friend,
then how to do it, meet them, make the friendships. Write for
my colleagues? What would I be proud for them to read? For
aging women, especially the single ones, the B.'s of the world?
Write a book of comfort for those in so much pain they don't
know where to turn. Write a book of joy, to brighten, help people
feel good—warm puppy stories. Why do people read? For infor-
mation, for inspiration, for a new perspective, for comfort, for
pleasure or distraction, for confirmation of what they believe . . .
I guess the biggest fear is that I'll be a junk writer. And, again,
that I have nothing of value to give.

Little did I realize that God was giving me, I was living, the story
that needed to be told while I blindly kept trying to direct my destiny.

I obsessed about identity and logistical issues, took care of current
events, and planned for the short September weekend in Paris. That
week, patients came on Monday, Tuesday, and Wednesday, before my
late-night flight to Paris, and, in between consultations, I practiced
computer skills, investigated modem and Internet options, and supported a friend who was running for local office. Finally, at 7:50 on
Wednesday night, I flew to Paris on a cheap Tower Air flight that
landed at Orly at 9:10 the next morning.

Reliably, David was waiting for me when I exited the customs area.
We both babbled about plans for the weekend, the upcoming move,
and the more general future as we followed the unfamiliar route
from Orly, south of the city, into Paris. Past Rungis, where the food
markets of Les Halles had moved. Through Porte d'Orléans. Across
the 14th arrondissement, past the church at Alésia, along avenue du
Maine. The golden dome of the church at Les Invalides came into
view. Across the bridge, and suddenly we were "home." Much easier
than CDG. David stopped for *croissants au beurre* and baguettes. He
treated me to breakfast, reunion lovemaking, and my jet-lag nap, and
then, when I awoke, we walked to the office. Mme. H. was about to

retire; this would be the last time I would see her. She had bought me a book of Robert Doisneau photographs. She wanted to say goodbye in a way that left us feeling like equals, my gift to her, of photographs of America, reciprocated. *Egalité. Merci.*

We were at the office when I realized that something felt just a bit "off." Using my clinical instincts, I let my associative thoughts settle on one potential source of discomfort.

"David, tomorrow night we are invited to dinner at M.'s home. I know she is the in-house lawyer you have worked with on one of your major accounts for years now—the woman I met at Terminal 1 when the two of you came back from the trip to Singapore—but is there anything else I should know? Anything else going on there? Or that did go on? Maybe you'd better fill me in on the history."

Yes, they had had an affair. But it was brief. And long over. She now lived with a man and was helping him raise his son. They would host us together. This was France, after all, and friendly encounters happened all the time. Wow! Did that ever make me nervous.

Saturday afternoon, we wandered across rue du Faubourg St. Honoré. Loris Azzaro, a boutique opposite the Bristol, announced an atypical September sale, prior to renovations, and David steered me inside. Two hours later, we walked out with a black-and-white woven wool skirt, a black silk blouse with ruffles and cowboy snap closures, and a black party dress, all folded neatly into the designer's shopping bag. David said he wanted me to have something new and pretty to wear on my recently slimmed-down body when we went to the Yale celebrations in November. I had never owned clothes like these. They fit differently and made me feel like a woman, a pretty woman, inside them and out.

When we reached the boat, the message light on the phone was blinking.

"You'd better call me, Mom. We'll be around." Danny's voice held a note of tension. I knew that he and Stefani were staying at the Signal Lane house over the weekend, so reaching him was simple. But he had never called Paris before, so I figured there must be a fairly weighty reason.

David punched in the Kallback codes.

"What's up, hon?" I asked.

"We have a bit of a situation here, and I thought I'd better tell you."

"What sort of a situation?"

"Well, we went downstairs to get something out of the freezer and . . . well, there's water down there. A fair amount of it. Seems to be coming from the hot water heater."

"Oh. Water. A fair amount. How much is that?" I asked.

"We've been mopping it up, but there's a pretty good cover on the floor. And it's leaking out into the hall by the wine rack. And through it into the storeroom. And in the other direction, into the den. And I guess there was so much overnight that it just spread into the bathroom and bedroom. The carpeting in my old bedroom is pretty soaked."

"Oops. Sounds like there *is* a bit of a situation. What have you done?"

"Well, we just found it a couple of hours ago. We've been mopping it up and putting pans under the leaking water heater, and dumping them into the lake when they got fairly full. And I figured we should call a plumber, so I did."

Good for him! I was impressed. I was also trying to sound casual, calm, cool. But by now my heart was pounding, my body temperature dropping, and my insides beginning to shake. I was grateful that Dan and Stefani were in the house and managing the crisis, but I could feel all that guilt and fear and self-doubt rising. "Do you need me to try to come home now, or can it wait for my scheduled flight on Monday?"

"It can wait, Mom. Things happen. We're okay. I'll keep you posted."

"Bye, Dan. And thank you again."

I hung up the phone, and the shaking escalated. The house was my responsibility, not Danny's. And I wasn't there to take care of it. The romantic, easygoing weekend Dan had hoped to share with Stefani had turned into a very different experience, while here I was, in Paris, with a man buying me designer clothes and feeding me *macarons* from Laduree, purchased impulsively on the walk home. It was as good a time as any to have a serious cry.

That night David and I drove to Enghien to have dinner at M.'s home. She greeted us at the door wearing one of those simple but incredibly sexy French combinations of perfect pants and a sweater with major décolletage. Her attractive boyfriend, who spoke virtually no English, smiled politely and receded into the background, as did I, while David and M. chatted about wine, work, and the wonders of French culture. She served us fresh figs with just the right cheese as a first course, but I did not know quite what to do with them. I watched David and my hostess for clues. When we moved on to the pork loin, the main course for dinner, she asked me point blank if I knew what I was eating, and, of course, I did not. By the time we left, after one in the morning, a whole shop full of Loris Azzaro clothes couldn't put my self-confidence as a woman back together again. And then there was my failure as a mother and homeowner to be faced when I got back to the boat and remembered the mess I had dumped into my son's unexpecting lap.

But Danny was handling it. He had left another message for us. The plumber had made the weekend call and shut off the water to the house and would contact me later in the week. Dan and Stefani had mopped and mopped and continued to empty the pans that caught the drippings, and things seemed to be under better control. I calmed down a bit.

David and I spent Sunday enabling me to reach more comfortable places, inside and out. He helped me with practicalities: how to craft an effective letter to a patient's insurer who was resisting reimbursement, how to understand the requirements of the French government and respond to them, how to think about and deal with the damage I would find in the Signal Lane house. He helped me with decisions: we would sell the Maine house now, and the Westport house would go on the market in April, when I returned to the United States for the bat mitzvah of the girl whom I had stayed with in 1996. I would close the practice December 30, and he would be with me for support and celebration. I would take the beginning of January to organize the move for Luke and me, allowing all my current attention to focus on the needs of my patients and practice and feelings about them with neither dilution nor distraction throughout December. And when David came to the United States later in the fall, he would help me file the French documents with the French consulate in New York. By the time we joined Jacques and Corinne for dinner at Du Côté 7ème, I felt far more able to carry on.

While I was busy dealing with housing emergencies and the announcements that I was leaving, David dug into his work, finalized plans for his October trip to the States, and began to plan a winter ski trip with his sons. Adam, still a student in the computer engineering doctoral program at the University of Colorado, had landed a teaching opportunity, and thus his availability was limited to Christmas into mid-January and to spring break. David intended to be with me from Christmas Eve until January 5 and was reluctant to commit to another period of absence from his office right after a trip to the United States. As for March, Adam's free week immediately followed the week my children were coming to Paris. So David had two challenges: explaining to his sons that I would soon move to Paris to live with him and would be included in any future travel plans, and acknowledging that my presence in his life impacted his immediate availability. He arranged a conference call with Scott and Adam. They heard his news, no comments, and arrangements for the ski trip became the topic of discussion.

Telling his sister was another matter, and he put off that conversation until the next day, knowing that he did need to relay the information himself, rather than wait until she heard the news of his upcoming change of status through his sons—or, worse, their mother, with whom his sister remained friends. Shortly after he did tell his sister, she called me, voicing concern that I would be unhappy living so far from my children. She was also "worried" about my missing my girlfriends, being comfortable in the limited physical space of the boat, finding work. She had a list of things that "could damage the relationship." I agreed that the geographical distance from Jennifer and

Danny, Steve and Stefani, was a serious concern to me but disagreed that it created a threat to my relationship with David. I have no idea what she said to David when they spoke on the phone.

His sister was not the only person who reacted to my news with caution or negativity. At least she was direct and forthright. One friend's husband reminded me that, as he saw it, I was taking all the risk. Another friend simply disappeared, refusing to return phone calls or even respond to a letter I mailed. My brother became inaccessible. Two other girlfriends offered horror stories of expatriate experiences with tax, residency, or other legal issues.

Perhaps the most painful change in a relationship following my announcement that I was moving to Paris came when one of my closest friends insisted I should not go to France unless I was married first. The conversation went something like this:

"You can have the wedding at my house."

"That's very generous of you, and I know it would be gorgeous, but the last thing I'm interested in now is getting married again."

"How can you go overseas without that extra bit of security?"

"I don't even know if we can live together. David has been single sixteen years. And I do not want to get married again."

"You are being foolish."

"You are not my mother. Please back off."

That remark hit a nerve, and we ended up yelling at each other in the middle of the diner, our other two friends watching in astonishment. I left in tears, and none of my future efforts was able to repair the rupture.

Meanwhile, I was making progress in closing the practice. Telling current patients was the most critical task, but it was certainly not the whole job. I wrote letters to former patients, letting them know I would no longer be available. To colleagues who might find the change of status useful information. To a few very long-ago patients to whom I still felt strongly attached. I did research on what notices needed to be posted in what newspapers and added posting them to my lists. With names of referrals for my current patients in hand, I made sure to identify backups in case a first contact did not provide the comfort level I hoped it would.

A double benefit came from the interview with the lawyer-publicist. He offered me a work-for-hire writing opportunity, short clips in a book he was assembling, for which I would be paid the same $300 that it cost me to talk with him for an hour. So I both recouped his fee and wrote my first pieces for a nonprofessional audience.

My major collapse came a week after I had come home from the September trip. After the flood. After dealing with a disaster recuperation service that came to halt the development of mold, dry out warped parquet floors, rip up carpeting, and prepare for installation of new. After throwing out the ruined contents of the cedar and luggage closets, filing insurance claims, and beginning home repairs. After beginning to close the practice. After telling my kids. And some patients. And friends. After imagining myself a writer. After negative reactions and cautions from others. After deciding I would write about "saying goodbye." Rambling through all my angst, I shared some of it with David:

> *I can feel the terror underneath everything: What if you can't tolerate saying goodbye to living alone? What if I can't? Though I am hardly alone. Funny, in some ways I think I'll be able to have more solitude—which I happen to adore. And I keep reminding myself of the data: the more I am with you, the more I love being with you. And whenever I've felt a need for psychic space, you seem to know and it's just there.*

With the help of David's constant encouragement, sympathy, and frequent faxes and phone messages, I calmed down, as I had known I would. I also learned that he could tolerate the way I reacted when my resilience wore down. In Paris, he said his own goodbye to the secretary who had worked with him for decades as she left for retirement, greeted and helped orient his new one, and dug into new client matters that demanded attention and intelligence.

Back in Connecticut, I called Renee. Looking beyond the upcoming Jewish holidays, we began to plan our Thanksgiving gathering, probably at her home in southern New Jersey. She assumed that we were including David's son Adam, as well as Scott and his family. They had other plans, but the offer was made and I felt good about and grateful for the expansion.

I signed up for the intermediate/advanced French course in Westport's adult education program, along with a couple of seminars on financial management, and continued my crash courses in Microsoft Office. Finishing the old, preparing for the new, living in the moment. Soon David would arrive and we would have ten full days of being in the present together. Reviewing the past year, preparing for the one ahead, a year that could change us both forever. This year, the Jewish high holy days were loaded with significance.

I began cooking, baking, and freezing plum cakes, the ones made with small, oval Italian prune plums, a once-a-year fall specialty in our home. Noodles and spinach, chicken with wild rice and mushrooms, a pound cake for dinner before Kol Nidre. Sausage and peppers for Sunday-night pasta with Scott and Stefanie. More plum cake, of course. And for the following Saturday night, with David's sister and her boyfriend, I planned to serve lamb, marinated and barbecued. Baked stuffed potatoes to accompany the lamb went into the freezer. David's sister was bringing salad for a first course. There was much to celebrate.

On Wednesday, October 1, 1997, David boarded Air France flight 006 and arrived at JFK around 3:00 p.m., just in time for us to wiggle across Manhattan and get to Glen Ridge, New Jersey, for dinner at Jennifer's before Erev Rosh Hashanah services.

18

Transitions and Possibilities

David arrived for the Jewish holidays in his high-energy mode. We had planned yet another full and complex week, one loaded with significance—Jewish moments shared with Jennifer and Steve, visits with Scott, Stefanie, and Sofia and with David's sister and her boyfriend in our home, and steps toward a new life for us both. My American Reform Judaism was very far from the Orthodox and conservative traditions David had grown up in. It was also quite different from our French "liberal" experiences of the year before. My "Jewish food" repertoire included a smooth pâté of chicken livers, rather than chopped liver; a low-fat noodle concoction that included spinach, instead of cinnamon-sugar and apples; and, of course, the plum cake, which replaced honey cake or rugelach or anything else I had never learned to whip up. I had no problem serving people Madeline's crabmeat-and-artichoke appetizer or *Silver Palate*'s sausage-and-peppers dish.

Services began promptly when stated, and people sat through them until their ends, rather than streaming in and out as their spirits moved them. Perhaps the biggest difference was that I had never "observed" more than one day of Rosh Hashanah celebration in America, although some Reform Jews *did*—and do—observe two days; in fact, I had thoughtlessly scheduled patients for the second day of the holiday that year.

David was geared up. As we left JFK and spun across Manhattan and through the Holland Tunnel, he driving the car as always, he worried that we might not make it to Jennifer's on time. He began complaining that he had landed at the wrong airport. I watched him with both amusement and a shudder as his temper erupted and he screamed at other drivers through our closed windows. David had this clear, resonant voice to begin with. To hear him yelling obscenities at the top of his lungs inside my small Honda both surprised and mystified me. It also caused enough vibration to rattle us both. Later I came to appreciate that these tantrums of his occurred under only three conditions: extreme frustration (most often with others' behavior that delayed him from pursuing or reaching his goals), severe anxiety (usually about his capacity to be "a good boy"), and, most reliably, when he was suffering unrecognized and unacknowledged guilt. Usefully, when the first two situations were missing, I had learned to look for the source of his guilt whenever I saw his fury erupt out of nowhere. In retrospect, I know he was kicking himself for not having flown into Newark. My challenge was to help him find a way not to feel too ashamed about what he felt guilty over, so that he could own his role in his distress. Alternately, as I did in this instance, I could just watch him have a tantrum. If we were going to live together, I needed to detach from David's reactions when they had nothing to do with me; I had already learned that lesson!

We made it to Jennifer and Steve's that afternoon in plenty of time for David to change out of his jeans, to enjoy the holiday meal that she and I had created, and to get to their new temple early enough to stake out seats where we could see the clergy and the ark. David participated, reading both Hebrew and English words. He sang the familiar chants that he knew, although they appeared within an unfamiliar prayerbook and were accompanied by radically different melodies. He had not attended services in any congregation in America for a very long time, and on an unconscious level it signaled the beginning of his slow march toward reclaiming his roots, all of them. For me, I was just thrilled to be sharing traditions I valued with the man

I adored, my beloved daughter and son-in-law, and an American Reform congregation.

We returned to Connecticut after the service. David slept off a bit of his jet lag, but we were due back in New Jersey early the next day. Jen and I had prepared a luncheon to follow the morning service, and she had invited a friend with her eighteen-month-old daughter, as well as Steve's father and brother and his brother's wife and their new dog, to join us. Luke stayed near home with my eight-year-old next-door neighbor, Valerie, and her mother.

Jennifer's meltdown came sometime after lunch. Her eyes kept watering, clearly suffering some kind of irritation. Finally, I failed to bite my tongue.

"Do you want to take out your contact lenses?" I asked.

Jennifer got angry. Jennifer almost never got angry. She got angry this time.

"I am a grown woman. I do not need you telling me what to do. Do *not* tell me what to do. I can take care of myself!" By now her voice was raised and she was fighting real tears, half sitting, half standing, looking as if she might hit the table in frustration.

I tried to apologize, to explain, to understand what was going on. The fight between us was uncomfortable, injecting a note of real awkwardness into idyllic moments, embarrassing us both on this holiday devoted to harmony. We managed to remove ourselves from the table and make it up to her bedroom, where we spent whatever time it took to get to the bottom of what she was feeling. As happy as she was for me on one level, at a deeper one, the little girl in her was aware that her mother was going far away. She knew rationally that she did not "need" me to take care of her anymore. But the emotional reality was something else. She was scared and angry and not sure she could cope without the easy access we had always had to each other. All those adult sleepovers in Westport since she had gone to work in Norwalk, all those long and so-comfortable dinners we had cooked or assembled, all those conversations on the phone or when one of us had returned from an errand, a task, a meeting, an event.

The walks on the beach. The giggling. All of it would change with an ocean between us, and she knew that, perhaps better than I. That extra step of needing to calculate time zones, of waiting for Kallback to call back, of not being able simply to get in the car and go in search of a hug or a face-to-face discussion. All the laughter we would miss, all the milestones in each other's lives. To say nothing of commenting on the weather. And we both were clear that we expected this move to be "permanent." Nobody could imagine David leaving France to return to live in the United States back then.

Much sobbing and clarity later, we had both said what needed to be said and cried tears that needed to be shed. We returned to the company in the living room with our arms around each other and smiles on our faces. We would manage to make it through, to do this. Our love for and commitment to each other were strong enough to reinvent ways in which we honored them.

David was both confused and impressed by what had just happened. His way of being with his boys was so different from the directness with which my children and I explored our conflicts, concerns, differences, demands, and expectations of one another—the process by which we rarely left behind unfinished business—and kept our understanding of one another at least relatively up to date as we all grew and evolved, managing our separate adult lives. In contrast, David and his sons seemed to have frozen one another in former states, expectations trapped in images from earlier times, begging for updating, potentially generating misunderstanding.

David and I spent a quiet day at home in Westport on the second day of Rosh Hashanah that year. No services. I did indeed see some patients, and David walked Luke at Sherwood Island, contemplating the moments we had just shared, the significance of the new year, the life changes that had been set in motion. We marketed and cooked, preparing for our guests to arrive the next day.

Saturday morning, the train from New York pulled into the station and Scott and Stefanie disembarked, bringing with them a portable playpen and stroller, an overnight bag, luggage loaded with baby equipment, and, of course, Sofia. We visited neighborhoods in Fairfield and Westport, drove around the area, took another serious look at the impressive community-built playground on Compo Beach. Eventually, Sofia napped, and by the time David's sister and her boyfriend arrived for the evening, we were all ready to relax and slow down. David's sister and her boyfriend returned to the city after dinner that night.

The next day, at Scott and Stefanie's request, we visited some open houses. We put them and Sofia back on the train after an early dinner. This visit had been a pleasant one, without any of the drama of the previous Thursday, a different kind of sharing, of intimacy, creating memories about the new, rather than grieving the loss of the old. David's and my decision to be together was already bringing each of us different balances of benefits and losses.

The week passed in a blur. Before we knew it, Yom Kippur was over and David was back in Paris, where he began to look at house and apartment listings. He was shocked at the inflation since he had been a young man starting out in America in the late '60s or a new arrival in Paris in 1972. He knew he needed to recalibrate his notions of the "simple life" so that we could live as we had been, retaining a level of comfort but also indulging in expensive pursuits from time to time. And there was that issue of housing. His bohemian boat was sexy and quirky, but tending to it was time-consuming and challenging. Besides, he had enjoyed sixteen years of its cocoon-like uniqueness, and maybe it was time to move on, just as he was inevitably moving beyond his loner lifestyle. Apartment living would be a lot easier. But first, it was time for a trip to Normandy—out of space, out of time, even out of the familiarity of complex Paris.

I continued to obsess about financial independence, on the one hand, and all those goodbyes, on the other. An income stream would be nice, beyond the interest thrown off from my assets, but the assets would be there and I could draw from them, especially early on, especially if the Maine house sold soon at a good price. I set aside the notion of retaining a pied-à-terre in the United States. No way to justify *that* luxury.

I tried to develop principles for thinking about the endings:

> *1) Identify what is being let go—what resources, fantasies, possibilities, opportunities; what history, memories, roles, responsibilities (the latter can probably be duplicated, the former maybe not). 2) What are some good exercises for acknowledging them? 3) And then be clear about what is important. Make patients the first priority, then the book proposal, then getting myself there—my cookbook for endings. What recipes? What essential ingredients? For sure I want a satisfied patron, so what is required? Savoring comes to mind, being there, experiencing each mouthful.*

I had found a metaphor for dealing with my challenges.

Soon it was time to count down. Ten more weeks, then nine, eight. What did it all mean! Make room for the new. Think in one year chunks, not eternity. I was buying a year of my life, a year without clinical work commitments. I was tired, wanted to sort it out, to rediscover my voice, to simplify. Jennifer was being an angel. She even figured out that she could keep a good eye on the house and help us both out at the same time. Commuting to Connecticut in the winter created a stressful work situation for her. She offered to stay in the house one night or more each week and make sure that plants were watered, bills were paid, and no major damage went undetected or unattended. My leaving could create opportunity and benefit for her, too. And there was that upcoming trip to Paris we were planning for March with her husband and brother and his girlfriend. She had turned the corner and was now comfortable with a new order of things.

Jennifer became invested in the photo albums that I had assembled since her infancy. She wanted a symbolic equivalent of the recipes I had put together for her bridal shower years before. The cookbook was an attempt to package and preserve memories of her then-recently-deceased paternal grandmother within spiral-bound pages wedged between plastic covers—an honored presence, but within boundaries. Because of the emotional power embedded within the photo albums, I felt a need to contain the history of our family and maybe differentiate us all a little bit, give each of us bits and pieces of the history that was his or hers or ours or mine.

We decided to break up the albums, and each of us—including their father when we distributed photos prior to 1979—would receive a selection, a representation, a concrete reminder of who we had been and moments we had shared. (How I wish I had imagined the potential for scanning photographs into a computer, preserving all the images in a way that enabled us all to share them and later to make our own choices about what to keep and what to discard.) I decided Jen and Dan could split up the photos I kept for myself after I died. Meanwhile, they would each have a "legacy" of their own, and it wouldn't just disappear. We are all entitled to the stories of our own past.

At the same time, David was ramping up his efforts to live his life with joy, delight, and sharing. With me. He made reservations for us for the following weekend at Château du Baffy, inland, between Arromanches and Courseulles, arriving *fin de matinée* on Friday, October 31, departing Sunday, November 2. He promised that activities were going to be casual, flexible, and sexy: strolls on the beaches or on bluffs, visits to small towns, drives on back roads (*route des moulins*), explorations of ruins and châteaux, villages of potters and painters. We would be in Normandy on La Toussaint, Day of the Dead, a celebration very different from its US twin, Halloween. Friday night we would dine at the château, typical Normandy cuisine, and

Saturday we would share a *plateau de fruits de mer*, saving the giant crab for last, at a restaurant overlooking Port en Bessin. Lots of loving in between. He reassured me that he would bring my curlers, walking shoes, and Wellingtons. And extra sweaters. I could travel light. He promised wine with dinners in Normandy, even Pommeau for aperitifs in the salon, in front of the fire. We were going to celebrate my upcoming professional talk at Gerontological Society of America meetings, our long-term future, a writing career, *anything you want*. Again, he insisted, *Choosing to do for yourself does not need to mean you "don't care" about others. Keep that straight.*

On early-morning walks with Hope, I reminded myself to actually see the sunrise, the leaf colors, the ice on the shore, the ducklings and goslings born in May that had matured by October. To remember to let yesterday go and live in today. If each day is well lived, then one doesn't have a lot of yesterdays dragging forward, pushing the burden of the past into today. Or filling psychic space with regrets. Just as important to keep the psyche uncluttered as the closets. Maybe more so. What legacy would I leave? I didn't care. I prayed only not to leave a mess and mindlessness, like my mother had. I needed to clean it up, clear it out, leave whatever remained in a tidy, transparent bundle.

Thinking of legacy, I began to wonder even then at the miracle of David's and my having found each other. In my journal, I mused.

> *Stuart, is this your gift to me? Did you find David for me? Shoot the arrows, make it happen? For sure, you would know the mind—recognize his level of energy, intelligence, soul . . . Paris a bonus. Haven't really let myself tune in to that yet. But the whole experience of finding him, being with him, the idea of creating a life together—all have that miraculous otherworldly touch. Did you send Luke to me as a test case and, when I passed, did you then send me David?*

After a long day of appointments with patients on their way to the end of their therapy with me, I boarded Continental flight 056 in

Newark, bought with my Visa frequent-flier points, bound for Charles de Gaulle Airport, where my lover awaited my arrival.

As always, David stood outside the doors to the customs clearance area, expectant grin on his face, jaunty hat tilted just right on top of his head, arms ready to hold me tight. He whisked me straight into the black Ford, and we made our way onto the Autoroute. Again, I slept a good part of the way to Normandy. Again, he stopped at Creully to buy me Badoit, coffee, and a croissant. And again we reached the channel, La Manche, cliffs and sea and islands and waves, all a delightful landscape reaching across the water toward England in one direction and along the shore to Belgium in another. We spent our stolen hours crushing mussels beneath the soles of our Wellingtons— nature's reflexology—and breathing deeply, letting the salt air fill our lungs and refresh our hearts, reminding us of how it felt simply to be alive and together.

On the return flight, after just three nights, I again babbled:

> *The screen says 5:36 p.m. in Paris and four hours thirty-three min. to destination. . . . I picture you at work, on a lunch break in the strange light, images of the arrondissements of Paris, the wood on the boat, the white trees at the Rond Point, the frost on the roof—and everywhere, David, David, David. Your being fills me up—and then I am aware that tu me manques. Yes, we've got a good thing going. Close up a life? Of course. Move to a foreign land? Of course. Do things I've never done before? Of course. All is possible. All is necessary—if I can be with you. Can't read my book, new Marie-Claire (en français), stowed in the overhead—too tightly packed to bother with. Movie probably a good one (Jack Lemmon and Walter Matthau) but no enthusiasm for much. Lunch okay, and I had to smile: yes, better than on the way over—and the Camembert took me right back to Normandy. The charming Château du Baffy with the soft murals and storybook bridge; the flowers freshly planted in November; the endless beaches and puzzling*

organisms on them. The fabulous food (plateau de fruits de mer like at Hôtel de la Marine almost compensation for the "R" months), and so it goes. Wellingtons and walking, the art lesson at Revier, the perfect church ruins and elegant Cabourg and a plate full of far too many chocolates after champignons beyond the highest hopes . . . Overwhelmed, I am, David—filled with you and the joys of sharing with you.

And so I returned to face the final stretch of living in Westport before my move to Paris in January 1998.

VI

Squirrels Crossing Utility Wires

19

Formalities

*E*verything seemed to shift after the Normandy trip. As soon as we began to plan together how to tie up the many pieces of my life in Westport, I knew what I needed to do: stay present and stay calm as events and emotions unfolded. Keep breathing. In the same way in which an enormous proportion of the work in therapy is done in the termination phase, an opportunity to grow was now presenting itself to me. I had to somehow rise to the challenges. In addition, I knew that this period of my relationship with David would be critical for our future dynamics. I had to be competent *and* set aside time for the inevitable disorganization as I struggled to feel and understand and ultimately let go of guilt, anger, grief, fear. I had to be strong *and* remain vulnerable, as I followed through on difficult decisions and faced conflicting alternatives in choices that had to be made. And I had to balance it all: do all the work that was on my plate, both emotional and logistical, especially when I didn't want to; find enough lightness to make it through with some kind of grace; and, in all that, manage to stay strongly connected to David and my children and, above all, to my patients. Both they and I deserved that.

November meant I would begin to "close down" my professional life—at least the part associated with clinical work. I would shut doors on routines, experiences, practices, habits of growing that had

nurtured me for more than two decades and walk away from an identity that had defined my professional status. In Paris, I would have
no need to be "Dr. Tower." Although I welcomed the change, I was
already grieving the loss of the relationships I had established with so
many of my patients and even colleagues.

My patients. My dear, courageous patients. No, I did not love them
all. To say I did—or even imagine that I did—would render the word
meaningless, suggest a lie to myself at best, fraud at worst. But I had
indeed grown to love many of those who had crossed the threshold
of my office, determined to become their truest selves as they looked
inward or examined their outward behavior, week after week, in my
"therapy chair." As they had allowed me to witness their transforma-
tions. Over time, as they shared their stories with me—with themselves—they became more and more whole. As they shed the weight
of their secrets and reclaimed their dreams and desires, the psychic
baggage and clutter that had accrued across time dissolved and permitted radiance to shine through. Sometimes I thought I could actually see the luminous spaces created within them, like open windows
with freshly ironed white eyelet curtains fluttering. allowing wind to
gently float through spaces on a spring day. New breath to solve old
problems, generate new perspectives, make changes in experimental
ways. As my patients learned to conduct their lives in acceptance of the
truths within, they came to trust that I, too, shared their wish for the
freedom to be and become who they were. I walked with them down
the roads of their suffering and recovery, cried with them through loss
and pain, and felt joy with and for them as they became themselves.
I was not neutral. I was rooting for them. And it was very hard work,
work that often left me exhausted, depleted, yearning for more time to
take care of myself. But I knew I would miss it. Even more, I knew that
I would miss them. And I would surely miss and regret not knowing
how their lives evolved.

Closing the practice brought more than imminent losses; at times
it brought what felt like unbearable guilt. How could I walk out
on people who had counted on me to be there and, in good faith,

expected my availability? They had grown to trust me—sometimes slowly and across much time, through crises, flashes of insight, quiet moments of assimilation. Worse, as I saw it, I was leaving them to pursue my own desires. With no *guarantees* of happy endings. I felt selfish, and sometimes foolish, for the risks I was taking. I reasoned that changes are a natural part of life. After all, I could have died and exited my practice that way, and anyway, I should not overestimate my own importance. The world was full of therapists, and there was no reason to believe that no one else could be as helpful as, or per-haps more helpful than, I had been. (By then, I was even thinking in the French double negative!) I appreciated that each person is unique and each relationship has inimitable qualities to it, but I knew that my role could be replaced, even if, for some patients, my absence would be specific and palpable. They would be forced to deal with a loss that had not been part of the agenda when they had first come to me.

As I struggled to manage the logistics and the emotional realities of closing the practice, I found the past and the future bearing down on me at the same time. Perhaps because Jen, Dan, and I had been redistributing the old family photos, images of my children when they were small and needed me kept flashing across my mental screen. Jennifer banging and splashing on her high-chair tray, eighteen months old, in the pigtails that I had finally learned to make for her beautiful, thick hair. Danny trying on the pink tutu I had made for his sister. Dying Easter eggs with the O'Sheas. Renee's son, Nick, and Jennifer tooting blue plastic horns nearly as tall as they were. Indian Guides and Girl Scouts, baseball games and Saturday afternoon hikes. More recently, the travels we had taken together and those when they went alone, inching toward independence. Jennifer's stories about Malaysia, Lyons, Cairo; Danny's months in London, on a remote Caribbean island, hiking and climbing out West. My own first day of graduate school, when I had found myself frightened, tears dripping cold against my cheeks as I walked down York Street, wondering what I had signed on for and wishing I could go home, and then realizing that "home" no longer existed as it once had—Danny and Jennifer were growing up.

Now, years later, as I was planning a move to France, my children, ages twenty-seven and thirty-one, were no longer children and did not need me anymore. Yet I was experiencing those same "I want to go home" feelings that Jennifer had labeled once when she was at summer camp: a mixture of sadness, anxiety, longing for what was familiar and comforting. Perhaps the best thing I could do for them, as well as for myself, was to seize this opportunity for a life filled with love. Joy. Beauty. Adventure. Whimsy. Pleasure. No more responsibility to care for others. Except David. And his needs seemed reasonable.

Whenever the weight of the present, with its demands, began to bear down on me and the challenge of reinventing my professional self felt daunting, I switched to the immediate future, especially the anticipated pleasures. First and most of all, I was going to get to live with David. And it *was* going to be in Paris.

David was David. He was fun and he was helpful, and thinking about him inevitably brought smiles back to my troubled face. I remembered watching him type on the little French Minitel. He was uncanny at identifying information that was worthwhile and that which was not—he'd be a natural at Internet research one day, if he got around to learning about computers. I felt confident that any resources I might need (for example, a superb hairstylist), he would be able to locate. My biggest indulgence (after the ballet): excellent haircuts. The investment that repays every day of my life. We would find a coiffeur.

I continued to obsess over leaving my children, aware that a part of the pain came from accepting that the childhood moments we had shared had ended. At first I focused on logistics. Putting the registration for my car in Danny's name. Insurance. The stuff that was stored in the house. Putting Jennifer on my bank accounts so that she could write checks in my name. Then I went looking for shared experiences, made plans to see *The Ice Storm* with Jen and Steve, pinned down a location for an upcoming dinner with Dan, looked forward to hearing news about the evening that Dan and Stef, Jen and Steve would share with each other at the benefit ball for the Good Shepherd Society, where Steve worked. Jen and Steve had earned an invitation through their volunteer efforts; Danny was invited to thank BMG for a significant donation of CDs. My children were sharing current events, just as they shared history. I loved that but also recognized that I would no longer be able to be a part of it, not only because I lived in a world that was a generation older, but because I was moving too far away. How I wanted to hold them tight, all the while knowing they had their own lives to live.

Two weeks before David was due to arrive for Thanksgiving, reeling from the emotional turmoil of closing the practice, the overload of practical details and decisions, and the pain of confronting distance from my children, I headed to New York to meet Danny for dinner. On the way out of the house, I grabbed the fax that had just come in and left for the station. On the train, I began to read David's plans for his upcoming trip. He was scheduled to arrive at Newark at one o'clock on a Saturday. On the previous trip, we had carefully shared the dates of his next visit with both his son and his sister. Our hope for his November trip was to drive directly into Manhattan, visit with Scott, Stefanie, and Sofia, then have dinner with them, his sister, and her boyfriend. But when David spoke with Scott to confirm the arrangements, he learned that neither Scott nor his sister would be available. She was hosting a birthday party in her home for Stefanie that same evening. Stefanie's sisters were coming, along with their husbands, perhaps another friend. There was no room at the table for us, and we were not invited. Scott would be happy to see David and me upon arrival, however, and perhaps walk with us a bit on the short trip from his apartment in the West Village to his aunt's loft on South Broadway. And, by the way, perhaps we could stop and visit Stefanie's sister's new store, the one she had recently

opened as a showcase for the Oriental furnishings she was import-
ing. The shop was on the way.

David's fax reported just the facts. In my emotionally vulnerable
state, I was stunned when I sat on the train and read his words. We
were excluded from an event that his sister had first planned weeks
after we had watched her enter the dates of David's next visit in her
Filofax. In ink. She was holding an event involving her brother's son
and his family. An event placing them at the center, but without her
brother.

David seemed to take this news in stride. He said he was relieved
that we could drive up to Connecticut and go to bed early. I realized, once again, that our ways of being in the world, especially in our
close relationships, were different. What would this mean? When was
someone included, and when were they excluded? And why? What,
after all, was "family"? And what was I getting myself into? I feared I
was in the middle of a game or dance that they all knew and I did not
and that at any moment David and I could be triangled out. The music
would stop, and all the chairs would be taken.

Having boarded an early train and thus with time to spare, I
decided to walk up Madison Avenue to the Whitney. I detoured into
Saks Fifth Avenue to use the bathroom and found myself wandering
around the store. Gradually I recognized impending panic, perhaps
similar to what David had experienced in Camden, Maine. All the
stylish women, especially those behind and in front of the cosmet-
ics counters, 98 percent dressed in black and 90 percent of those in
black pantsuits, intimidated me. Feeling drained, I made my way to
the ladies' room to sit, meditate, and call home, hoping that David had
phoned in and left a message. I was afraid to call him, because I didn't
want to scare him with my shaky voice reflecting my shaky frame of
mind. But I would have loved some reassurance that he genuinely was
not as disturbed by his family dynamics as I was.

No message, but a bit calmer, I made my way back to Fifth
Avenue, to a beautiful church I'd never been in before, Fifth Avenue
Presbyterian. In contrast with always-bustling St. Patrick's and St.

Thomas, this church was nearly empty, a single couple sitting in a pew. The organist and a trumpet player practiced hymns. The walls, paneled with warm wood, created a perfect "holding environment," and I prayed my distress away (thank you, God), observing the chemistry of fear dissipate while I breathed.

I wandered through Bendel's, then walked east on Fifty-Seventh Street, which had begun to look like a version of Paris: Chanel, Hermès, Dior. Across Madison, right onto Park Avenue, down to Fifty-First Street, then left into St. Bartholomew's, perhaps my favorite New York church, definitely my favorite midtown church. I stumbled into a service. Perfect. The combination of beauty, meditation, and movement worked their magic, and I returned to sanity and serenity.

By then it was clear to me that the stylish women in Saks Fifth Avenue had nothing at all to do with my reactions. I was afraid of entering a world of interpersonal dynamics that threatened everything I believed in, everything I had worked to build with my own children and close friends. David and I would need to talk through our differences in perspective. Posing as an optometrist might help.

By the time I met Danny half an hour later, I was in good shape and very proud of myself. I knew there might be many such moments in Paris for a while, moments of disorientation and discomfort, of feeling overwhelmed or uncomprehending, and I felt reassured that I had taken care of myself in a healthy and effective way. Dinner with Dan was just the wonder I needed it to be. My son talked and talked, mostly about his work and the role of work in his life, and I had the privilege of listening. We talked about how sometimes it's foggy and sometimes it's clear—and once in a while it's scary, but skip the fear stuff. I could see how much happiness Stefani was bringing to him and silently thanked the woman who had become the focal point in his life.

The weeks ahead were busy. The Connecticut Psychological Association breakfast I had so tediously planned finally happened, an aide attending as a last-minute substitution for the congressman. I monitored details of closing the practice. Renee and I made Thanksgiving plans.

My brother was turning sixty, and, perhaps because I had been steeped in my own transitions, history, and photographs, I decided to make him a scrapbook filled with as many markers of the memories we had shared as I could assemble. I also included photographs that preceded my birth, found among papers I had received from my mother when she shipped her desk to Connecticut before she moved into a nursing home in San Francisco. Even though his response to my imminent departure from the United States had brought little but cautions and negativity, I was hoping the scrapbook might return our relationship to a more regular and respectful framework. So, in the middle of everything else, I created page after page of reminiscence, bought a leather album to contain it all, and managed to get it in the mail in time for his big day.

Obviously moved, he called. "I didn't expect ever to see some of those pictures again." I was proud of myself, and so happy that I could bring him a smile through the memories I had shared.

Stan sent me the government ranking for my grant application. His e-mail informing me of this long-awaited response was perfect in the current context:

> I have good news and bad news. The good news is that your life just became a bit simpler. The bad news is that the priority score on the FIRST is too low to think about the possibility of funding on this round. The score is 260, and the percentile is 50.7 percent. We will have to wait for the pink sheets to see what the reviewers said.

With that tacit permission, I could let go of any off-site scientific-research aspirations that had been going to accompany me to Paris. Things did indeed get much simpler. God running the show again?

I was relieved, and so was David. Now we could just focus on closing the practice, on getting Luke and me over there, and on my sadness at leaving my children behind, without the additional layer of constructing a way to do work in the United States while I was living in France.

I continued to have occasional phone conversations with Adam and spoke often with Scott. Danny sent me CDs of Gregorian chants, Christmas carols, and sacred hymns of colonial Latin America. Jennifer slept at the house at least once a week.

David continued to work on identifying and completing any additional papers, beyond my formal application, that the bureaucratic French government might request or require.

I still did not have a departure date. Who was stalling here? On the one hand, David intuitively glided through life, assuming he could and would have what he wanted when he wanted it and that everything would just work out. But was he ambivalent about the intrusion Luke and I represented? Or was I dragging my feet, unsure how long I would need to put myself back together after the shock of closing the door on an important part of my life? I kept making lists of details, struggling through current and former patients' episodes of rage and grief, several of them suddenly coming in when they had received my letter about leaving. Wanting to leave a minimum of "unfinished business," the scourge that led to a cluttered mind, I worked to tie up loose ends of commitments and relationships. But I did need to decide when Luke and I would get our "final" United States haircuts, to arrange for him to have all his official papers, and to finish my holiday shopping before the end of the year.

One night David and I had a long conversation, trying to think through good timing. I had continued to hope I could leave Westport with some prospect of a new professional direction for my life in Paris. Now that the grant proposal score was causing me to turn away from collecting new research data, I focused on becoming a "real" writer. I rewrote drafts of proposals for two books, *Saying Goodbye* and *Making a Difference*, and faxed them both to David. He responded with insight and support. I incorporated his suggestions into the revisions, then faxed them back to him.

On Saturday, November 22, he arrived at Newark at 1:15 p.m. on Air France flight 004. Again, our eager embraces fogged up the windows in the parked car before we left for the Holland Tunnel. When we arrived at the Archives Building, we visited for a few short minutes with Scott, Stefanie, and Sofia, and then walked them over to David's sister's building, where they took the elevator up to her loft for the birthday party for Stefanie. David and I then drove "home" to Connecticut. We had all day Sunday to ourselves, a chance for Luke to purposely ignore and then nuzzle up to David, and for the two of us to survey progress toward the transition in a quiet and orderly fashion.

Jennifer arrived to sleep over on Monday and Tuesday nights, and on Wednesday we all traveled to New Jersey, laden with my contributions for our Thanksgiving feast and David's gifts for our hostess. After a Wednesday afternoon in Moorsetown filled with the warmth of reunion with our relatives of choice, Jennifer and Steve continued on to Baltimore to celebrate Thanksgiving with Steve's family. David and I were returning to Westport the next night, after Thanksgiving dinner, with Dan and Stefani.

The next day, as planned, David and I drove to New York for the "big trip" to the consulate. It was closed for a long weekend. Apparently, even in New York and for a holiday that was not their own, the French decided to *faire le pont*, "make the bridge"—take an extra day of vacation when a holiday fell near a weekend. We digested our disappointment and managed not to mention it to David's sister and her boyfriend during the pleasant afternoon we spent with them, wandering around SoHo and then sharing dinner at a restaurant. David and I were determined to maintain some kind of connection with them, even if his sister's "concerns" and worried behavior—not including us in the birthday party was only one example—had suggested that she was less than enthusiastic about our plans.

Saturday night, still anxious about the incomplete French government formalities, I took David to Bridgeport Cabaret's performance of *A Chorus Line*. We breathed through a tense Sunday until we could return to New York on Monday morning, prior to his early-evening flight home, in the hope that we could complete our official business at the consulate before he needed to get to the airport.

On Monday, December 1, 1997, David and I sat in a parked car on Madison Avenue while we waited for the French consulate to reopen its doors following the long weekend. I turned to him and said quietly, "You are signing on not only to provide housing for me, you know. You are filing papers saying that you will take care of me. Is that okay?"

He smiled that amazing smile, looked into my eyes, and took my hands in his. The tiniest of nods. "Yes, that's okay."

Tears began to tumble down my cheeks. First one or two, then a trickle. Soon I began to sob, my chest heaving as the enormity of making this particular dream a reality sank in. David was offering to "take responsibility" for me. Only once before, during my too-brief time with Stuart, had I felt that someone not only wanted me but wanted to take care of me. David took me in his arms, stroked my hair, held me tight, and dabbed at my wet cheeks with his freshly ironed handkerchief.

"It's okay. It's really all okay. We want to do this. We want to be together. Shhhhh." His clear, resonant voice was uncharacteristically soft, quiet, utterly comforting.

Within minutes after the consulate opened, David had worked his magic with the powers that be inside the townhouse that, to me, had seemed so mystifying and daunting the month before. We left with smiles on our faces and reassurances that the application would be expedited, and that I could, indeed, expect to be able to leave for France with a properly executed *carte de séjour* within six weeks. David and I decided that I would book my flight for January 17. On that Monday, December 1, we reached Newark in time for his 5:20 p.m. departure on Air France flight 003, back to Paris. About six weeks more to go.

20

Saying Goodbye

December was a whirlwind of trying to live consciously as I navigated the waters of emotional highs and lows and entertained fantasies about the directions my life might take. After David returned to Paris, I again gave my bereft and disconsolate puppy some extra TLC, did laundry, returned phone calls. A woman I volunteered with on Yale Alumni Fund projects, with whom I had become increasingly friendly, had a background in publishing. She was a Francophile who enjoyed hearing about my romance and adventures, and, after I told her that I hoped to write following my move, she offered to put me in touch with a literary-agent friend of hers.

The practical side of me thus addressed, I turned to the more intuitive part, the part that was acutely aware of the mystery and unexplainable energy behind my relationship with David. The part for whom the angels and demons were as real as the material data of bank accounts and appointments on the calendar. I scheduled a "reading" with my favorite psychic and, as a birthday gift to myself, an update with an astrologer. Both announced that the scary steps I was taking were on track. I reported on the reading to David:

> *Not an easy transition but a necessary one and enormously*
> *rewarding once complete. She sees Jen as extremely happy for*

me—pure, clear, just pleased for me—and Dan as not caring about the house but missing me, needing me to call him, really stay actively in touch for a while. Message is to let go of all unnecessary baggage. Need to travel light. She also sees me writing children's book(s?) or a book about children (the one on how to become or raise a parent from the child's perspective?). And she sees me lecturing in Italy. . . . You comfortable "driving the car" and me loving every moment of it.

So much to look forward to; so much encouragement to let go of the shore.

Jennifer continued to sleep at the house one or two nights during the week, allowing us to share healthy dinners and long talks. My daughter, with her impeccable integrity, admitted to having sad moments about my going, now that she had begun to imagine how "it is going to be different." For the first time, she told me that I had been one of the reasons she had moved back to the tri-state area. And, echoing the major theme of my life, I voiced genuine surprise that I still meant so much to her, that she believed I had something unique and of value to give to her. She was so able, resilient, resourceful. And loving. I had thought all she needed—besides Steve, of course—were more opportunities to grow, develop, create, thrive.

These conversations were among the most difficult but necessary, critical moments on the road from there to here. Because of them, I knew we, both Jennifer and I, would make it, remain close. Besides, she *did* have Steve and they were *both* good travelers.

I remained more concerned about Danny. He was so quiet, so even-tempered, so intent on being generous and positive. He said nothing negative. His concerns were all a bit under the radar, and I wasn't sure how to read them. And perhaps I wanted to credit his own love affair, growing stronger day by day, with more sweeping power than any one relationship could ever have. I needed to give him space, to not intrude, but at the same time stay energetically connected. What great training for loving my adult child into his future!

David had much work to do when he returned to Paris. Old matters, new matters, the current events of his daily life, and now the task of preparing for our arrival, both mine and a dog's. While tending to these practical demands, he provided a constant stream of moral support—faxes, phone calls, information; smiles, laughter; commiseration with me when I needed to cry.

I booked Air France's early-evening flight to Paris on Saturday, January 17, 1998. Tentatively, the kids and I made plans to share a "farewell" dinner on Friday, which would give David all of Saturday to get ready for our arrival on a low-traffic Sunday morning. Responding to my announced plans, David got up in the middle of the night to make one of his precious "dark zone" phone calls so that I could go to bed with his presence close to my ears, close to my heart.

My patients were following through on contacting and meeting with the therapists to whom I had referred them, and they began to make orderly transitions. Friends and colleagues called to schedule a farewell meal or concert. Jennifer and I put a specific holiday baking night on the calendar.

In Paris, David began to make plans for our life together after the move. He invited me to concerts and the ballet, events that both of us could enjoy. With me in his life on the horizon, he was willing to put commitments on the calendar.

David also described long conversations with his sister. I observed, "Seems she and you never discuss your process or what's between you, only other people." I asked him to please not talk about me with her, but rather to let me speak with her directly if she had any questions or wanted to have information from or to share information with me or otherwise to develop a relationship. I did not want them discussing us, him and me, and so had some sense that I might be disrupting a dynamic that had the force of a lifetime behind it. I again described the dangers of "triangling," my determination to avoid it, and a commitment to managing all my relationships directly. Two people discussing a third who was not present spelled danger.

And there was, of course, the matter of a middle-aged woman and her dog moving onto a small and compactly organized converted barge floating on the Seine. David spent more than one weekend sorting through his things, filling cartons with clothes for donation to the American Church in Paris's winter rummage sale, and packing others with books that he then donated or took to his office. He wrote:

> *Cleaning out stuff: a good occasion/reason to triage (how 'bout that), give to the needy, throw out worn/torn/junk, and move other stuff/papers/old correspondence to office, where there's more room and more appropriate. No, you are not intruding. We are gonna make home together. 'Nuff said.*

My Air France flights were confirmed. I would pick up the tickets in person at the airline's midtown office, just a few blocks from the Yale Club, where later that week I would be attending my last meeting of the Alumni Fund Executive Committee, complete with a working lunch that just happened to fall on my fifty-fourth birthday. My heart was thumping away.

Danny seemed happier about it all. One weeknight when Jennifer was away on a business trip, I drove into New York to take Dan and Steve to dinner at Benihana. After swordplay and steaks, we made our way across town in a jolly mood. All seemed to be right with the world. An event starring Kenny G. in which Danny had been involved had gone well. The holidays brought a whirlwind of artists to town, events and parties along with them, and he was thoroughly enjoying the perks of his job, the idiosyncrasies of the recorded-music industry. Even better, he had been able to bring Stefani into his BMG world by including her in his holiday invitations. He was quick to agree to come home for dinner January 16, and then, giving me much joy, he asked if he could drive Luke and me to JFK on January 17. Best of all, he announced, "I'm starting to get ready for France. I bought *Wine for Dummies* yesterday. Ordered first bottle last night, and everyone liked it!"

I began to imagine placing a few of my furnishings on the boat;

perhaps the embroidered pillow I had bought in India, the cream-colored one with the green and gold animals on it, could sit discreetly on the sofa. Or a set of my fluffy towels might hang on the hooks near the painted sink. Perhaps just a few favorite kitchen tools and utensils could fill a pretty pottery canister that I could bring specifically to hold them. But none of this in January. Only my clothes and computer in January. And Luke, of course. We were going to live on a houseboat moored in the middle of Paris. I admitted to David:

> *Maybe I will be somewhat "emotional and scattered" for a while in France—the pendulum was so far in the other direction that a temporary swing on the way to correction would be okay. I'm really not afraid of a thing—it's all going to be part of the process. At this time I feel so strongly about you and me and what we are together that I can only believe any "trials and tribula-tions" in the future would be just what they have been in the past: opportunities to understand each other better, be closer.*

Besides, my ability to effectively manage my anxiety attack before Thanksgiving had reassured me that my coping skills were in place. David responded with relief and typical understatement: *Glad you are aware your pendulum had "gone too far in the other direction."*

We experienced a minor setback when David went to the *service des étrangers* at the Préfecture de Police to confirm the documentation required to legally bring me to France. He was told that I *did* need to obtain the visa personally in New York and then, within eight days of arrival, obtain the *carte de séjour* at the *préfecture*. At first, the woman at the *préfecture* insisted I had to stay in the United States and wait for my visa, but finally she relented and actually suggested that there was no reason I couldn't enter France on a normal "tourist visa" (i.e., my passport), while waiting for a *visa long séjour*. But she was concerned that I be back in the United States when "convoked" by the consulate in New York to collect my visa.

David studied the information sheets again and concluded that it was just *her notion* that I needed to be there to follow up. Given the Christmas holidays, always disruptive of office procedures, and the uncertain timing of my visa, we faced potential conflict at best and departure delay at worst.

David was dealing with his own bureaucratic nightmare, the details of which he had kept to himself. The City of Paris had recently passed new standards concerning the boat communities on the Seine. David had known that a formal set of regulations had been created; he dreaded confronting the papers that were required to document his compliance. Indeed, every time he attempted to open the packet, he found some other matter more compelling. He finally admitted:

> *Brought in docs re: boat registration and inspection and new regs but just can't face it (been stalling since my return from the United States). I look at papers (folded) on desk and just get sweaty and nervous, panic or anxiety attack. I stall. Things I know are not controllable or just annoying, so I hide, avoid, delay . . . Maybe tomorrow. Or maybe later this afternoon.*

I tried to offer helpful suggestions, invoking the Premack principle for managing anxiety, that one can make him or herself do anything by pairing it with a less attractive alternative, but David assured me he would handle the matter himself, in his own way, and then faxed me a birthday card that included detailed instructions:

> *This was the best way to get birthday wishes to you first thing on the right day. 1. Go back upstairs. 2. Go into my closet in bedroom. 3. On shelf on the right (above bar), my Bass shoes. Under the shoes, a shoebox (Bass). 4. Inside the box, a home-made "card" and a package. Both are for you. Happy birthday, my love.*

The forethought. The planning. The surprise! The card. And the gift: a necklace of multiple strands of tiny pearls, complete with a unique gold clasp. Simple. Elegant. David's impeccable eye for beauty again. I felt like a princess. A spoiled one, at that. I called him immediately to express my delight.

The same day, I went to my working lunch at the Yale Club. After saying my goodbyes, I was presented with a cake, my first birthday cake in several years, devil's food with black-cherry filling and coffee buttercream frosting. The chairman of the fund promised to find an active role that I could play in supporting the university from Paris. I again thanked my friend for the referral to a literary agent. And then walked the few blocks to pick up my airline tickets.

While David continued to make room on the boat in preparation for our arrival, I said more goodbyes. Patients were "terminating" their therapy with me, as we had agreed, and I was bidding farewell to my own friends. Some patients and even some friends felt betrayed. Some were furious. Occasionally jealous. Sometimes sad. Not all of them. Some seemed to understand and were thrilled for me. Many brought me gifts that were thoughtful beyond measure—the set of French-language tapes and the Tiffany keychain with an airplane on one end and a globe on the other went into service immediately. One woman, who worked in a mental health field herself, brought into the room as a therapy issue her deliberation over what to give me. By the end of our discussion, she asked what I would like. After reflection, I suggested a photograph of her and her children, a testimonial to how much she had grown since I had known her, to remind me of the integrated, reflective, sober, and loving woman she had become. There were many other gifts as well, all meaningful.

The Sunday that David carted boxes back and forth, I worked on my personal relationships. A local performance of the *Messiah* offered an opportunity to clear the air with one of my closest, most longtime friends. She explained that she had felt torn in the middle when another friend had begun passing judgments about me and I had refused to allow her to be a messenger between us. She came to understand that I dealt with *all* of my relationships directly and not through a third person. We let go of unspeakables, declared discussion of a nonpresent person off-limits, and reestablished our friendship.

Another synchronicity, which seemed in general to surround me at that time: I had wondered if a favorite former patient whom I had not heard from might be at the concert, given that it was held at her church. She was not, but when I got home, there was a message from her. Yes, I could see her the following week.

That night I attended a dinner party at Madeline and Bill's—beautiful and lots of fun. I reported to David:

> *The couple from London they were "honoring" have a daughter, and also a son who lives in Paris. He is the editor of a French computer magazine, and his wife has a Vietnamese restaurant. Bill and Madeline send lots of love. They've been saying glowing/wonderful things about you.*

France and French connections seemed to be everywhere. David tried to send support across the ocean as I trudged through painful ending after painful ending with both friends and patients, often filled with tears, both theirs and mine, and sometimes accusations of abandonment or deception. One patient urgently "needed" to schedule an appointment during hours when I never worked, on a Friday night, reassuring herself that she was worthy of special treatment. She arrived forty minutes early, leaving me scrambling to open up the office, turn on lights, contain Luke in the bedroom, and put on lipstick and my jacket.

David continued to discuss dates for his March ski trip with Adam. It *would* take place, and I *was* included, but Adam had two requests for his father: 1) that Adam be able to "bring a date, too," and 2) that he and his father spend time together, just the two of them. Adam was not then in any relationship. Neither David nor I was pleased that he seemed to consider me to be a simple "date"–as if I was just arm candy or a source of convenient sex for his father. Of greater concern, to me, anyway, were Adam's thoughts about having time *alone* with his father. Of course I wanted them to spend private time together. I wrote to David:

> *Just as I certainly don't expect you to be with my kids all the time, I don't expect to be with you and Adam. As for skiing, I may not even have the guts to do it again (do they have cross-country, touring?)—or I can be a tourist and write. Dinners no problem. He'll have as much "alone" time with you as he/you want. . . . Thrilled that he is talking to you.*

By the week of Christmas, with David due on Christmas Eve, I had written an invited manuscript review for *Acta Psychiatria Scandinavia,* we had decided that I would maintain my disability insurance policies and that David and I would both look into medical insurance coverage for me, and I had ended my own therapy. That week I had fewer than twenty patient appointments scheduled, almost half intended to be last sessions, and thus I expected only ten clients the following, final week of my private practice as a clinical psychologist. Yes, they could write to me. I handed out business cards printed with the Paris office address and telephone number, along with final invoices. Yes, they could call me if they were in Paris. I was not dying, or even disappearing; I just could not be their therapist any longer.

As the departure date drew closer, so did my children. Jennifer spent more time hanging around the Connecticut house, and Danny dropped in unexpectedly for surprisingly direct conversations, as well as his favorite made-by-Mom cereal-and-nuts mix, followed by a steak and baked potato. I had promised myself to allow whatever feelings came up in me to have space, to be worthy of acknowledgment, to have some kind of appropriate expression. And so it was a time of love and tears, of sharing secrets and hugs. Of practicing breathing.

21

Closing Doors

avid's last trip to the United States before my move to France was intended to be a social and supportive one. Scott and Stefanie had organized a party on Christmas Eve for guests, including her parents, who were visiting from Michigan; her sisters and their husbands, now happily domiciled in the New York metropolitan area; and David's sister and her boyfriend. David's plane was scheduled to arrive at 1:15 p.m. at Newark, and the party did not begin until six or six-thirty and might run late.

Christmas Eve, traditionally a heavy drinking holiday, was not ideal for driving, especially when reflexes are running six time zones beyond the clock. I decided to treat us to a room at the Marriott Courtyard near the airport. We would check in directly after David's arrival. After our reunion, he could nap and then shower, and, as a bonus, after the party, we could drive back through the nearby tunnel and spend the night in comfort, then make our way to Westport in the clarity of daylight the next morning, Christmas Day. Danny and Jennifer and Steve were planning to sleep at the Signal Lane house on Christmas Eve, so they could care for Luke.

The plan promised to work well, especially once we found the road to the strategically located motel. Great sex, restorative sleep, a hot shower, and a trip to the city, all bright-eyed and bushy-tailed.

Stefanie's mother had prepared traditional holiday dishes that she had learned during her childhood in Germany—linzer torte, glazed ham, home-baked bread. Add Stefanie's own delicious potato pancakes, complete with a choice of applesauce or sour cream, and we shared a feast fit for an extended family on the most central holiday of the winter. We even found a parking spot on a side street just a block away from their apartment at the intersection of Greenwich and Christopher Streets.

That was not our best decision. Luckily, David had left his briefcase and luggage in the motel room, so when the Honda was broken into and ransacked, his belongings were not there to be taken. We discovered the vandalism after the party, around midnight, and had to wait another hour before AAA arrived to help us open the jammed doors and bypass the blocked ignition. We limped through the tunnel back to the New Jersey motel. Another insurance claim. More repairs. What was the transcendent message about leaving my cluttered American life?

The next day, Christmas, was extraordinarily sweet. My gifts to Dan, Jen, Steve, and Dan's Stefani centered on their scheduled week-long trip to Paris in March, the "real" gift. Guidebooks. Notebooks. Travel-size toiletries. Jennifer and Steve gave me a small jewelry box, because I was going to live on a small boat, and a four-by-six-inch photo wallet to protect pictures of those I wanted to keep with me. Carefully selected CDs from Danny. I don't remember what else. I do remember that we visited the O'Sheas in Fairfield and made it to the Community Theater to view *Titanic* before picking up our Chinese takeout, and that we made a fire in the fireplace, worked on a jigsaw puzzle, and were grateful to be together.

David and I went back to the city on Sunday to take Scott, Stefanie, and Sofia to dinner at the Cowgirl. The following week, I saw my last therapy patients. In each session, one relationship at a time, we ended work in which we had each invested our hearts, minds, and souls. We reviewed the roads traveled together, the paths they had taken while I walked alongside, the triumphs, the detours, the discoveries. Often we cried. Tears of joy over the learning we had shared, painful milestones softened by the comfort of being able to speak truths, express fear, rage, and grief, to be heard and understood. Tears of sadness at ending the special partnerships we had forged.

As each of these sessions ended, I moved closer to my own emerging reality, one that would bring a new professional and personal identity. I had been wise to put everything except closing my practice "on hold." The emotional demands of remaining "present," fully emotionally available to myself and my clients, left no room and no energy for dealing with details like selling or closing a house. Or even packing up for the move. Logistics could so easily have provided an excuse to avoid facing the reality of what I was doing and the agony of all the mixed emotions. Luckily, David was there to hold me at night and Jennifer came to sleep over on Monday, as usual.

One beloved patient brought me a gift that remained posted on the refrigerator until I sold the house. She had carefully colored in the black-and-white images in a *Hagar the Horrible* cartoon by Dik Brown, dated 4/1, from what I can only guess was 1997:

Frame 1:   Hagar and Ernita talking. Hagar: "Boy, I envy you, Ernita."

Frame 2:   Hagar: "You have a home, a husband, children, security."

Frame 3:   Hagar: "All I have is my career, travel, an occasional adventure, fending off suitors . . ."

Frame 4:   Hagar: "But you have a real life. . . . Ah, well . . . I shouldn't complain."

Frame 5:   Hagar is off the picture; a small girl stands alongside Ernita, who holds a baby in her arms. Hagar: "So long! I'm off to Paris!"

Frame 6:   The little girl: "Mom, where's Paris?"
            Ernita: "Shut up."

On Tuesday, December 30, I saw my last patient in the Signal Lane house. I waited for the person who was supposed to follow her. The man scheduled for my final clinical hour never showed up. When I reached him by phone, he said, "I guess I forgot." This was the first time ever that he had forgotten. He never did pay his final bill. I guess, even after all our work together, that was the only way he could express his feelings about my leaving him.

That night, David took me out to dinner to acknowledge the milestone. This was for real. I had actually ended a number of extraordinarily meaningful relationships with people I cared about deeply. I had let go of my primary and only regular source of income. I was going to depend on him, both financially and emotionally, at least for a while. I remained terrified of the burden he might feel upon the assumption of responsibility for me, but there was no other way to do it, at least not in the near future. Three more questions faced me: At age fifty-four, did I still have the resilience to adapt well to a new culture? Could I tolerate living so far away from my children and friends? And, after sixteen years of happily living alone on his boat, could David feel nourished, rather than suffocated, when he had permanent company in his home, in his life, in his heart? Could we actually live together in peace, harmony, and joy?

Once again, days felt surreal. We rang in the new year at home, another couple joining us to cook together and toast our new lives. We went shopping for a crate in which Luke could travel comfortably in the cargo hold of the Air France jet. We joined David's sister and her boyfriend in New York for a somewhat awkward meal, given their lack of enthusiasm about what we were doing. And Scott and Stefanie and Sofia brought Stefanie's parents to Westport for a festive brunch during David's last weekend in Connecticut. Her father, an expert in plants and trees indigenous to climates like ours, generously surveyed our landscaping. He could identify the exotic yellow azalea, my personal favorite among the specimens that Stuart had lovingly and carefully planted fifteen years before, and helped me better appreciate its heritage. I remembered that such gifts often come when they are least expected. Embracing origins, although not essential to marveling at beauty, can deepen appreciation of it.

On Monday afternoon, January 5, 1998, David boarded Air France flight 003 from Newark, scheduled for a 6:20 a.m. landing in Paris. He needed to get back to all those open files, as well as to his preparations for Luke and me. I treasured the time I would have to tie up loose ends. Hope and I took our last walk on the beach one foggy, misty, almost ethereal winter morning. She promised that she and Alvin would visit us in the spring, when their youngest daughter would be studying in Prague. A neighbor's husband, on his way to Paris, had volunteered to deliver a suitcase to David, so I packed and dropped off one to him. There were dental X-rays to collect, and I needed to FedEx Luke's International Certificate of Health to the state veterinarian in Hartford for official signatures. There were lunches and dinners with nearby friends, long talks on the telephone with those who lived at a distance. Seemingly infinite computer tasks to prepare for working on the laptop indefinitely and on 220-volt electricity permanently. Finally, I was ready to lose sight of the shore.

22

A Hug Worth Waiting For

When David returned to Paris on January 5, 1998, he took with him the largest suitcase from my house. I had filled it with bulky winter clothes and summer shoes. In addition, he carried my laptop onboard—one fewer item I would need to bring with me in the cabin of the plane.

He struggled to clear space where I might arrange my "things." He bought a rack to hold hanging garment bags and a shoe organizer and installed them in the second cabin, as he began to turn the space where his sons usually slept into an oversize closet. The Saturday before my arrival date, he went to BHV, a large Parisian department store renowned for home-related products, and purchased four unfinished wood pieces, each with three drawers. He had carefully measured the space on a shelf alongside the long corridor from the living room to his—our—sleeping cabin, and they would fit perfectly. In an act of love, commitment, and insanity, he carried the four small but very heavy wooden chests, two tied together and hanging from each arm, all the way home, the length of the Seine from the Hôtel de Ville to Concorde, from BHV to his boat. This feat was one of those amazing shows of strength, impossible under any normal circumstances, now rendered essential by his focus on a goal. By the time I arrived a week later, the little drawers formed a bank of orderly personal protectors awaiting my most private belongings. They looked like built-ins along the hallway that led from the living room to the master cabin.

The following day, David went to the Marriott on the Champs-Élysées to retrieve the suitcase that my neighbor's husband had brought to Paris. He lugged it home, then emptied a dizzying array of socks into a hanging shelving unit he had bought. He was emotionally ready and becoming physically prepared but was getting nervous. All those socks were a little scary.

Back in Westport, I hung up my suits in the closet, climbed into jeans, and turned my attention to computer details and my hopes of becoming a writer. I contacted the literary agent who was a friend of my friend. She agreed to meet me at Starbucks in Greenwich for a half-hour conversation. Gathering all my ideas and possibilities, written introductions, outlines, and notes, I arrived at the meeting anxious but brimming with enthusiasm and potential directions my writing could take once I was in Paris. The allocated half hour expanded into most of that Friday afternoon, and I went home with an author-agency contract to sign and return to her before I left for France ten days later. How little did I appreciate the ways in which living in Paris with David would gently mold me, turn me into a woman who inevitably walked down new paths, following a sense of internal direction, a compass pushing me toward new definitions.

That night, Danny played in the alumni basketball game held each January at his high school. Stefani joined me as, perhaps for the last time, I watched my son play on the court I knew so well. It was my final full weekend in the Signal Lane house that winter.

Saturday night, Renee and Matt and both of their children arrived for a gathering before we might be—expected we would be—hopelessly dispersed. They brought gifts. Annie's hunter-green watering can symbolized all the "watering" that I had done through the years as I had nurtured her and others, helping them grow into whatever their own sort of flower might be. Nick gave me a hand-woven scarf, the many fabrics and colors reflecting the composition of my own life, now integrated in a beautiful whole. I promised to return should an important life event take place—hopefully a wedding or a birth—and Renee and Matt promised that they would come visit us in France.

David was running out of things he could do to prepare for our arrival. Late that Sunday, he wrote:

> *Moved your picture from counter to TV to make counter less cluttered (more room for two) and 'cause next week I'll have you in person to look at over breakfast. Hermès windows gorgeous. Tea shop rearranging its window. So much to see and share. Just can't wait.*

And the next day:

> *Next Monday maybe we'll sleep late together, have a leisurely breakfast, walk the dog on the quai for his first morning in Paris, then stroll to the office with Luke on leash (now that is gonna be an experience). We'll ease into new routine. And no longer need to get to office early to read fax from my sweetie and to respond. No time zone calculations. . . . Mme. M.* [David's new secretary] *(asking about my preparations, weekend chores, etc.) joked about my "last week"—"take advantage." All I want to do is be with you, here, finally. I love you, Roni Beth.*

I worked on tax returns, supervised the handyman as he finished repairs from the fall flood damage, and carefully monitored documents. Just days before my departure, the precious French visa did arrive. So did Luke's International Certificate of Health and my birth certificates—originals, newly obtained from Ohio authorities. I got an international driver's license, extra passport photos, and a AAA map of France. Where *was* Tignes, where we were going skiing with Adam in March, anyway? I packed up and sent a fifty-seven-pound carton of books and papers by boat. I was momentarily concerned that it might not reach its destination, especially since I had no receipt, but I reassured myself that the post office did tend to come through, remembering that my first poorly addressed love letter had reached David on his boat.

David had located an apartment to rent in Val Claret, a village in Tignes that he knew and liked, and booked it for us and Adam March 22–28. He made reservations for the three of us on the high-speed train from Paris. He set up Kallback accounts and numbers for Danny and Jennifer so they could call me in Paris at no expense. He wrote:

After this one, only two more morning faxes to you (unless I come in to the office Saturday), and only two more evenings for you to fax me! After that, it's "good morning, Roni Beth," in person and in bed.

On Friday night, January 16, 1998, as promised, my children came "home" for a farewell dinner. We cooked and ate, drank and reminisced, laughed and cried. They all slept overnight. The next day, Danny drove Luke and me to the airport in plenty of time for our flight to Paris. He left us and my nine suitcases at the curb and went to park the car. When I checked in, the man who did the honors said that we could keep Luke with us until shortly before boarding, so that he would not need to be in the hold any longer than necessary.

We took the escalator to the waiting area, Danny carrying Luke in his bulky but sturdy crate. Then there we sat, in the Air France boarding area at JFK, sharing what were to be my final moments of living in America. Together. Sweetly. Tenderly. The unspoken richness of our love for each other spilling out all over. Nothing left to say. Simply the joy of being in each other's orb, next to each other's energy, our deep awareness that we each had a life to live and that, for now, we needed to move in different geographical directions.

The flight attendant called my row. A crew member took Luke in his crate for careful placement in the hold. I stood to board Air France flight 007, bound for Paris, France, David, and the person I would become. I felt like a squirrel I had recently watched strutting confidently across a telephone wire. Instincts were guiding me to my destination. No fear of falling. Doing what I was meant to do and capable of doing.

When Danny returned home to garage the car, he found a fax waiting for him and his sister:

January 17, 1998—Paris
Dear Jennifer and Danny,

Thank you for letting your mom come live with me in Paris. I promise to take good care of her (and "the dog").

Between faxes, e-mail, Kallback, and bargain plane fares, you will discover the distance isn't that great. And both your mom and I want to stay close, so we will.

Looking forward to sharing my (soon "our") city with you in March, when you will be able to confirm to your satisfaction that Mom is just fine (that'll take about half an hour, plus quick visit to check out her office), and then you have free time to do what you want—with or without us—in this fabulous city.

I expect we'll inaugurate new Kallback numbers and speed-dials tomorrow.

David

The Air France jet landed at Charles de Gaulle Airport, Terminal 2C. I handed my passport and new documents to the immigration officer. With a smile and a stamp, he sent me in search of my luggage. I stood in the baggage claim area, watching the nine suitcases tumble onto the carrousel. Suddenly, a familiar hand was rubbing my shoulder. I heard the soft yip I knew so well. I turned. There was Luke, sitting next to his crate, and there, beside him, stood David, holding his leash.

"We're in the restricted area! How did you get in here? How did you find Luke? I don't understand." I was crying, babbling, filled with love and joy. And confused.

Using his resonant voice, his deep grasp of French culture, and his

wicked grin—and perhaps the perfect cap on his head also helped—
David explained, "I told the customs agents that they just *had* to let
me come in, *à titre exceptionnel*. My girlfriend was coming from the
United States to live with me, she had nine suitcases and a little white
dog—a bichon, for goodness' sake!—and she needed help. So they let
me through." And with the embrace that ushered in the years that
have followed, David murmured, "Welcome to Paris, my love."

Postscript

I hope that lessons learned through my life and this love story may inspire you to live with courage, joy, and integrity. I hope they give you permission to feel the fear and "just do it" anyway; to allow pleasure and the desire it can evoke; to experience all of it, the entirety of existence—the good and the bad, the clear and the confused, the pride and humility that come with understanding. I hope they nudge you to take time for stillness, allow space for internal direction, opportunities for reflection. My story is less about the healing power of love than it is about the powerful forces of destiny, the way our lives push us toward lessons we need to learn to become the people we are meant to be. It is about the necessity of choice in the context of inevitability, the ways in which we create possibilities in our lives and then are free to decide how to respond to them. My story of two people helping each other along the paths of our souls is the gift that has been given to me and that I joyfully pass along to you.

Acknowledgments

iracle at Midlife: A Transatlantic Romance emerged through a series of synchronicities. An earlier and longer manuscript, written to tell the story for our children and grandchildren once we were no longer around, sat on a shelf for five years. Gratitude for bringing it from there to publication goes to Christine Chen, for her chanting workshop at Yogaworks, which opened my mouth; to Linda Novick, for her art course Unmasking the Soul at Kripalu, which told me to stop being invisible; to Susan Tiberghien, for her class on writing love story memoir at the Hudson Valley Writers' Center and for sending me to literary agent April Eberhardt; to April, for agreeing to meet with me at the Unicorn Writers' Conference, for her enthusiasm, and for introducing me to memoir guru Brooke Warner; to Brooke, for assigning me to Annie Tucker, my angel-editor.

Thanks also go to the team at She Writes Press for a cover we love, for shepherding the manuscript into concrete book form, and for a community of authors, my late-life virtual "mommy group." Special thanks to Cait Levin, project manager, and to Crystal Patriarche and her publicity team.

I thank the friends who have been cheerleaders for my writing for years, especially those who have encouraged me to go public with it. Thanks go to Yogaworks for a stable of teachers who have kept me balanced throughout, to Woodlands Community Temple members for dedication to compassionate values, to the Yale Alumni Fund staff and board for years of helping me grow and serve and for modeling excellence. While I was writing and revising, three angels, people I loved who have left this world, sat encouragingly on my shoulders, whispering words of wisdom when I needed them: Stuart Lowenthal, Richard Hackman, and Stanislav Kasl.

And, of course, David. Without David, there would be no story to tell, no book. David, you have understood my need to write since we walked across the meadow at Banff Conference Center in August 1996. Thank you for never letting me abandon the dream, for clearing in our lives the space that following it has required, for graciously giving up the countless movies we did not watch, and for providing wise counsel on everything from manuscript editing to contracts to decisions about priorities. Your love and our story remain the miracle that continues to transform us both.